Blue Saint

Annie M. Cole

To Nikki,

May you always leave behind a trace of grace.

Annie Cole

Renaissance
Valley Publishing

Published by Renaissance Valley Publishing

Copyright © 2021 by Annie M. Cole

ISBN 978-1-7367947-0-8

Published March 2021

Chapter 1

God moves in mysterious ways, sometimes too mysterious to notice until they bring you back to some remembrance, to home, to memories of a sanctuary you thought you would never see again.

The sultry mid-summer night in New Orleans marked the passage of Leta Purviance as she walked home on a side street. The sidewalk bordered a decrepit building, bounded on three sides by a spiked iron fence. High above the overgrown lot, wide-mouthed stony creatures stared down from their perches where they squatted as if ready to pounce on their unsuspecting prey.

The sound of footsteps echoed in the night and seemed to come from every direction. Leta quickened her pace, carefully surveying the enclosed yard. A squeak of hinges intruded into the silence, but the sound ended almost as suddenly as it began. A man appeared out of nowhere and stepped from the darkness to block her path. Chilling fear washed through her, and in one quick movement she was seized by strong, musty hands. One pressed hard against her mouth, the other, like a vice, tightened around her waist. He hefted her up and dragged her through the iron gate, completely in control of her movements.

Cold, congealing horror gripped her heart as a broken chain was lifted from a door and thrown to the ground. Free of his grip, she struggled to get loose, kicking against the hard body until her assailant regained dominance, then pushed them through the doorway until they were quickly swallowed up by darkness.

A deathlike stillness permeated the room and the old walls seemed to moan in sorrow for the girl's impending doom. Leta struggled against the grimy fingers at her mouth, but the struggle seemed to amuse him. Darkness hid the face of the demented soul that held her captive, but his guttural laughter filled her with terror.

A deep-chested cry of outrage sounded from the doorway as the door crashed open, banging against the wall. Leta was thrown aside as the outraged invader ran toward them. Her attacker pulled a gun from the back of his pants, but in one swift movement the weapon was knocked out of his hand and landed squarely at Leta's feet.

"You'd best keep your dirty hands off that girl—or I'll kill you with my bare hands!"

"Reck!" Leta yelled, recognizing the unmistakable voice of the man. She snatched up the gun and was about to toss it to him when the attacker pulled a steel blade from his boot. A look of cunning crept into the wild face of the man as he drew back, ready to plunge the knife into the heart of Reck.

A deafening blast sounded. The attacker fell forward. The knife disappeared into the press of his body.

Moments later the whole area began to wail with the sound of sirens and flash with blue and red lights. First responders crowded into the room. Reck shielded Leta with his body as if expecting her to be hauled off and carted away. Much like a small child viewing some great disaster, Leta could only stare dumbly. She remained motionless, giving no outward sign that she was affected by incident. Then, she uttered the words, "I killed him."

***

The countryside was quiet, almost hushed as Leta Purviance drove along the backroads of Quay, South Carolina. Old, abandoned houses scattered the landscape and were no more permanent than those who had built them, but the wisteria remained, tangled in the trees and by ghost walls, holding up nothing.

The land grew familiar, and soon the SUV rolled to a stop near an undergrowth of blackberry bushes. The thorny dense shrubs rambled on either side of a rutted-out lane, forming an almost impassable thicket in the wild, untamed woodland. Leta inhaled, releasing her breath like a cool cloth of grace had just been draped across her forehead. The document clutched in her hand certified, in straightforward terms, that she was now the owner of three acres and one small house. And not just any house, but Stone House, the only place she had ever known as home. And if it's true that a place belongs forever to the one who loves it the hardest, then some part of Leta had always lingered within the walls of the old stone dwelling.

Word had filtered down through the Purviance family that Bess Purviance, known affectionately as Grand Bess, had grown old and senile and could not be trusted with financial decisions any longer. But a more dignified explanation as to why Grand Bess had gifted the old gardener's cottage to Leta Purviance was told by Bess's husband, Royce. He had stated, without apology, that his beloved wife's actions were simply an outpouring of her benevolent nature and that anyone possessing such divine qualities must never be questioned, only submitted to.

Much to the displeasure of one Purviance heir, however, it was a great humiliation to learn that the love child of Bess and Royce's prodigal son, Rod, had been counted among the beneficiaries to Purviance land. Edwina Purviance had made it her mission in life to paint Leta as a wild and worthless outcast. Edwina, her opposite—the pampered debutante of a prosperous family.

The property in question was prime real estate which ran along the banks of Sweet Grass Creek. The estuary wound its languid way through the marshlands and spartina grass, until it melded with the sea near the small coastal town of Quay.

A rain-sweetened breeze flirted with Leta's hair as she stepped out, her small hiking boots sinking slightly into the soil as she stared at the entrance. Sandy ground molded intimately around the deep dirt drive, appearing as though it had been rubbed into the earth by a potter's thumb. The familiar old sweetgum tree, with its star-shaped leaves and gray-brown bark, towered at the edge of the entrance and seemed impervious to the passage of time. She ran a hand down the deep furrows, remembering the small holes in the bark where her grandfather, Patrick, had said the yellow-bellied sapsucker and woodpeckers would lap up the sweet sap. She took a deep breath of it, then turned in search of a form through the trees, knowing by heart the lines of the slate roof, jutting up from the overgrowth.

Keenly aware of the surroundings, her senses were heightened as the wind carried the scent of freshly plowed earth, pluff mud, and rain. Flowering dogwoods, strewn throughout the woods, stood stark white against an ominous sky, darkened to a gunmetal gray by the approaching storm. Only a gentle breeze and the faint drone of a few erratic bees disturbed the silence. Leta felt loose, free, no longer confined by the closeness of her surroundings in New Orleans or assaulted by the nightmarish memories or endless distractions of noise and flashing lights. The spell of that city was broken. Carried away on the wind. She was finally home.

The old gate barring the entrance moved ever so slightly in the breeze, making a haunting sound on its dying hinges. She grabbed the wobbly frame, forcing it wide through the heavy weeds. A truck could be heard nearing, rolling its load over the road. A moment later an orange and white U-Haul came into view, squeaking to a stop as it approached the gate.

Leta held up a hand to the driver. "Hey guys. Here's the key to the door. Just back up and start unloading."

The driver plucked the key from Leta's hand and accelerated, signaling out the window with a wave of his tattooed arm. The truck bounced and churned through the deep soil of the lane, evidence that no one ever drove through there anymore.

Following behind the movers on foot, Leta stepped high over bent grass in the center of two ruts before sinking into the soft dirt of the tire tracks. As the house came into view, she noticed the screened door hanging precariously from its hinges. Her heart went out in a surge of love and pity from the tattered look of the place. She supposed everything in the house had long since been sifted through by pilferers and what was believed to be of value, carted off long ago.

The jumble of tree limbs and tangled vines littered the yard with the proof of neglect. Pushing aside the tall grass, she began clearing debris, intent on staying out of the way of the movers.

"Hey!" Leta called out. "Either one of you guys have a lighter?"

One of the men hopped off the back of the U-Haul, shuffling his feet toward her, but didn't answer, just tossed a Bic in her direction. She caught it as the thought occurred to her that she must've hired a couple of mutes.

"Thanks," she said, watching the guy plod his way back to the van.

First, she collected the paper that littered the yard, then placed it in a pile and lit it. She tossed in a rickety chair with a dry-rotted bottom, followed by several old tree limbs, cans, and an odd collection of matted mops and frayed-out brooms. She kept one old broom and began clearing a path around the fire. The fire roared up suddenly, scorching her face and driving her back a step. Red-hot flames licked up the dried wood and debris, sending up a plume of gray smoke. It was hard and slow work, and that was good for Leta. It helped clear her mind, sweat out the poison of her bitter past.

The slam of a truck door broke Leta's concentration, and she turned toward the sound, slapping the grime and ash from her hands before brushing the hair out of her eyes. Guardedness fell into place as she watched the stranger approach. Ever since the incident, her father had stressed the precaution until it was a natural reflex. She straightened to full height, all five-feet-six inches, as the man stopped a few feet away. Neither the remote setting, nor the threat of a storm, gave her the same tense feeling as seeing a strange man on her property. Her life hadn't had a whole lot of goodness in it for a long time. To Leta's way of thinking, strangers never brought anything but trouble.

The man stood with his hands on his hips in a perfectly worn-in pair of jeans, boots that looked like he'd never give them up, and a broken-in canvas field jacket splattered with mud. His skin was turned-earth tan, his close-cut beard as swarthy as a pirate's. A silent air of self-reliance sat across his shoulders, but it was his dark eyes that held her attention. They seemed capable of drawing out answers to questions he didn't have to ask.

Looking the guy over, she was beginning to have second thoughts about her plan to stay the night in her recently acquired home. The man before her had a fresh-off-the-battlefield look about him. A certain untamedness that unsettled her. Leta had seen men like this before. The places she and her father had frequented were full of them. More times than she cared to count she'd been confronted by one of her father's business cronies with all their liquored-up courage. The last thing she wanted to deal with here was that kind of man. A slow uneasiness began to seep in and settle around her as she watched the stranger.

Then a voice, rich like molasses, but clear and strong, broke into her distrustful thoughts. She squinted from the smoke into the stranger's eyes as if not understanding the question.

"I was just asking if you're the one moving in?" he repeated, eying the U-Haul truck. He looked over his shoulder at the backs of two gangly young men who were struggling to get a kitchen table through the narrow doorway. Turning his attention back to the girl, a half-smile crossed his lips as he found himself meeting eyes of bright gold set in a face washed by dust and sun. He took in the longish, light-brown hair, pieces of it sticking to her cheek like seaweed on a seashell. The rest of her hair hung loosely around her face from the haphazard way she had tried to confine it in a cloth band. She had generous but unsmiling lips.

Being questioned by the man didn't sit well with Leta. There was something about the way he had asked the question, or maybe it was the inflection in his voice, whatever it was, she didn't like it. She bit down on her teeth until her jaw hurt. Feeling her boot heels press farther into the ground. She answered the man. "I am." *Not that it is any of your business,* she thought.

His keen eyes narrowed, and she read the caution in them. "I need to warn you," he pointed up, "you've got a pretty nasty hole in your roof. A limb fell from that oak over there—during a storm. Happened a few weeks back. Heard it all the way over on my place." He ran hand across his beard. "Meant to let somebody know."

"*I* know." Her chin came up a notch, even though she had no idea whether there was a hole in the roof or not. She dared him with her eyes to say anything else. *Who does he think he is, anyway?* He looked at her as if she'd lost her mind, then smiled in a way that made her want to plant her size seven-and-a-half boot in the center of his backside.

"Well, seems like you've got it all figured out." He glanced at the fire, still rubbing his beard as if undecided, then turned to leave.

She felt insulted by the stranger's response, but a thought kept nagging at the back of her mind. Maybe the guy understood more about her present situation than she did. She conjured up all kinds of creatures that could be inhabiting the house. Things that slithered, slipped, or scurried through that gaping hole. Things that could be living inside, hidden in the crevices and cracks. It *had* stood empty for quite some time. With a quick shake of her head, she reigned in her fearful thoughts. Come what may, she was staying. And if there were any creatures lurking about, well, they'd just have to scoot over.

Before the man had reached his pickup, he turned around and began walking back toward Leta. Fumbling in the pocket of his jacket, he produced a business card and handed it to her. "My number. In case you should need anything." He raised his hand toward the road past the gate. "If you follow the road around, the entrance to my place is just past the clump of cedars. I'm Tru Ransome—your closest neighbor."

Tru Ransome? What kind of name is that? A made-up name, she imagined. "Leta Purviance, and thanks…I'll keep that in mind." Taking the card, she stuck it in the pocket of her jeans, catching a whiff of tobacco and sawdust coming from his jacket. She turned without another word, but not before seeing the nearly black eyes widen at the mention of her name. Annoyance crept up her spine as she walked to the door and away from the man. She'd been the target of gossip and contention from the Purviance family most of her twenty-six years on earth. Not to stand high in the opinions of one's own family was as humiliating a thing as could happen to a person, especially in a tightly knit community like Quay. It was a place where everyone knew everything about everybody.

Leta heard the pickup crank, then the ping of sticks hitting the underside of the truck as he pulled away.

Without turning around, she stopped until the sound faded into the distance and the rumble of thunder carried above all others.

Before they had settled in New Orleans, Leta and her dad, Rod Purviance, had lived under so many roofs, in so many towns, that a home of her own had been the one thing she'd desired most. Her father had purchased a well-known bed and breakfast called The Hideaway, nestled in the heart of the oldest portion of the city, where Leta had an apartment. Never once had she ever imagined that the only place on Earth where she had a history of home would be handed over to her on a silver platter. She reminded herself that no matter what lay ahead, she was home. And nothing, not the warnings from a neighbor or the threat of critters, could keep her from what she'd wanted her entire life—a place to call her own.

"Hey guys!" she called, waiting as one of the movers appeared in the doorway. "Got an extra tarp in the back of your truck? I'll buy it from you?"

"Dub," the guy shouted into the house. "We got an extra tarp we can spare?"

Dub yelled back from somewhere upstairs, "Yeah! She's gonna need it—there's a big hole in the roof! Need to cover it up before the rain gets here! Grab it and shimmy on up here, Injun—fasten her down!"

Happy with the order, Injun whistled little snatches of songs as he walked back to the truck to get started on the task. Leta figured he'd been given the name due to his ruddy complexion and high cheek bones. His poker-straight raven hair fell to his shoulders, putting the finishing touch on the entire persona.

Looking out over the landscape, the fresh new green

of spring sprouted around the house making it look shabby and worn by comparison. Built as a gardener's cottage, Stone House was located near Sweet Grass Creek and was surrounded by once lush gardens and fertile fields. A scattering of trees graced the yard close to the house, their branches hovering over the quaint two-story dwelling like the protective arms of a mother. Leta had always thought the nestled position of the house near the creek gave it the appearance of having popped from the pages of Thoreau's *Walden*.

The timber-framed structure was a study in contrasts. Relatively simple in style, the gabled house was nevertheless charming. It was clad with stone on all four sides and set with deep, well-placed multi-pane windows that surrounded the house. A solid wooden front door, of undecided color, stood open and leaning. A brick chimney punctuated the slate covered roof near the gable where the hole gaped open beside the flashing. She ran her hand down the surface of the house, feeling the coolness of the stone beneath her fingertips as she watched and waited for the final piece of furniture to be unloaded.

Strange as it seemed, she wanted to explore her new home alone, without anyone standing by or shuffling past her with boxes or chairs or anything that might take away from the moment she'd dreamed of, longed for, for so long.

After walking the men to their truck, she thanked them, paying them a little extra for their trouble.

"If you need us, call again. We do all kinda work, don't we Injun?" said Dub, pulling himself into the cab of the truck.

Injun nodded. "That's right…we can fix that roof too,

when you're ready for it." He slammed the door and threw up a hand.

She watched as their truck dipped into the ruts and disappeared down the road. With a tightened throat against a flood of emotions, she turned and entered Stone House. As her eyes adjusted to the dim light, she saw the crowded room full of boxes and furniture and took in the enormity of the job ahead of her. She accepted that it would be some time before she would get everything in order. There was much work to be done in the gardens and fields too, if her plans were to take shape as she hoped.

The bare wooden staircase hugged the wall near the entry and tugged at the corners of her memory. Across the room the large multi-paned window stood there like an old friend. It captured light from a break in the clouds and cast the movement of the creek to the ceiling in glittering waves. Much of the room was taken up by the stone fireplace, flanked on either side by floor-to-ceiling bookshelves. It spoke to her feeling of comfort by flooding her senses with scents of ash and wood, filling her mind with remembrances. Somehow this anchored her.

For the first few moments she'd felt like a trespasser. Then the house seemed to live, to breath, as if the thump of a heart began to pulse beneath its wood and stone. Leta knew the house held secrets—most old homes did—but the house, like any good Southern woman, presented a carefully poised, sugar-spun manner of charm that invited you in and welcomed you. But the truths this home had witnessed, the old gal guarded. Because at the heart of Stone House was a winding tale of both love and loss, tragedy, and triumph—the substance of life.

Chapter 2

Since the day Tru Ransome first laid eyes on the property, the place had been heavily on his mind. It had been a summer's day in his boyhood when he had come across a scattering of long-standing buildings, tenant houses, and one old general store. Out exploring, as young boys do, he had stumbled upon the place quite by accident. They had been visiting his mother's people nearby when, bored with the talk of his relatives, he'd wandered off and crossed the creek where a natural bridge had been made out of a fallen tree. Now, it was with a sense of pride and contentment that he looked over the land, his land.

Molly Ransome, Tru's mother, had been instrumental in persuading her son to make the move to Quay. Reluctant at first, Tru soon realized that making the decision to plant his flag here had been a good one.

He guided his truck onto the rutted-out dirt road that cut all the way through his property to the creek. The road looked more like a run-off ditch than a driveway. Still, he managed to navigate the pickup through the ruts and channels until it ended near an old church called Shiloh.

The clapboard church sat peacefully at the end of the

road. It was just over the property line on a narrow jut of Purviance land. He lowered the window, breathing deeply the aroma of violets which grew in profusion about the chapel. Just passed the church in a small clearing, beneath the cool depths of age-old cedars, a small cemetery rested with headstones covered over in silver lichen and gray-green moss. Tru made a mental note to return to the graveyard, explore the area more carefully, and clear it of fallen limbs and debris. He put the truck in reverse, wheeled around, and headed back toward a broken sign dangling from a post that held the faded letters, *Landrum's Boarding House*.

Walking toward the house on a dirt path, he tossed his keys in his hand. At the end of the porch hung a slatted swing, set to motion by the wind, causing the rusted chain to creak in the breeze. Life seemed to slow down here. There was this sense of peace about the place, like being transported back to a simpler time. Like a gentle rain falling on hard-packed ground, it had taken time to sink in, to soften the hard edges of his life.

Smoothing his beard, he leisurely took in the rising wind and watched it linger in the branches of an ancient oak. It played along the ground and through a swath of sweetgrass that rolled up quietly from the creek. The land created a cathedral-like quiet that spoke to the man's soul. He whispered, "Ransome Land."

For a time, Truman Ransome—who people called "Tru" because Truman never fit the man—had lost himself. He'd lost direction, purpose, even the one thing he had believed he could always count on. He had become just another guy with a remote in his hand most nights, whose life had emptied out to nothing. Not long after he had stumbled upon the property, his thoughts began to jell into a firm belief that perhaps this might be his chance for a new beginning.

"How'd that sweet-talking real estate agent girl convince you to buy this place?" A masculine voice, Southern smooth, spoke from behind Tru.

Recognizing the unmistakable accent of his uncle, Tru slid a key into the front door of the old boarding house and turned his head slightly. "Thoroughly, J.D., very thoroughly." Tru caught his smile, but not before it lit his eyes. "Where'd you come from?" He forced the door open with a heavy thrust and motioned for J.D. Redman to come inside.

"Parked at the road and walked down. Didn't want to risk those ruts with my new tires."

Tru regarded his mentor with fondness as J.D. walked past him into the house. He was tall and lanky, and Tru had always thought his uncle had the manner and appearance of a young Gregory Peck. A touch of gray at the temples made him look more like a high-dollar lawyer than a preacher. Of all the men Tru had known in his life, his mother's brother had been the one person he'd felt he could trust. People respected J.D. and thought the sun asked his permission to rise. Tru knew the man lived what he believed.

"Now that I'm here, I wouldn't be opposed to coffee," J.D. drawled, arching a brow as he looked over his nephew. "You look no worse for the wear. Your mother said you looked like ten miles of bad road." J.D. scanned the man once more briefly. "Molly said you got this place for a steal. How long have you been out here now, anyway?"

"Three months and I have no regrets. This place fits me."

15

J.D. knew instantly the reason for Tru's isolation and the ache that gnawed away at his heart. To stand alone when facing loss and rejection seemed to J.D. the worst of all possible situations.

For the past several years, Tru had been second guessing his judgement on nearly everything that mattered. It was natural enough, he supposed, after what he'd been through. But seeing his uncle stand in front of him, looking every bit as solid and sure as he'd always been, caused him to think that maybe, just maybe he'd made the right decision in coming to Quay.

Looking around, J.D. noticed the sparse furnishings: a chair or two here and there, a table, a cluttered bar having once served as a guest registration counter with stools on either side. The cabinet on the wall behind the counter was divided into eight numbered cubbyholes filled with an assortment of keys and small leaflets of paper. "Well, it's evident there are no women within a mile of this place."

Tru choked and had to cough to clear his throat. "What do take me for?"

"A man," he stated, bluntly. "Coffee first. I never discuss anything without coffee."

Tru pushed a stool away from the bar with his foot. "Sit." He pulled out two mugs and slid them on the counter before pressing a button on the Keurig. As the coffee brewed, the aroma permeated the room with the warm, comforting scent of fresh java. He placed a cup in front of J.D. "Sometimes, all it takes for me to unwind around here is a good cup of coffee and a—"

"Goo Goo?" J.D. finished for him, remembering his nephew's fondness for the treat and the reason behind it. He snatched a Goo Goo Cluster candy bar from a basket near the Keurig. "I'm glad to know drinking fifty dollars' worth of booze isn't everyone's definition of a good time." He took a swig of coffee.

"We all have our vices," Tru said, snatching the bar from J.D.'s hand and tearing open the wrapper. "I have these things shipped in from Tennessee—but they're worth it."

"Seems like most people I council these days have some sort of an addiction or another. You'd think that'd be something you'd deal with in a large metropolitan area, not a quaint little town like Quay."

"Let's go sit outside," Tru said, between chews. He grabbed his coffee and headed for the back screened door.

The rockers squeaked in protest as each man adjusted his weight in the chairs, holding on to their coffee cups as if their very lives depended on it. From their vantage point, they could see everything around the little-less-than community. Tru propped his feet on the porch rail and sat back to enjoy the changing weather of the evening.

"Nice place you've got here," J.D. said. "Not too far from where your mother and I grew up. If memory serves me," he pointed across the creek past a stand of loblolly pines, "we lived just over that small rise." He sat back and studied the area. "Hard to believe they're all gone now. Doesn't seem to matter how far you go, home will always be the place you first started out in life."

"True enough for most, I guess." He swallowed down the last of the candy bar and wadded up the wrapper, shoving it in his pocket. "Wish that were true about drugs being only a city problem. No place seems immune to the epidemic these days. Drugs and crime go hand-in-hand."

J.D. raised his gaze from his cup and appeared somewhat confused. "You mean you've had trouble—here? This place is tucked so far off the beaten path I'm surprised anybody could find it. It's an almost forgotten piece of land. The townspeople steer clear of it because they think it's haunted. Besides, what could a thief possibly want to steal out here?"

"Copper. It's in the pipes." Tru's cheeks flexed with irritation. "I've chased off more than a dozen in the past three months. No more than boys, most of them. Young, desperate, directionless boys."

It was past time for Tru to sort it all out in his mind. He needed a new vision. A purpose for being. Other attempts had resulted in nothing more than loss of sleep, at best, and a waste of money. More money than he cared to remember. After so long, the predicament had led to a desperate place just this side of crazy. If he were to ever get out of the blue fog that shrouded him, he knew he had to find a true purpose for his life.

J.D. motioned with his cup and asked, "Where's that smoke coming from?"

He arched a brow, then slid the blue cotton sleeve of his shirt up past his elbow. "My new neighbor."

"You met him?"

"Her, and yes." He shifted uncomfortably.

J.D. nodded and gestured calmly toward the neighbor's property. "It's all about looking closer than other people will and looking farther into their history. Must I remind you that people are in our lives for a reason? Even people who may be hard to look at."

Tru looked at him for a moment without speaking. His jaw flexed. "I never said she was hard to look at."

J.D. suppressed the amusement on his face and changed the subject. "What's your idea for the place?"

Tru turned his thoughts onto a fresh track. The plan was loose, to the point of being undefined and flexible. "I want to use it to focus on men. Men who might not, for whatever reason, feel like church is the place for them. Guys who don't look like your regular church goer. You know who I mean."

The man's gray eyes widened considerably. "What— like a men's retreat?"

"More like a fish camp…thought we'd have one of those big firepits or something. I don't know. Maybe some Adirondacks to surround it." He flung up his hand casually. "If I've learned anything, it's that when there's a group of men sitting around smoking cigars or pipes, they tend to get honest with each other. I see that as valuable."

J.D. paused with his cup in his hand, lost in thought. "Unconventional…very, unconventional. An admirable idea. I would expect nothing less from you."

Tru shrugged. "Like I said, these are men that the church hasn't reached. I've rubbed elbows with a lot of them…and you have too. My clubs are full of them."

J.D. nodded. "Ah, your cigar clubs. How's that going?"

Tru ran a reflective hand over his beard. "I've sort of been missing in action lately. Got a great staff, though. Keeps things running smoothly. But I can tell you this, most of those men are just looking for purpose. Something to live for, fight for." His dark eyes narrowed. "I think I can help. God knows I want to."

J.D. drummed his fingers on the arm of the rocker methodically as he stared straight ahead. "Makes sense to start where you are." He seemed to be talking to himself and mulling over the idea for what seemed like a long time. He looked over at Tru with considerably more interest. "Show me what you've got so far. I'll look it over, see if it's something I can bring before the leadership of the church…garner some support."

Tru finished his coffee and set the cup down. "I need plenty of that—prayer too."

J.D. gave a strange look. "Tru Ransome, that's one thing you've always had from me. Even when it's landed me in hot water." He smiled broadly, then winked. "Let's go inside and see your plan."

They stepped to the bar where Tru swept the top clear. He grabbed a cardboard cylinder from the corner and dropped the blueprints on the counter. "Where do you want to start?"

J.D. stuttered in surprise. "How-how long have you been planning this? And more importantly, why am I just now seeing it?"

Giving no answer, Tru, once again the businessman, spread out the drawings and held them in place with a tape measure and a bottle of water. Snatching a pen and notepad from the end of the bar, he began jotting down notes and explaining his ideas. Minutes turned to hours as the men poured over the plans.

J.D. bent his head over the drawings and squinted. Tapping his finger on the paper, he asked, "Why is there no mention of women in your vision…anywhere? You've specified men only for all your positions." He rubbed the end of his nose with his knuckle and looked at Tru. "Are you not an equal opportunity employer?"

Tru's brows drew together, and he was silent for a moment. "Women are like exotic animals—better admired from a safe distance."

"Oh, I see. Once bitten, twice shy." He raised an eyebrow. "Does that go for Edwina Purviance?" The question hung in the air until he saw a slow grin spread across his nephew's face.

"Especially Edwina Purviance."

When J.D. had questioned Tru about his social life in one of their phone conversations, Tru had thought it best to relieve his uncle's distress and let the man know that he had, in fact, been seeing someone recently. Someone he'd met by chance outside of Quaytown, the local coffee shop. A woman he'd often admired in the early days of his youth when he'd spent summers with his mother's family.

"What are you afraid of? Interaction between the sexes?" J.D. asked bluntly.

Tru glanced down at the drawings, smoothed out some of the wrinkles. "Well, there's that."

J.D.'s laughter echoed through the room.

Patting his chest, then his pocket as if he'd forgotten something, Tru glanced around. "Have you seen a chain around here? It has those keys on it." His questioning eyes turned to J.D. who shrugged in bewilderment. "The ones you gave me, remember?"

"I do. Those keys are an important reminder," he admonished. "I'll help look for it."

"Nah, it'll turn up. Probably on my dresser. Anyway, I was hoping to give you a tour of the grounds before this rain moves in."

"Got a name for the place? Names are important, you know," J.D. remarked, leisurely examining the plans in front of him.

Despite himself, Tru smiled as he watched J.D.

hovering over the blueprints. Something about the place intrigued his uncle… he could tell. "I wanted to name the place Shiloh, after the old church; but that's not what the people around here are calling it."

The people of Quay liked to name things: boats, trucks, houses, land. Some of the names for the places around the area were not their current names, but their ghost names from the past, what they used to be. Like Hickory Nut's Barbeque would always be Hickory Nut's Barbeque. It didn't matter that the sign above the joint flashed Big Ed's in bright neon green. The name Shiloh never took off, and never really had a chance, either. It was Ransome Land from the get go.

Immediately Tru's face changed from one of mild interest to that of complete attention. He tapped the drawings with his pen. "In fact, during my research I discovered that Shiloh was once considered to be one of the holiest places of worship in all of South Carolina. It was where the early settlers of the land assembled, set up a community, and divided up the land. There are still direct descendants of the original colonizers living around these parts." He nodded in the direction of the church. "Shiloh had a magnificent beginning. But now it's just a lot of faded lumber, held together by prayer in a field of weeds. An empty shell of a place."

J.D. stared off for a long moment, then picked up his cup and gestured with it. "What happened to Shiloh could happen to any place or anyone. When a person or a place no longer inspires a walk of faith or fails to walk out that faith in love, it can very quickly become just an empty shell in a field of weeds. It's good for both of us to be mindful of that." He held up his cup in a toast, then swallowed down the rest of his coffee.

Looking back on his life, Tru was astonished at how little he had known of the evil workings going on all around him. For more than seven years he had been deceived, and not by just anyone, but by the one he'd promised to love, honor, and cherish so long as they both lived.

Searching for relief from his tormenting thoughts, one night he'd pulled out his cell phone and made a call to his mother, Molly. After the call it had taken Tru less than a week before he'd fled the city of Charlotte, North Carolina. Taking little with him, he had made no plans beyond a final stop at the cemetery where his father was buried. After that, he simply drove away from the past and all its reminders, but the ghosts of that shadowed life remained, still.

Chapter 3

Life had a way of changing too quickly for Leta Purviance—changes she struggled to come to terms with. She had been raised by grandparents whose circumstances had been altered by the loss of their only daughter, Heather, in childbirth—Leta being the result of that birth. Leta's father, Rod, had had every intention of rearing his daughter without the help or interference of his family. And for the most part, he had succeeded. The only allowance he'd made was to Heather's parents. Empathetic to their grief, he'd found it almost impossible to take the baby from them once he'd decided to leave the area to pursue his own interests.

Rod had little experience with babies. And certainly not one related to him. The thought of a baby relying solely on him and in need of his constant care and nurturing was a little frightening to the man. He had never been warned about what to expect from his own emotions in these matters. So, in this reversal of life, Rod made his first decision based on what he thought was in the best interest of someone else, his daughter. He chose Heather's parents as the sole parental guardians of his child, and they had remained her primary caregivers throughout her young life.

All had been going well with the arrangement until the day Leta's grandfather, Patrick, drew his last breath. A mere three months later, Mae joined her husband in death by what was classified by many as a broken heart. The aftershocks of losing Heather seemed to have lasted years for Rod. It caused him to develop a type of nomadic existence, moving from place to place, never settling down. Somewhere along the way he'd picked up a few bad habits in the business world, namely, risk-taking with other people's money. From a worldly perspective, he had been somewhat successful, until the day came when death made it necessary for him to assume his role as father to his now fifteen-year-old daughter.

Leta's mind traveled back to the last conversation she'd had with her father before leaving New Orleans. "Leta, sweetheart," Rod had said, with the icy control of a gambler, "My advice to you is to steer clear of Tremont. In fact, stay away from anyone bearing the name Purviance. You've been through enough already."

Leta had not answered at first. She saw no reason to justify herself or her decision to her father. She might have argued that she was not a child anymore but a twenty-six-year-old woman! And on top of that, the land she had been given *was* where she had grown up and it *was* Purviance land and she *was*, after all, a Purviance! Those arguments would have had little effect, however, on a man like her dad.

Rod's reputation was well known to the residents of Quay, and most especially, to his family. They knew and remembered the wild times, the reckless wanderings, the disgrace he had brought on the family when he'd fallen in love with the groundskeeper's daughter. But the final straw that knocked the camel flat came when Rod and Heather had conceived a child.

"Do I look like I'm made out of spun sugar?" Leta had said to her father. "I won't break into pieces the minute I face trouble. Besides, I wouldn't have made it this far *with you* if I weren't made of tougher stuff than that. I can handle my own. You're no picnic either, you know."

Rod had given his daughter a sly smile and leaned back in his chair. "I almost wish I could leave New Orleans and be there to see it...almost."

***

Tremont was a peaceful place, with a meadow all spread out and green, dotted with white sheep. This grand, almost stately plantation was picturesque, to be sure. White peacocks strutted haughtily out of the way of Tru's truck as he drove slowly up the lane toward the house. Gnarled fingers of roots, twisted with age, bowed and cracked around the ancient oaks flanking the path leading to the front steps. The home sat high and raised from the ground under the quiet trees. It stood there silently dripping from a recent rain, as if mourning bygone days.

Walking up the steps to the gallery, he brushed the rain off his jacket and stood before the solid oak doors, admiring the carvings. Without thought, his hand ran across the smooth surface of the wood and came to rest at the center of the door on a burnished fox head. The fox had a brass ring in its teeth and kept its sharp eyes fixed straight ahead.

He lifted the brass ring and was about to knock when he heard voices coming from beyond the door. One of the voices was shouting, another begging, arguing, and one voice was breathy and halting, barely a whisper. That one voice was so unlike the others, he strained to identify it.

The quiet voice spoke so directly, so matter-of-factly, without emotion. Glancing through the beveled glass of the sidelight window, he saw the back of a woman standing perfectly still facing a room that was beyond his vision. Her hands were clenched together behind her back and her back braced, as if ready for something bad to take place. He grasped the brass knocker and rapped three times.

Edwina Purviance was long-limbed and sleek as a cat. Her porcelain skin and perfectly cut flaxen hair made Leta tuck a stray wisp from her own fly-a-way strands behind her ear. She watched her cousin glide across the room toward the door with such grace that the princess of Monaco would have been envious. All Leta could do was stare, thinking, *in twenty years of charm school, I could never move like that.*

As the door came open, an attractive man with a dark, close-cut beard paused at the door, stomping the rain from his boots and wiping his feet on the door mat.

"Tru!" Edwina said excitedly. "Come in! When you told me you were coming out, I knew I had to leave Mount Pleasant immediately and come straight to Tremont." She leaned into him and smiled into his eyes.

"I hope I'm not interrupting," he said, meeting the woman's enthusiastic embrace. He glanced in the direction where he had seen the unidentified woman.

Edwina pulled him forward with a graceful arm. "Not at all. We were just discussing some family matters. Come on in, Grand Bess loves visitors." She walked the man past Leta without notice, treating her, as always, like an underbred. The thought of being in the same room with such an inferior person as Leta embarrassed Edwina, down to the roots of her hair.

Grand Bess remained seated but extended her hand, like a queen surrounded by her court. "Truman, always so good to see you." A portrait of a much younger Bess hung on the wall directly behind her chair, as if the seating in the room had been designed specifically with that in mind.

Tru took in the kind blue eyes, faded with age and the touch of rouge on her pale cheeks. Her stature seemed to have grown plump with the passing years, and her auburn hair was streaked with gray. She wore a spring dress of flowered peach and matching shoes with kitten heels. He responded in the gallant fashion of a gentleman by reaching for Grand Bess's hand. The thought briefly crossed his mind that he should kiss it. Taking the frail fingers into his grasp, he gentled squeezed them. "You look lovely, Mrs. Purviance. It's so good to see you."

"Have you met my granddaughter, Leta?" Grand Bess asked, fluttering her baby blue eyes.

Tru turned to face Leta, but before he could speak, Leta took the words from him. "Yes…we've met." She looked up at him, feeling exposed somehow under the scrutiny of his deep brown eyes.

Edwina's eyes widened in surprise as she shifted her gaze from Tru to Leta. "My goodness, you don't mean to say that you two know each other." Her beautiful face, remote and cool as a stone.

White teeth gleamed in a reckless smile as Tru responded. "We have. It's good to be on friendly terms with your neighbors."

28

Leta watched the exchange between Tru and Edwina. It was obvious he admired her cousin, looking at her like he was gazing at a Rembrandt—not flipping through the sales insert of a newspaper. She had his undivided attention.

"I'm sure Truman would enjoy something cool to drink, Edwina. Be a sweetheart and go get something for your guest," Grand Bess said, discharging her from the room. "And let your grandfather know he's here."

Conscious of her cousin's distress, Leta stepped away from the wall to let her pass. *This might turn out to be fun after all.*

Grand Bess smoothed her dress over her knees and said, "I'm sure a man of your discernment has picked up on a wee bit of tension in this room. The least we can do is try and explain as best we can. I wouldn't want to leave you with a bad impression. You'll go away thinking we're the rudest family you've ever met."

Tru shrugged. "No explanation is needed, Mrs. Purvance. All families have discussions. It's not my concern."

Grand Bess looked straight at him. "Let's not be so formal. We're neighbors, after all. Call me Grand Bess." Her eyes lingered on his handsome features. "You see, Edwina disagrees with one of my recent decisions. In fact, she's informed me quite often that a person is never too old to make a bad decision. What do you say, Truman? Do you agree with Edwina?"

The last thing Tru wanted to do was get into the middle of a family dispute. Especially when it meant going against Edwina. "I can't imagine you ever making such a decision. It's been my experience, more times than not, that wisdom comes with age, the same as

29

beauty."

Leta fell back against the wall with a thud and rolled her eyes in total incredulity. *What a charmer, this guy.*

In one fluid motion Edwina breezed into the room and placed a tray of drinks and an assortment of cookies on the ottoman in front of Grand Bess. "Here you go, Grand. I couldn't remember which cookie you liked, so I brought a variety of the freshest."

"And what of our guest? What's his choice?" Grand Bess picked up a butter cookie and began nibbling.

"Why, whatever he wants," Edwina said, sliding a flirtatious glance in his direction before taking a seat.

Tru shifted on his feet uncomfortably.

"Sit down, Truman, please." Grand Bess indicated a chair. "Leta…take a seat across from me and let's have some refreshments. We can all talk while we wait for your grandfather. I think he has some business to discuss with Truman." She handed Leta a glass of iced tea. "What's your choice of cookie, dear, sugar?"

"Anything chocolate." She forgot her aggravation for the moment and looked over the choices, selecting a chocolate chip cookie from the tray as she took a seat.

Tru sat down, resigning himself to a wasted day. It was rare enough to have an afternoon off, even for a few hours. When he'd been summoned by Royce Purviance earlier in the day, he'd called Edwina asking her to meet him at Tremont. He had hoped to spend some private time with her, but now that seemed out of the question. He relaxed back on the couch next to Edwina, listening to her chatter on about giving aid to some charitable cause for orphans.

Edwina, by innate instinct, moved her hand lovingly over Tru's arm as it rested beside her. Her back was turned away from Leta, effectively dismissing her. Still, Leta couldn't help but admire her cousin's style. Well-dressed no matter the occasion, she seemed "right" without effort. Leta knew she'd never been, and probably never would be, put together like that. But that didn't matter much to Leta. What she wanted was to be calm without mental fear, that's what she wanted. She sought a safe place to call home. And that's what she hoped to find at Stone House.

Grand Bess's rasping voice interrupted Leta's thoughts. "Leta, tell me about Stone House and your plans for the place. A little birdie told me that you plan to live there right away."

For the first time since she'd arrived at Tremont, Leta could take a moment to consider her grandmother. There was a twinkle in the soft blue eyes that time could not dim. A dusting of powder touched the finely creased cheeks and lipstick, the color of a shiny penny, feathered into the line around her wide mouth.

"The bird was right." Leta said, tasting her tea.

"Will you need a few supplies to get started? Maybe something nice for the home? I can send one of my girls over to help clean?" An elegant brow raised, waiting for a response.

"I have all I need but thank you." She winked. "If I have a twenty and a dollar store, I'm pretty well set."

Edwina missed the mild sarcasm and turned to look at Leta, appalled. "The dollar store—really."

Grand Bess straightened in the tall-backed chair, completely ignoring Edwina's comment. She squeezed a slice of lemon into her glass before carefully placing it on her napkin. "That's fine, dear…just fine." She picked up a spoon and methodically stirred. "I remember those lush gardens your grandmother Mae kept for us. No one was better at coaxing the Earth to surrender her bounty than Mae." She swallowed hard. "What was it you used to call her?"

"Ma Mae," Leta answered, then smiled as she fondly remembered the woman.

"I seem to remember seeing you as a child, walking between the rows behind your grandmother…you were never more than a few steps away from her. Tell me, do you garden?"

A wistful look came over Grand Bess, and for a moment, Leta felt sorry for her. She'd heard from her father that in her later years Grand Bess had expressed regret over the lost years of Leta's childhood. She blamed herself and her stubborn pride for allowing the unwritten code of conduct to dictate whom she could associate with and whom she could not.

Remembering back, Leta smiled tenderly. "Ma Mae was quiet and taught me a lot without saying a word. I learned how to garden through her actions. Learned the importance of canning, giving too. She had this coffee can up on a high shelf. One day, when she wasn't around, I pulled it down and found that it was stuffed with money. I asked her whose money it was. She said, the Lord's."

The room became quiet, and she glanced around, meeting the dark eyes of Tru. Uneasy beneath the man's regard, Leta shifted in her seat and sipped her tea, then cleared her throat. "My plan is to have a flower farm. In fact, once I clear the weeds, I believe I may have a pretty good start with the flowers that are already there. Ma Mae must've planted some hardy seeds; there're blooms all over the place."

A clatter of China drew their attention to the coffee table where they saw Edwina's hand hovering over a plate of strewn cookies.

"My goodness...did I hear you say you're planning on having a flower farm?" Edwina turned in her seat toward her cousin, an incredulous look on her face.

A smile curved Leta's lips as she stood to her feet. "You did." A pause followed while she let her cousin consider this. "You know, Ed, I've always found it helpful to face people when you want to be in on their conversation. Might want to try that next time. It's good form." She raised her tea glass in salute to her grandmother. "Thank you for the hospitality, Grand Bess." Leta placed the glass on the tray, then reach over and touched her grandmother's hand. "I just wanted to come by and personally thank you. I hope to make a home here and get to know you better."

The watery blue eyes looked up at Leta and she smiled, patting Leta's hand. "I want that very much." She dabbed her cheek with the back of her hand. "I'll be right here for you, dear. Come often and stay long."

Angry at her own powerlessness, Edwina stood to face her cousin. "I'll see you out. How's that for form?"

Tru placed his glass on a coaster and rose from his seat. "If you need help fixing that hole in your roof, I've got my tools in the truck. Found some old slate shingles around my place. Be glad to try them," he offered.

The response came back clear from over Leta's shoulder. "Thank you, but not necessary...the movers are coming back to patch it soon."

Edwina moved to the door and opened it for Leta, then followed her out on the porch, gently closing the door behind her with a soft click. "Why don't you go back to where you came from? You're not wanted here…surely you know that."

Leta glanced back at Edwina, startled by the venom that spewed out of such a perfect pair of lips. "Does your pastor approve of your evangelistic methods?" She grinned at the humor of it, remembering how tirelessly her cousin had always worked in the church. "When you see Lou, please tell her to come see me…I miss *her*."

"I'm sure my sister would appreciate your comments. But Louisa has matured, changed from the girl you remember her to be."

Leta had to rummage deep within herself to find any remembrance of the loathing she had always had for Edwina. Now, she felt only a slight aggravation. As children, they'd had a natural dislike for one another. Edwina had always made Leta feel as if she were the stuff she'd stepped in out in the pasture.

"Oh, I'm sorry to hear that about Lou. And she was so nice too." Before Leta could say anything else, Edwina turned and slipped back inside the house.

Leta didn't regret coming to her grandmother's house, but the whole time she'd been conscious of a sensation in the pit of her stomach. It lay there like a hard rock— she knew it was fear. Not fear of her grandmother, but fear of seeing disappointment on her face—or worse, pity!

Chapter 4

Gray moss swayed in the air beneath the oak branches as Leta's car disappeared down the lane. Tru stared out the window, lost in thought. Most of the Purviance women were easy on the eyes, and the girl, Leta, was certainly no exception. But a different breed altogether. *A bit feral*, Tru thought to himself, *nothing at all like the more refined cousin, Edwina. Or even the childlike, Louisa. No, this girl was a variation all her own.*

"Truman Ransome," called a voice that sounded like gravel rolling around in motor oil. He turned to see Royce Purviance standing next to Grand Bess as she held on to her husband's arm like a drowning woman would grasp a rope. The man was thick of neck and his body squat, like he'd been packed in a can too tightly.

"Yes sir." Tru crossed the room and extended his hand. "You must be Royce Purviance."

"I am," he stated with the confidence of a king. He grasped Tru's hand in a firm grip, meeting his eyes squarely.

Tru had been warned of the man's status as the supreme head of the Purviance dynasty. He made the laws, dictated them, and everyone abided by them. He ruled. His one weakness…his love for his wife, Bess.

"Please, step into my office." Royce glanced at Edwina. "I promise not to keep him away from you too long, my dear."

Tru followed the man into the study. A first glance around the room told him it was decidedly masculine. A large oak desk sat at a slant in the corner of the room near the floor to ceiling windows. Books occupied massive rows of shelves against one wall. In front of the hearth, a leather couch and two chairs sat on top of a vintage rug around an overstuffed ottoman covered in periodicals.

Royce gestured to the seat across from his desk and maneuvered his heavy girth around to his seat. The chair protested in a series of loud squeaks as the man's considerable weight settled into the chair. "I have two reasons for asking you here today, Tru. The first reason is I want to see if you're interested in the little jut of land that joins your property." He tapped his fingers on the desktop. "It's just a sliver, but a fine piece of land...waterfront. Has an old, abandoned church on it near the water."

"I'm more interested in the second reason?" Tru angled his head, watching the sharp fox eyes in front of him. The thought crossed his mind that the door knocker must've been crafted after the sly old fox in front of him.

Royce smiled. "You're a suspicious man, Tru Ransome. I've heard about you...from folks around town. Some say you're a tyrant when it comes to running things your way. Say you have your fingers in a lot of do-gooder enterprises scattered all around. If I can be frank, seeing you now, I just can't picture you as some kind of uptight Christian. I hope that doesn't offend you."

"It doesn't. What do you want?" Tru leaned back in

his chair, studying the man, looking for the angle he knew was there.

Royce picked up a snow globe from the corner of his desk and began twirling it. It seemed a habit, a stalling tactic to help him think. "You have some pretty elaborate plans for that land of yours. Seems to me you're going to need a lot of help getting things underway."

"I have a good crew."

"Have you ever considered women?"

A slow smile spread across his bearded face until it reached his eyes. "Is that a trick question?"

Royce chuckled, enjoying the exchange of words between them. "Let's cut to the chase."

"Thank you," Tru said, a little too quickly.

The old man raised an eyebrow at the response before proceeding. "I want you to hire my granddaughter."

He leaned forward in his chair, elbows on his knees. "To do what?" Before Royce could respond, Tru shook his head. "I don't want Edwina near the place—it's for men—exclusively."

"Not Edwina." His head pulled back at the absurdity of the thought. "She's a different kind of lady. I'm talking about Leta."

"Leta!" Tru shot the man a skeptical look. "I hire a person for their skill, no more, no less. I doubt I'd have anything for her. Besides, I'm not comfortable with the thought of having a woman around the sort of people that will be working for me. Rough necks, everyone." Royce opened his mouth to retort, but Tru cut him off abruptly. "The answer is no."

Royce drew a deep breath and released it, slowly. "Bess will be disappointed." He pinched the bridge of his nose with his fingers.

37

Tru shook his head in rejection of the statement. "I don't follow you. Why would that upset your wife?"

He volunteered the information freely. "My wife has a special…" he waved his hand in the air, searching for the right word, "fondness for the girl. Now that she has her home, she wants to keep her. To Bess's way of thinking, the only way to do that is either through a good marriage or a good job."

"Well, surely she'll understand my concerns. See the wisdom in not having her granddaughter around a bunch of hard-ankle men. I wouldn't consider any of them good marriage prospects, either."

As if the words finally appeased them, the two men quieted, then the silence was broken by Royce clearing his throat. "It's no use, son. Now that Bess has her reasons, she'll only work harder to prove us wrong. She's stubborn that way." He looked away and smiled. "Just like most Purviance women. Edwina is my pride, Louisa my joy, but quite frankly, Leta is a mystery to me. A bit of a wild one it seems. A product of an unfortunate situation between one of my sons and the groundskeeper's daughter," he hissed.

Rubbing his chin, Tru considered the man's words and his proposition, usually preferring to handle his business affairs on his own terms. But the biting comment about Leta angered him to the core. He stared at the smirking face in front of him. He'd seen men like Royce Purviance before. Their arrogance made them the worst sort of person, a fool.

"I can see you're considering my offer?" Royce stated, feeling smug.

Overseeing a flock of anything was where Tru Ransome soared; it was right in his wheelhouse—but managing a crew with a woman in the mix? Still, something about the situation intrigued him. The property appealed to him. He would love to get his hands on the old, abandoned church and be within his rights to oversee the cemetery. He'd let the idea simmer.

Royce faced Tru squarely. "If we could only think of some way to engage the girl in an occupation—some pursuit…"

Tru dragged his fingers slowly across his cheek, then glanced up in mild surprise. "She wants to start a flower farm on her property. I could help her get started. Loan out some of my men to break the ground, clean up the place."

Royce slapped the desk. "Good. You do just that. Keep a record of what you do for the girl. But, make no mistake about it, if she is anything like her father, she is headstrong. You'll have to persuade her to let you help her. If you figure out a way to do that, we'll come to some financial arrangement on the land."

Chapter 5

White curtains floated playfully on the sweet night air above the kitchen sink. They sucked toward the screen and out again, like little blithe spirits. Lightning cracked the silence, followed swiftly by a tumbling thunder. Moments later, the steady patter of raindrops began to hit the windowsill, a prelude to the storm that would soon sweep down upon Stone House.

Leta wiped her wet hands on a kitchen towel, then reached over the sink to snap the window shut. Bone tired and sore from unpacking and moving pieces of furniture for most of the day, she longed for a good hot soak in the tub and much needed sleep.

A fragrant steamy bath was a simple luxury Leta gave to herself on a consistent basis. Spicing the bath with a recipe of Epsom salts and carnation oil, she gradually lowered her aching body into the water and let out a sigh. The therapeutic waters felt like warm velvet, caressing her skin. Sinking back, she closed her eyes, letting the heat seep into her tired muscles.

Long moments passed before she reached for a towel and patted the wetness from her rosy skin. Pulling an oversized nightshirt over her head, she tiptoed to her room and tossed back the coverlet, slipping between the freshly washed sheets.

The house popped and creaked as it cooled from the rain and night air. Most nights, in the depths of the quiet, she heard the familiar sounds from her childhood: tree frogs, crickets, and sometimes, way off in the distance, the haunting sound of a ship's horn; but not this stormy night.

Her room, the same second-floor room she'd had as a little girl, wore the slope of the roof as a ceiling. The window was cut in among the stones. From there she could see across the fields to the marshes and creek below. Farther in the distance, across the wetlands, the spire of Quay Community Church rose in splendor and could be seen, most days, shining with the brightness of the sea behind her.

A bolt of lightning streaked across the night sky, and the rain washed down the window in sheets. Adjusting the pillow under her head, she rose up to listen. Had she heard a noise in the house, or could it be the storm?

Leta eased from the bed to close the door, then halted abruptly. This time she could not mistake the creaking of the wooden planks on the floor below. Something seemed to be methodically crossing the boards, planting each step carefully. But it was raining hard—she couldn't be sure.

Her heart began to pick up speed as she gripped the doorknob, twisting it indecisively. She scanned the room, spotting the rifle in the corner. Snatching it up, she held it close, and without a creak she stepped along the darkened hallway. With the wall at her back, she moved soundlessly down the stairs toward the kitchen.

The outline of a child formed in the dim light, and Leta gasped. A girl no more than six or seven years of age stood in the light of the open refrigerator. She wore pink pajama bottoms, ankle-length and splattered with mud. A dingy wet T-shirt at least a full size too small clung to her thin body, exposing her midriff and outlining her ribcage. Clinging to her back was a stringy, badly snarled braid. Every so often a shiver ran through the child.

The slight noise from Leta's gasp caused the girl to jerk her head around. Seeing Leta, she froze. The gaunt, tiny face was smudged with dirt and expressionless, like a small wild animal staring at a threat.

Leta held firmly to the rifle as she glanced through the dimly lit rooms. The chairs she had wedged under the doorknobs were still firmly in place. "Are you by yourself?" she asked, in barely a whisper. She did not want to frighten the girl.

The little head nodded once.

"How on earth did you get in here?"

The girl pointed past Leta toward a back room.

Stepping back cautiously, Leta pushed the door of the spare room wide. It had a strange, untouched look about it. She turned on the light and caught a slight stirring of the curtains. Reaching the window, she pulled aside the sheers and saw the answer to her question. Slamming down the window, she fastened the lock securely, making a mental note to have a security system installed as soon as her funds improved.

Returning to the kitchen, she noticed the dark eyes had grown enormous with panic and the little girl had drawn back, crouching in the corner beside the refrigerator. In nervous apprehension she appeared to have made herself even smaller.

Leta fell back on her own upbringing. She had never

been abused, physically, but in later years with her father, there had been times when she'd had to rely on her own survival instincts. Protecting herself from harm in sticky situations had become a natural habit. In her life she'd known fear, and the displaced feeling of not having a home, but never hunger. The girl's shabby appearance alone could rip the heart out of anyone capable of having compassion for another living creature.

"I would like a closer look at you, young lady. I think you owe me that, since you've scared the wits out of me." Leta's voice, though soft, was firm, and would not stand for disobedience. "Come here, I won't hurt you." She propped the rifle against the wall.

Reluctantly, the girl inched closer, small steps at a time until she was in front of Leta.

Leta pulled a chair out from the kitchen table. "Sit," she said. "We'll deal with a few of your most pressing issues first. Now, how about a nice piece of chicken pot pie and a glass of milk?"

The girl's chin came up a notch and the glint of pride in the small one's eyes did not go without notice. Leta had, in fact, a similar disposition. She understood it.

"Well then, I suppose I could call the sheriff and he could come get you. At least I'll know you'll have a meal in jail. It makes no difference to me whether you eat here with me or with the inmates down at the county jail, but either way, you're going to have a hot meal."

With the terms spelled out for her, the little girl had no other option open but to surrender. She nodded, reluctantly, and slid her slight weight into the chair.

"Good," Leta said with satisfaction. She opened the refrigerator door and drew out the partial pan of chicken pie—full of carrots, chicken, potatoes, and peas—cut a large wedge, and topped it with a slice of cheddar cheese. Sliding it on a plate, she popped it into the microwave. "If you eat all of this, you can have a piece of chocolate cake," she said, pouring a glass of milk and handing it to the girl. The child's eyes widened as she took the glass, then as the plate was placed before her, she reached for the fork in Leta's hand and ate her meal in silence. For all the girl's hunger, she seemed to find it difficult to eat in front of Leta, so turning her attention away from the child, she lifted the glass cover from the cake plate and cut a nice piece of the chocolate cake, placing it on a paper towel.

With her backed turned from the girl, she heard the quick scrapes of a fork across the plate and paused, wondering what might have happened in the child's life to bring her to this desperate place. Then, in one quick movement, the cake was snatched from the counter and the little girl fled to the back door, yanked the chair away, and darted out into the rain-soaked darkness.

A cool drip of rain ran down Leta's back as she leaned over the porch rail, peering into the darkness toward the creek. The cotton of her night shirt fluttered against her bare legs, and she felt strangely alive. She would never be sure whether the little girl had escaped, or Leta had let her go. The truth of it all was that Leta Purviance, in many ways, was that little girl.

Chapter 6

The day was Monday, and in their usual custom, the crew working for Tru Ransome had gathered at first light under the old oak tree near the road. This was a time meant for the men to get their instructions for the day, see about their materials, and air any concerns they may have for the job ahead.

Tru had barely begun the work of assigning orders when he noticed the attention of his men directed behind him toward the road. Following their eyes, he found the source of the distraction getting out of an SUV he recognized as belonging to his neighbor, Leta Purviance. As Leta approached, a few of the men grinned or spoke to her. Tru noticed she didn't seem the least bit put off or intimidated by them, but spoke cheerfully, making small talk about the good weather they were sure to have.

Tru calmly folded the papers in his hand and waited. He saw a quick flash of white teeth as she approached him. Staring down at the young woman, he took in the small work boots, jeans, and faded blue T-shirt. Her hair was gathered in the same messy bun he'd grown used to seeing on her. Not wanting to get too involved with whatever she was up to, he hoped she hadn't shown up for work. Nothing aggravated the man more than having his men distracted, still, he was led to do the kinder thing. "Good morning, Leta. What brings you out so early?"

"This is not a social call. And I know you have work to do, so I won't take up too much of your time. I'd like to know if any of your men know a family around here with a young girl. She's around six or seven years old? Brown hair, hangs in a braid down her back, kind of thin and tan." Despite herself, Leta felt responsible for the child. Even after she had reported the child to the authorities, she hadn't been able to sleep.

Tru nodded and was about to turn toward the men when Leta laid a restraining hand on his arm. "She's not in trouble. I just want to know that she's safe. She showed up at my house last night—and left in the storm, headed toward the creek. The sheriff hasn't been able to locate her."

He thought a moment before putting the question to his men. "Any of you men seen a young girl wandering around out here? About seven, brown hair, thin and tan?"

"Sounds a lot like ol' Flat Squirrel's young'un." One of the men said, with his feet spread, shoulders back and his thumbs hooked in his belt. "Heard tell he's been keepin' them kids over at the Dew Drop Inn since their momma done gone crazy and left 'em all. His wife plumb scared the life outa ol' Flat Squirrel, a-threatenin' to shoot 'em all in their sleep. He was hidin' out there— 'course, everybody knows Flat Squirrel can't never make a decision. Probably wandered off someplace and got confused…left those kids alone or sumpthin' and they up and wandered off. They's kinda free range young'uns anyway. Everybody in town knows Flat Squirrel. If he were any more stupid, he'd have to be watered twice a week!"

Another man chimed in. "Yeah, I saw him in town the other day. Seemed agitated—more than usual, like some hand hung over him pulling his strings. As for the kids, we ain't got nobody around here to take 'em in 'cept those Jackson's. All they do is use them as child labor to work their rental property. The state pays them to boot! Foster parents my—"

"That's enough, Mumford," Tru warned, knowing the old white-haired man's habit of spitting out profanity like a dirty-faced juvenile boy.

Leta was suddenly glad she'd followed a hunch to ask the men about the child. She had heard that Tru was developing his property as a men's retreat and hoped that somebody at the site might know something about the girl's whereabouts.

Leta tucked her hair behind her ear and looked around. "I appreciate the information, guys. I'll stop by the Dew Drop Inn and see what I can find out."

"It's just on the other side of Sweet Grass Creek...on old highway 100," Mumford said, then spit out a stream of tobacco juice, wiping his stained, white-bearded mouth with the back of his sleeve.

"Thank you." She smiled at Mumford before glancing at Tru. "Sorry for the interruption."

Tru had waited patiently for Leta to make her inquiry, his hands clenched the paper behind his back with his legs braced apart. It was obvious he was trying to be tolerant of the disruption, but he was ever mindful of the fact that the clock was ticking. "Hope you find the girl," he said, abruptly.

With a forced smile, she added, "Too bad you're not building a sanctuary for needy children, Mr. Ransome...sounds like this town is certainly in need of

47

one."

Tru straightened, nodded briefly, then turned his attention back to the men.

"Wait," she said, spying an old vine-covered tenant house on the land. "Mind if I look through a couple of your houses? Looks like a good place for someone to hide out for a while."

"Help yourself." He waved his hand in that direction. "Now, if you're finished," he said, in a less than pleasant tone, "we'll get back to work." It always aggravated him to have a delay at the start of a day. "Men—get on with your assignments," he ordered gruffly. "We've had enough interruptions for one day."

Leta nodded, then mumbled under her breath as she brushed past the man.

Catching a few of the words and not liking the implication, Tru raised a brow at the girl. "Did you say something?"

She stopped, turning around to face him. "Yes. I said you'd think that anybody who builds a place for men to get to know God would be a nicer person."

With that statement, Tru's mouth came open. He looked as if she'd just slapped him.

A moment passed before the impact of her words sank in with the crew. There was the sound of throats clearing and shuffling feet as the men struggled to keep their composure. It wasn't everyday someone got the best of Tru Ransome.

Leta continued down the path, coming upon one weed-choked sidewalk after another leading to small, washed-out houses in various stages of disrepair. She saw the familiar old store with faded white lettering etched on the windows that read, *Fresh Pies, Dry Goods*.

There were several more buildings scattered under the trees and a church near the creek, all of which made the area look like a little lost town back in the woods. Walking up the steps to the first house she carefully tested the porch boards with her toes before crossing it. Pushing open the door, she glanced around the abandoned room, seeing no signs of life. In fact, nothing looked like it had been disturbed in the room for a very long time. Cobwebs stretched across the doorways and there were no footprints in the thick covering of dust on the floor.

***

Nearly an hour had passed before Leta walked up the lane of the compound, holding the grimy hand of one dirty little barefoot girl in pajamas.

Mumford stopped working and leaned on his shovel. He pulled a rag from his back pocket and mopped his brow like a preacher during revival. He called to Tru, "Hey boss!"

Tru tossed an armload of wrapped shingles to the ground and turned to the voice, seeing Mumford nod toward the lane. Looking in that direction, he saw the pair walking up the road. "Sweet merciful heavens!"

When Leta reached the end of the lane and was loading the little girl into the SUV, she glanced back over her shoulder and found Tru's gaze on them. Those dark eyes burned with something other than the aggravation she'd sensed earlier from the man, something she could not quite define.

Chapter 7

The child was silent. Like a sleepwalker she numbly followed Leta around from place to place. First to the Dew Drop Inn where the proprietor informed her, in whispered tones, that Mr. Littleton had walked off in a daze after paying for a week's lodging some two weeks ago. She had learned that the little girl, Journey, and a boy that goes by Abe, disappeared from the place after he'd mentioned contacting social services.

The hard truth of it, Leta knew, was that after you get abandoned, you can't get unabandoned. No matter how much you cry and carry on about it. Nothing can change the fact that you've been left. So, the sooner you accept it, the quicker you can move on to greener pastures. The hard part comes when you wake up one morning and realize that everyone you've ever known and loved has disappeared from your life.

***

The week drew out, and on a bright and clear Sunday morning, Edwina Purviance confronted her cousin Leta after service on the front steps of Quay Community Church.

Leta had been talking to some of the church members, asking if any of them knew or had seen the boy, Abe

Littleton. She'd gathered what information she could from the congregation, making mental notes of all she'd heard.

At first Edwina observed from some distance, watching Leta as she went around making her inquiries. Then she proceeded to pull her aside and tell her what she believed were the standards of behavior for any well-respected member of the family.

"As a Purviance, there are certain ways to conduct yourself," Edwina reminded her dryly. "You have obligations now to the community, to the church. Maybe you should *attend* services, and not just harass people who come out of them. There is a standard you're expected to keep. You can't go around to every trailer park picking up strays and dragging them home and expecting good people to know about them." She slid her hand into the crook of Tru's arm as he walked up on the conversation. Edwina smiled knowingly, as if waiting for his stamp of approval on the little discourse, knowing he'd heard every word.

Before Tru could comment, Leta stated flatly, "You're dead wrong. In fact, you're just plain dead...spiritually speaking, I mean." Leta reached down and took the hand of Journey, the detached expression on the child's face told her all she needed to know. "Even *I* know that." Growing madder by the minute, Leta marched down the steps and away from them, fumbling in her shoulder bag until she pulled out her keys.

As Tru watched them go, he had a wild impulse to run after them, question Leta about what she'd meant. But the thought died when Edwina opened her mouth to speak.

"She's not like us, Tru. Never has been. I honestly

51

don't know what Grand Bess was thinking when she gave her Stone House. That's what brought her here, you know." Edwina matched his steps down the brick stairs. They walked across the parking lot toward the truck. "Before long she'll have that house packed out with riffraff from all over the county. People just like her. It'll look like some kind of-of reject daycare or a refugee camp for runaways." She pulled her hand loose from his arm and faced him. "Can't you see what a hopeless creature she is, family or not."

Tru wore his jacket loose against the brisk air and stood there a moment in a pool of sunshine; he tossed his keys in his hand. "Experience has taught me that those who have suffered in this life will always be a little different from the rest."

"Different? That's a nice way of putting it," she said blankly. "You don't have to be kind because of me. I know what she is. What she has always been. An embarrassment to the family."

Faced with a choice, Tru paused a moment then, as if coming to a decision said, "The hurt that comes from rejection can make a person…different. She's brave for what she's doing, and who knows, maybe even a little bit heroic."

"Heroic!" Edwina said, disbelievingly. "Oh honey, you have no idea."

"At any rate, being different from the rest is not always a bad thing. Especially when that person happens to be right and the one schooling her is wrong," he replied mockingly. "How did she put it? *Dead* wrong."

Edwina looked up at him with confusion, uncomfortable, but not quite sure she understood the rebuke. Anxious to change the subject, she said, "Why are we wasting time talking about all of this and spoiling our Sunday together—let's go have dinner. I'm starving."

***

The sun had dipped low in the sky when Leta, with Journey in tow, walked a path of uneven flagstones around the house and up to the porch. Lifting a pot of basil from a little metal table, she removed a house key and unlocked the door. After spending most of their Monday morning and half the afternoon trying to untangle a chain of events that had led to their present circumstances, Leta made the decision to call it a day and try again tomorrow.

Since Journey had come to Stone House, she had responded readily to the firm but loving ways of Leta. After an initial reluctance to bathe, the child had grown used to the vigorous scrubbing of her caregiver and had, in fact, grown to enjoy being cleaner and sweeter smelling. Leta had purchased for the child several things: shorts with matching tops, little cotton dresses, flip-flops and sneakers, and a soft lavender nightgown with a light robe and slippers. The little girl delighted in having those things. Leta routinely tucked her into bed without so much as a whimper and recited a small and familiar bedtime prayer before kissing her fingers and placing a kiss on the child's forehead.

In the short time since they'd been together, they'd already formed routines. There was comfort to be found in the ritual of simple tasks and ordinary habits. They seemed to have a way of pushing out fear and anxiety and establishing some reassurance that the pattern of life would hold.

Looking down at the little bundle under the covers,

Leta's heart felt a surge of pity. "We're a pair, the two of us," she whispered. "But at least we now have a home."

Leta gave a last pat to the fresh sheets, smoothing them. The movement sparked a distant memory of her grandmother, Mae. Ma Mae had quite a mothering instinct. She was the kind of grandmother who made you pick your switch when you were in trouble and then let you choose the flavor of Popsicle you could have afterwards. Leta remembered being lifted onto her warm, pillow lap and the scent of dusting power settling over them. She'd found a haven in those cradling arms all those years ago. Of all the people who'd passed from her life, she felt the loss of Ma Mae the deepest.

As Leta reached over to turn off the light, Journey's small voice whispered in the room. "I know where my brother is. I'll show you, tomorrow." With that said, she turned over on her side, pulled up her knees, and went to sleep.

Chapter 8

Early the next morning, rather than being confronted and questioned by Tru Ransome at every turn, Leta decided on a sly maneuver of her own design to reach the place where Journey had said her brother was staying.

Holding tightly to Journey's hand, they made their way toward Sweet Grass Creek and turned south, following an old rabbit trail she remembered from her childhood. They passed through a dense grove of scrub brush and weathered pine, sawgrass and sweetgrass, and more blooming blackberry bushes than she'd ever remembered. It had been too long since she'd smelled the damp mossy aroma of the creek bank. The water was still and glassy in the morning sun, undisturbed by even the slightest breeze. She felt the warmth of the sun on her back and smiled, knowing this moment would be imprinted on her memory for a long time.

When they reached the property line where Leta's land joined with Tru's, she shaded her eyes and looked closely up the dirt lane where she was sure the workers had gathered for their morning meeting. She spotted no one wandering about in that direction so they moved purposefully along the trail to their destination. The church called Shiloh came into view.

As they reached the church, Journey walked up the steps with her arms crossed guardedly across her chest. When Leta came up behind her, the girl raised her eyes with a curious expression of childlike expectation.

Leta asked, "Is he in there?"

Journey nodded without speaking and gestured inside.

Moving past the girl, she turned the knob, pushed hard on the swollen wooden door, and went inside. Journey seemed to take a chill that made her shiver, as though the thoughts of what lay within the abandoned old church might suck the very warmth from her bones.

They stood there for a moment, breathing in the smells of dust, old plaster, and decay. Something resonated within Leta as her eyes rested on the familiar words written on the wall above a rough-hewn cross. *Love Even Through Anguish.* She felt it in her chest—the exquisitely painful words that were both beautiful and gutting.

She breathed the scent deeply and tried to fix the long-forgotten memory of it in her mind. In a strange way, it was as if the words had been selected and placed there especially for her.

Journey pointed to a side door at the back of the church, and Leta made her way to it. The door creaked in protest as it opened slowly. A boy, wild looking and filthy, lay fully clothed on a mattress that looked as if it had been dragged inside and stuffed in the small room. He wore a T-shirt, ripped jeans, and tennis shoes too mud covered to determine their color.

He sweated upon the stained and sagging mattress in the middle of the floor. His dark, matted hair stuck to his forehead, hiding his eyes. He was quiet and obviously suffering from an illness. It seemed to zap his strength, but he managed to lift his head off the pillow slightly and look at them with heavy eyes. As Leta stepped forward, his weak and hooded eyes focused on her.

"I'm Leta Purviance," she whispered, giving a tender smile. She placed a cool hand on his forehead.

The boy's face tightened at the touch, but he nodded slightly.

Frustrated at her own helplessness, Leta took in the fevered face, ashen with a far-off look in his eyes. "Don't be afraid. I'm here to help."

The words lightened the boy's anxious appearance, and he dropped his head back on the dirty pillow. An expression of relief replaced the caution on his face.

Leta turned to find Journey standing silently in the doorway. "Go up the road and find Tru Ransome." A name which always sounded to Leta like it was to be heralded after a trumpet blast. "He should be near the big oak, close to the main road, or in the old boarding house. Tell him it's an emergency and to bring his truck."

Journey said nothing but rushed out of the room, set on her course of action.

The air was stale and stagnant in the small room. It filled the motionless air with a sour smell like a damp mop. Assessing the boy once more, she sought to reassure him. "Tru is a friend of mine and will be able to help us. I trust him completely." She saw a shine of sweat on his reddened face as he rested. He lay as still as death except for an occasional shudder that ran through his limp body.

She scanned the room for a source of water to cool his face. Without any luck, she decided a little fresh air might be helpful. Rattling the knob on the back door, she gave it a quick jerk, loosening it from the frame just far enough to get some fresh air circulating.

Glancing through the door, she saw the shadowy line of trees behind the cemetery and her thoughts traveled back in time. She found herself straining to hear the haunting sounds that even today sent a chill through her body.

Her earliest memory from childhood was hearing someone hum soft and low from the deepest part of those woods. It happened on several occasions while she played under the privet hedge that grew along the stone wall near the cemetery. When she had questioned her grandparents about the hums, she had been told by her practical grandmother that it was nothing more than the sound the wind makes blowing through the stones and the trees. But her Irish grandfather had a more mystical explanation, telling her it was the spirits of the saints of Shiloh "callin' out to help ya along life's journey." The little nameless melody played slowly through Leta's mind, and she began to hum it as she waited quietly for Tru.

The old church yard and desolate village held no attraction to the people of Quay. Few had the desire to wander around the abandoned town or dally too long among its ruins. Some folks believed it to be haunted. So, the little creek town remained unvisited by most and quiet, for the most part, until the low and haunting sounds of the hums intruded upon the silence, its melancholy tune drifting on the breeze.

Tru stopped at the threshold of Shiloh church and turned his head to catch the faint notes of a familiar tune coming from within. *The Ash Grove?* The old Welsh song had been sung to him as a child, bringing forward in his mind a picture of his mother. Delicate, beautiful, and a bit carefree, the young mother had spent many afternoons with her fatherless child on a porch swing, singing the winsome song. Tru was surprised by the emotions that were stirred within him as the song echoed within the walls of the abandoned church.

Journey had followed closely on Tru's heels until he had stopped suddenly in the doorway of the church. She tugged on his sleeve. "They're back there," she said, pointing to a door at the back of the church.

As they entered the room, Tru grimaced at the sight. He pushed back his cap and forced a smile as he looked over the boy. A movement in the corner of the room caught his eye, and he glanced over his shoulder and saw Leta. He turned his attention back to the boy, taking in the situation.

The young boy's eyes flinched and narrowed suspiciously in Tru's direction. He tried to rise up, but his weakened body proved to have the greater need, and he surrendered to it without a struggle.

"I'm Tru," he said, looking directly in the boy's weak eyes. "This is what we're going to do. I'm going to lift you and place you in my truck. I'm taking you to the ER in Quay. Don't worry about anything. You're going to be fine."

The boy did not resist as Tru slid his hands under him, lifting him from the mattress without effort, and began walking out of the church.

Tru spoke over his shoulder to Leta as she rushed to keep up with his pace. "There's room in my truck if you and the girl want to come along. It might make the boy feel better to have his sister close by. She is his sister, right?"

"Yes, Journey, and her brother's name is Abe," Leta replied, rushing past to open the church doors ahead of them. She hurried down the rickety steps and opened the truck door, anxiously standing by as he settled Abe into the front seat. She helped Journey into the backseat and climbed in after her.

The truck dipped slightly as Tru got in and started the engine. Leta stole glances at him as he pulled out, making a wide turn to the rutted road. The truck smelled masculine, like leather, tobacco, and motor oil. He drove slowly over the dips and bumps, navigating carefully through the sawgrass that swished beneath and against the sides of the pickup.

When Tru glanced at Abe, Leta saw a tightness in the man's jaw. Feeling a need to thank him, she said, "I appreciate the help. I don't think I could've lifted him. He's almost as tall as I am."

Tru glanced in the rearview mirror and didn't answer right away. "How long has he been like this?"

The voice seemed deeper, accusatory. She felt his gaze on her. "No idea. Journey said she would show me where her brother was…this is the first time I've seen him. All I know about the children is that they belong to a Mr. Littleton and that they've been staying at the Dew Drop Inn." She thought for a moment. "Or at least they *were* staying there. Seems like these kids may have been holed up on this property for a while. I caught this little girl," she rubbed the top of Journey's head, "rummaging like a raccoon through my refrigerator."

The dark eyes fixed on her again. "What are your plans for them?"

"Well, I'm not turning them over to the state, if that's what you mean." She blew the hair out of her eyes. "I don't have it all figured out yet, but I'm willing to keep them until we can locate one of the parents, or grandparents. Then, we'll see." She looked out the window, still feeling his penetrating eyes on her.

They drove the rest of the way in silence. The motion of the truck rocked Abe's head as he leaned it against the headrest. Journey was silent too. Leta reached over, giving Journey's small hand a reassuring squeeze. "He's going to be all right. Don't worry."

***

Nearly two hours passed before a llama-faced orderly opened the double doors of the emergency room and pushed the stretcher bearing Abe to the elevator. "I'm taking him to the fourth floor." A red light flashed, then a ding sounded as the elevator door slid open. "Give us some time to get him settled before you come up." He motioned with his combed-over alpaca head toward a cubicle. "That's the desk where you'll need to sign him in. Oh, and here." He tossed a plastic bag to Tru. "The boy's clothes."

As the elevator door closed, Leta turned to Tru. "Do you think he'll be okay?" She snatched her purse from the floor. "Did he say what was wrong?"

"We'll know soon enough," Tru said. "At this point, we can only pray." He pulled out his phone and checked his messages. "Getting hungry?" He looked up and saw his answer in Journey's eyes. His cell phone rang, and he excused himself for a moment, walking off down the hall. Thirty minutes later he returned with a brown bag and a cardboard cup holder carrying drinks. He placed them on a table in the waiting room. "Hope you like turkey sandwiches and plain chips." He pulled three Goo

Goo Cluster candy bars out of the bag and held them up. "And the piece de resistance. I can't believe they have them here. They're usually pretty hard to find."

"I see you're a man who knows his chocolate." She walked over to the table and began separating the food. "Better not risk those peanuts, though. I have no idea what she's allergic too."

"Good point. We're kinda flying blind here, aren't we? Coffee?" he offered, handing her a steaming cup of French roast. "It's actually pretty good—for hospital coffee."

Leta inhaled its fragrance, closed her eyes, and smiled before turning her attention back to Tru. "How long before we know something? I'm in new territory here." She took a sip of coffee then glanced over her shoulder toward the desk. "All I know about the boy is his name and I think he's about twelve. She turned to look at him again, her eyes wide in fear. "What if he's allergic to some medication? What are they going to say when I tell them I don't know anything about his medical history?"

"I have someone on it," he said, his voice softening a little. "I'll handle the paperwork. Someone's coming from the church with clothes and some other things for Abe...I checked his sizes before I threw out his clothes. Nothing worth saving," Tru explained. "The smell alone made me think twice about burning them."

To Leta's immense relief, a smile tugged at the corners of his eyes. This was a new experience for her; a man who knew how to take care of business. Rod Purviance had always allowed Leta to make decisions for herself—telling her all the while that he was building self-reliance in his only daughter. Some part of her believed that her father just didn't want to bother with her, especially when he was busy gambling with someone else's money.

Leta drew a deep breath and exhaled slowly, enjoying the sense that she was not alone in this. "Will you ride with us up to the fourth floor?"

"Of course. I'm not going anywhere. Not until I know the boy is going to be okay."

***

"Severe dehydration," came a bird-like voice from somewhere near the hospital room door. "Once we get the IV fluids into him, he'll bounce back to health in no time."

Leta slid Journey off her lap and leaned forward in the vinyl chair to meet the voice. She saw a tiny woman with feathered gray hair. Most of her face was obscured by eyeglasses, which perched on the end of her beak like nose.

"I'm Doctor Gregan. Are you the parents of this boy?" the little woman asked, her dancing and magnified blue eyes darting back and forth between Leta and Tru.

Tru had been leaning against the window ledge but stood to his full height. He extended his hand. "I'm Tru Ransome and this," he gestured toward the chair, "is Leta Purviance, the temporary guardian of Abe Littleton and his little sister, Journey."

"Well, I can certainly see the *need* of that…given the circumstances." She crooked a finger, calling Leta to step out into the hallway. "May I speak with you a moment?"

"Of course." Leta got up and followed the doctor into the hall.

"We're doing all that is necessary for the boy

physically, but there seems to be some underlying issues here. I get the sense that Abe may be suffering emotionally. Keep an eye on him and if you don't see a marked change in his mood, behavior, I'd like to see him in a week or so."

"Whatever you think is necessary, doctor." She was surprised to see the wide smile that infused the older woman's face.

"I was hoping you'd say that. How long have you had Abe in your custody?"

"First day."

Doctor Gregan's twinkling blue eyes winked. "You have my prayers."

As the doctor walked away, Leta clutched her arms to herself, willing her body to stop quivering. When Tru's firm hand clasped her shoulder, she swallowed hard against the tightness in her throat. The gesture seemed to impart some strength to her soul, and she began to feel an infusion of hope. Embarrassed to have her fears displayed so openly, she tried to lighten the mood. "Does everyone in this hospital resemble some sort of wildlife…or is it just me?"

Tru squeezed her shoulder before releasing it. "It's just you."

Chapter 9

The kitchen window was open, and the scent of privet hedge floated through the screen along with the nightly sounds of crickets and croaking frogs singing their evening benediction. Reaching into the sudsy dish water, Leta pulled the stopper, wiped her hands on a dishtowel, then reached for her glass. She took a long cool sip of ginger ale, comfortable with the silence in the room in the absence of Journey's continuous chatter. With Abe's presence in the house, the little girl had found her voice, acting like a cast-off doll with fresh batteries. Bedtime had brought with it a much needed reprieve.

Masculine laughter drifted across the yard from beyond the woods which separated Stone House from Ransome Land. They were familiar sounds. Since Tru had opened-up the camp, she had learned to recognize the men by their voices rather than by sight, like the hidden creatures in the trees and underbrush. "On a night like this," she whispered to herself, "I'd like to be right out there with them."

She shook the remaining suds from her hands and wiped them on a dish towel, listening intently to the low conversations in the night. She'd grown used to the sound of Tru's voice and his deep resonating laughter.

She could pick it out of a crowd. The men seemed to be settling in for a long discussion. With her glass in hand, she moved across the room, bumped the back-screen door with her hip, and crossed the porch to Ma Mae's old wicker chair. She settled into the comfortable hollow, swirling the melting ice in her glass, surrounded by the pulsating life of the low country. After the sun set, the night sounds always seemed to settle her soul. But this evening, something was off. A restlessness took hold of Leta, and she struggled to calm herself.

The children had been in bed for about an hour or so, and she felt no compulsion to go there herself, even as bone tired as her body felt. Getting used to having two children to care for was taking a while. But after Abe had been released from the hospital, Leta had established a routine, one Ma Mae had established with her years before at Stone House.

The children seemed to thrive within the structure, but reestablishing school habits had been another matter entirely. With less than two weeks left of the school year, Leta was determined to catch them up on their work to prevent them from repeating the grade. With the help of a sympathetic school principal, Leta had done just that.

The evening wind, light as featherdown, blew across Leta's face as she rocked rhythmically in her grandmother's creaky chair. Upstream, she could see the pale lights from Ransome Land reflected in the creek like watery stars. The last of the brief twilight had faded, and Leta was alone with her thoughts. "Blue twilight," she whispered, remembering what her grandfather Patrick had called it. This melancholy time of the evening was both a relief and a sadness. Her grandfather, whom she had called Pop, told her that it was normal to feel blue once the light faded. Then, she'd watch with keen interest as Pop would pull out an old wooden shoe polish box and place his boots next to his easy chair. There, he would sit down with an old towel across his lap and polish them. He liked to watch old westerns while he rhythmically brushed and buffed his boots. The warm smell of shoe polish and leather had a way of lingering in the room hours after he'd left it. On occasion, Leta thought she could still catch a whiff of the scent on the air. She rested her head against the back of the rocker, lost in thoughts of her childhood and the people who had loved and cared for her.

In the growing darkness, out from the trees, a shadow began to take form, moving by degrees into the dim light. Leta eased out of the chair and, without taking her eyes off the phantom, began to slowly make her way toward the screen door.

"Leta!" Tru called out from across the yard. "Is Abe still awake?"

A breath of pure relief passed silently between Leta's lips. "No, he's asleep. Why?"

"I tried to call." He ducked under a trellis of fragrant wisteria. "We're having a campfire cookout for some of the men and their boys...thought Abe might want to come along. But if he's asleep..."

The screen door banged open and slapped shut as Abe rushed through the door. "I'm awake! Can I go with Mr. Ransome? Please!" His eyes pleaded with Leta as his body twitched with excitement. Light from the doorway spilled out onto the porch, highlighting the nose peeling, boyish face wearing a crooked grin. He seemed anything but depressed.

"Not barefooted—go get your shoes," Leta said, "and

don't slam the door; your sister is asleep."

Abe scrambled toward the door, then stopped and gently opened and closed the screen door, before tearing off toward his room.

Plopping down in her rocker, she shook her head. "That boy. Can you tell he's feeling better?"

Tru braced his hands on the wrought-iron gate that separated the garden from the swath of grass encircling the house. He stared at the flagstone path leading to the porch several long moments before he stepped closer. He cleared his throat. "Anything I should be aware of— where the boy's concerned, I mean. I'm not that experienced with kids."

Even in the dim light she could see a shadow of a smile playing across his lips. "He's a bit clumsy, unsure on his feet. But I think he'll grow into them, eventually."

"Clumsy? How?"

"He stumbles a lot. Fell on the rocks down by the old ice plant when he was six—he told me. His grin is a little bit crooked because of it and his face marked from the cut. But, if you can look past all that, the true value lies within that child." She smiled and rocked back in her seat. "He's a good boy."

The more Tru listened, the more he needed to hear. All at once he found himself standing on the porch steps, leaning against the railing, waiting for the woman, whose voice was like a vanishing wisp, to speak again. He was certain now that the decision to grant Leta Purviance temporary custody of the Littleton children had been a right one. He had his friend J.D., and his many connections, to thank for it. It was clear that the children in this woman's care were loved and well cared for. She was born years before her time, or so it seemed to Tru on that night. He had to admit, if only to himself, that Leta Purviance was a rare and perplexing woman.

The evening mists began to rise from the creek, and a cool dampness worked its way up the path. Leta asked, "Do you think he'll need a jacket?"

"It's a little cool." He glanced sideways at her. "It'll be all right. The fire is nice and warm."

"Abe will enjoy it. It's nice of you to ask him." She looked at her hands. "You'll make a good father one day."

Tru stared at her, totally caught off guard by the comment. He was not quite sure how to accept the compliment. "What makes you say that?"

She shrugged. "I just know."

"Well, I'm not in any hurry to find out," he said, dryly.

She realized with embarrassment that she had spoken too freely. She had been doing too much sitting and thinking lately. It was high time she got up off her rear-end and got started on plans for her flower farm. There was much work and research to be done and the fields were there, waiting. She got up. "I'll see what's keeping him."

Chapter 10

The days grew warmer into June and the land around Stone House grew lush, erupting in vibrant color under the cultivating hand of Leta. In a few short months, she had turned an enthusiasm for digging in the dirt into a thriving flower market that served the people of Quay and the surrounding areas.

The career path had been intentional, but the quick outcome had been a complete surprise. The venture began as she uncovered, unearthed, and untangled a virtual treasure trove of flowers on the property, both wild and domestic. She then began separating, sorting, and arranging them in the galvanized buckets that she'd discovered in the potting shed. She'd filled two large wheelbarrows with flower buckets, made a sign that simply said, *Flowers for Sale* and pushed them to the road outside the gate. The unexpected success of her business provided a boost to her dwindling finances and allowed her some breathing room until her first crop.

Without a formal vision for her market, Leta planted vegetables in a small kitchen garden along with flowers and supplemented her inventory by buying, at a discount, fresh seasonal produce from a trusted local farmer. Strawberries and peaches, tomatoes and peppers, even honey. Pretty soon she had a somewhat profitable business on the side of the road three days a week with regular customers and grateful people who began to spread the word around the community.

Midmorning found Leta in the garden. Every shovelful of dirt felt heavy and difficult as she looked down the long open field of grass. She pulled at her dampened shirt, catching a breeze to cool off from the heat. "At this rate," she said out loud, "I'll be pushing up daisies long before I drop the first flower crop."

She knew Tru Ransome had a tractor and a tiller, still she couldn't bring herself to ask the man for help. Her cousin, Edwina, had been spending more of her time at Ransome Land lately, and that was the last person she ever wanted to encounter. So she decided to save her money and rent a tiller as soon as her funds would allow.

***

A sharp heavy rap of a fist upon the door pulled Tru Ransome from his cell phone. "Someone is at the door. I'll call you later and firm up plans for the weekend." With that, he slid the phone into his back pocket and reached for the door. Giving it a yank, he opened to find Mumford and the boy, Abe, standing stock still in front of him.

Mumford paused a moment and grew uneasy.

"Well?" Tru demanded.

"Caught the boy stealing your tractor," Mumford said. He spit a wad of tobacco juice on the ground. "There's some rope up in the shed. Best keep him tied up there, don't want the others getting at him when they found out what he's done." He said the words calmly enough, but his eyes darted to the Abe.

71

Tru stood still. Nothing but his dark eyes moved as he considered the boy. "Stealing my tractor?"

Abe took a gulp of air before swallowing hard.

"I'm not going to beat you, boy," Tru said. "At least not yet." His whiskered cheek flexed in irritation. "What were your plans for my tractor?"

Abe swiped his sunburned nose along his sleeve, then sniffled. The words burst out in a flood as he explained the situation in an anxious rush. "You see, Miss Leta's been working herself to death with a shovel on them fields. I was just gonna borrow your tractor to help her 'cause I know all about tractors from my papaw. He's got a pecan grove. Before he got old and sick, he used to let me drive it. Anyway, I ain't never seen her so put out and tired, Miss Leta, I mean…thought if we had a tractor, we'd have time to make the first plantin'. That's all she wants—to make the first plantin'. I was gonna bring it back, directly. Honest."

"Slow down, boy," Tru said with his hands stretched in front of him. "I'd like to get this all straight. Did Leta send you here to get the tractor?"

"Naw—I decided to do it myself. She's over there now just hittin' that hard ground with a shovel." His voice began to pick up speed again as he watched the man's dark eyes squint in suspicion. "That's all I was doin', tryin' to help her out. And your tractor was just sittin' there by the tree, doin' nothin'."

Something in the boy's tone struck Tru, and instead of questioning him more, he narrowed his eyes and thought about his words. The conversation he'd had with Royce Purviance came back to him in an instant. He shook his head, berating himself for forgetting. He had had every intention of helping Leta with her fields, but in his single-minded pursuit in getting Ransome Land up and running, he'd let it slip his mind. "Mumford! Have the boy work off the offense. He can start by mowing the grass around the old store. Turn him loose at quitting time, but make sure he comes back tomorrow. No sense getting the law involved, *this time*."

"Will do," Mumford replied, turning to Abe. "And don't you worry none, son." He led the boy off the porch by the shoulders. "I got my snake bite kit handy if'n you should need it. Did you know they used to call this here piece of land copperhead row?" He slapped Abe on the back as they walked down the steps.

***

Leta had succeeded, to a small degree, to dig a somewhat straight row through a tangle of Queen Ann's Lace. A large bucket sat near the furrow, loaded down with the lacey flower. She had just cut a handful of the long-stemmed flowers when a shadow fell across her path and she looked up to see Tru. She dropped the flowers into the bucket and straightened, wiping the dirt from her hands.

"Hey," she said, smiling as she shielded her eyes from the sun. Leta caught the uneasy, almost unnoticeable hesitancy. "Is everything okay?"

"I owe you an apology," Tru said.

"An apology? To me? For what?" She blew the hair out of her eyes and swiped a hand across her brow.

He ran a hand behind his neck, kneading the tense muscles there. "For not being a very good neighbor."

"I don't understand." The topaz eyes sparkled in the light as she searched his face for meaning.

"I've been so distracted with my own work; I wasn't

paying attention. I have a good tractor just sitting there. It won't take long to get this field plowed for you. You'll be ready for planting in no time."

Leta shook her head. "Oh no, I—"

He held up his hand to halt the answer. "I insist."

Her eyes narrowed and grew a shade darker. "I appreciate the offer, but no thank you. I can't afford to pay you. Besides, you have your hands full with your own project. I can manage."

Tru's mind was working quickly underneath his calm exterior. "Well, I was hoping to do a little trading."

"What kind of trading do you have in mind?" Her manner changed from one of mild interest to strong suspicion. She crossed her arms as she waited for his answer.

"I've been considering the possibility of hiring someone to mow and weed around the structures on my property. Thought Abe might like a summer job. I would pay him a fair wage *and* plow your field." He ran his fingers under his chin. "Might do the boy some good. Teach him some responsibility."

A spark of hope ran through her, and she had to wait a moment so as not to seem too eager. Abe had troubled her. She knew the importance of a man's influence on a growing boy. Glancing up to the porch, she saw Journey quietly playing with her old rag doll she'd found in the attic. She scanned the area briefly, looking for Abe.

"Are you sure you know what you're taking on?" she said, the low, velvet soft voice nearly sent shivers down his spine. Even perspiring, she seemed to give off a fresh scent, like chilled carnations.

"Of course. I know better than most the importance of early direction, since I severely lacked it." The corners of his mouth lifted briefly.

"I bet your father had his hands full with you."

"No, but my mother sure did. My dad died when I was young."

"Oh, I'm sorry to hear that." Leta smiled and extended her hand. "It's a deal, then." She looked around. "That is…if I can find that boy."

Chapter 11

The town of Quay had been relatively active in recent months, but in the drowsy heat of summer, few had the desire to wander the glaring sidewalks or dally too long in the hot sun. So, the seaside shops and narrow houses, decked in colorful blues, greens, and corals, huddled close against each other, offering shade to the few who ventured outside their air-conditioned sanctuaries.

Well cared for gardens were visible in courtyards and behind intricately crafted wrought iron gates as Leta drove through town. With the windows lowered to keep the air circulating, not wishing for a single flower to wilt in the heat, the heady scent of magnolia blooms mixed their fragrance with the briny air. It whipped through Leta's hair as she neared the wharf. Before turning into the lot of the open-air market, she stopped a moment and glanced up at the church steeple. Quay Community Church had always seemed to her like a beacon of hope, perched atop the small rise...even when the sea was wild and came leaping up to smash against the rocks of the seawall, the church stood firm, unwavering and secure.

Life at the market seemed to go on as usual, slowing in the heat of the day. She had heard about the market from a customer. And, as her inventory increased, quickly decided to move her business from the roadside to a place where she could meet the rush of tourists and the influx of summer travelers.

Flowers and vegetables had sold well all throughout the day and were liberally disbursed to be enjoyed by all. It had been what Leta had always dreamed of, but now the edge was gone from the achievement. Something felt hollow, missing.

The wind churned up the threat of a storm, turning the calm sea choppy with whitecaps. Darkness invaded, overtaking the sun as streaks of lightning splintered the sky farther out at sea. Leta chewed her lip, watching as the storm gathered steam over the water. Then, a bone-jarring clap of thunder pierced the air, sending vendors scurrying for shelter.

"I'm scared," Journey cried. "Can we go back home?"

Home Leta let the word settle over her like a blanket. "We sure can, sweet girl. We sure can." She packed up everything as quickly as possible, turned the SUV around, and headed toward home.

***

Bracing his hands on the porch railing, Tru leaned outward, staring into the rain as he watched an SUV navigate the mud runnels and potholes of the drenched road. Pulling up close to the porch, the window lowered on the passenger side of the vehicle as Leta shouted over the noise of the rain.

"Looks like the storm chased you home too." The rain was now a steady drumbeat on the roof of the vehicle.

"It did—but not before it soaked me to the bone!" Tru glanced around. "Guess you're looking for Abe?" He waved his thumb toward the door. "He's inside. Come in. Coffee's on!"

"Sounds good!" Leta raised the window and reached behind her to unfasten Journey's seat belt. "Are you ready to make a run for it?"

Journey nodded eagerly, a grin spreading wide on her face. She leapt to the front seat and waited for the door to open.

"Here we go!" They dashed from the SUV and hurried up the steps. Leta brushed the water from Journey's slick arms and smoothed back her hair. "This rain is a soaker."

Tru reached for the door. "At least with the rain, the ravenous mosquito attacks have dwindled. They've been bad today. I sent Abe inside to clean out one of the upstairs rooms just to get him away from them." He twisted the doorknob, giving it a firm push. "Got his work cut out for him. That last tenant must've been a hoarder. I've never seen so much junk. There must be hundreds of canning jars up there and all kinds of useless stuff." Though a hint of humor showed about his dark eyes, there was a trace of sternness about them too. "Know anybody that can use a bunch of junk?" He moved behind the front counter and began pulling out cups for coffee.

She cocked her head thoughtfully as she considered his offer. "What will you take for them?"

"What, the canning jars? You can have them." Tru propped an elbow on the counter and raised a brow, unable to resist the question. "You collect old canning jars too?"

"They make great vases for my flowers. The blue colored jars are my favorite." Leta ran her fingers through Journey's damp hair and spoke in a teasing tone. "Guess it didn't take much for us to pull up stakes and run for home, did it Journey. We were kind of looking for an excuse not to work today."

Tru watched her closely as he rolled up one of his drawings and tapped it into the cylinder, clearing the bar. "Why is that?"

She shrugged and changed the subject. "This place has potential." She ran her hand across the smooth time-worn wood.

Journey pulled on her arm. "Can I go help Abe?"

Tru slid a bar stool back for Leta and answered Journey. "Sure thing…just be careful where you step. I wouldn't want you to get hurt." He turned to Leta. "Now, how do you take your coffee?"

"With cream." She took a seat and waited, listening to the sound of Journey's steps until both voices were heard upstairs.

"You seem to enjoy being home again," he half questioned, almost hesitantly.

"I do," Leta assured him. "A little too much, I'm afraid."

"How's that?" He stirred a dollop of cream into her coffee and slid it toward her.

She shook her head. "It doesn't make sense."

"Try me."

"Okay," she said, slipping into a deep drawl. "What kind of a person would be less than thrilled with a thriving business. A business that practically fell in their lap." She tucked a stray hair behind her ear. "I was given land that is covered up in flowers. I cut them and sort them and sell them—period. Now, I can hardly make myself leave home. All I want to do is stay out here and

79

work in my fields and never leave. Not even to make money that I certainly need."

Tru took a swig of his coffee and swallowed it down. "I know what you mean. There's something about the air out here that seems to change us all. One of my Native American friends told me that the land out here is covered with some sort of sleeping plant. Says it's supposed to have a calming effect on people." He met her attentive eyes and gave a lazy smile. "It seems to be working."

"Well, that explains all the naps I've been taking lately." Her soft laughter filled the room. "I thought I was getting lazy. Now I know it's just a result of the drugs I'm breathing in."

Tru looked up from his cup and remarked dryly, "I'm sure having two kids has nothing at all to do with it."

The sound of footsteps on the porch boards drew Tru's attention to the door. It came open with a gust of wind and rain as the startled eyes of Edwina fell on them.

"Hey, Edwina! What a nice surprise!" The coffee cup banged on the counter and Tru crossed the room to greet her. He took her umbrella and helped remove her raincoat, placing it across the back of a chair. "Want some coffee? We were just having a cup."

Leta's nerves stretched taut with tension as Edwina entered the room. Sharply aware of her own damp and haggard appearance, she folded her arms over her shirt and smiled at her cousin as she approached the bar. The woman was the epitome of cool and collected and dressed the part for every occasion, even a pop-up thunderstorm.

Smiling, Edwina attached herself to Tru's arm and allowed herself to be led to the stool next to Leta's. "No coffee for me. I just finished a water."

"You two girls catch up while I go check on the kids. They seem too quiet for my peace of mind." He winked. "I know from my own personal experience what that can mean."

As Tru disappeared up the stairs, Edwina straightened and turned her frosty stare on Leta. "Well, you certainly waste no time going after what you want, I'll give you that." Her voice had an undisguised sneer in it. "You fooled Grand Bess, and now you've set your trap for Tru. But it won't work—not with me. I'm not a senile old woman. I know your little games." She tossed her keys carelessly on the counter. Her face hardened, and there was pure hatred in her low voice. "Now, get out." She pointed a perfectly polished fingernail toward the door. "Get out before I embarrass you and those filthy little beggars you think are your children."

Leta shrugged unfazed at the stern lecture. Edwina's breath smelled like strong Altoid peppermints, and the scent burned her nose. Holding on to her coffee cup, she slid off the bar stool and went to the foot of the stairs. "Hey kids, come on down. We're going home."

"Home?" Edwina laughed. "That's not your home and those aren't your children. A home needs a family, and yours is made up of bits and pieces nobody else wants."

Leta's survival instincts kicked in and her need to fight for everything she valued came rushing to the surface. She took a deep, steadying breath. *Your cousin is not a target; your cousin is not a target.*

The century-old floorboards creaked beneath their feet as Abe and Journey came down the stairs with Tru following closely behind. "Why are you leaving so soon?" Tru said, looking confused.

"We've got to get back." She patted the top of Journey's head. "Thanks for the coffee." She handed Tru her cup, grateful to release the temptation to fling the thing across the room at Edwina.

He gave her a faint frown and opened his mouth to object, but Edwina interrupted. "Oh Tru, let them go. Can't you see they need to get home? I mean look at them, they're wet and filthy. Don't embarrass them anymore by insisting they stay."

"They look fine to me." Tru warmly made the comment. "That's the joy of childhood, to not be concerned about keeping up appearances."

"I'm not just talking about the children," Edwina stated flatly, then smiled.

He paused for a moment, leaning on the banister. "I'll have Abe load up those jars for you tomorrow when this rain clears out. Want them in the garden shed?"

"That'll work." Eager to get away, she hurried the children to the door.

"Might even take him fishing afterwards, if it's okay with you."

Abe wheeled around to face Leta with a hopeful expression. "Can I go fishing? Please?"

Listening to the exchange, Edwina raised a delicate eyebrow.

"You heard Mr. Ransome," Leta said. "Finish the job and I don't see why not. But for now, we need to get home." Opening the door, she turned around and found Edwina glaring at her. Each woman stared at the other with something less than delight. Leta forced a smile. "Bye Ed. And, if you ask me, I think you need more fiber in your diet…might help your disposition."

A quick and deep laugh spilled out through the open door behind Leta, causing her to glance over her shoulder. Tru covered his grin by scratching the stubble at the side of his jaw.

As soon as they were in the SUV, Leta let out a ragged breath, trying hard to control her temper and hold her tongue at the same time. There was something about having your children insulted that made all your protective instincts come alive. "Come on, kids. Let's go make dinner."

***

Now that Edwina knew Leta was stopping by to see Tru, she tried her best to visit him more often, just to make sure her cousin was nowhere around. She made it a point to drop spiteful hints and insinuations of Leta's conduct in the past. Retelling stories she'd heard about the life Rod and Leta had shared after the passing of Leta's grandparents. Actively hoping to sway Tru's respect for Leta, she told a string of half-truths and bold-faced lies she'd fabricated about how the pair had lived like gypsies, roaming from one town to another, stealing, cheating, and running around with disreputable people.

The relentless attacks on Leta's character continued. By week three, Tru had come to the definite conclusion that he had had enough of this constant assault on his neighbor's character.

"Have you ever considered praying for your cousin?" Tru questioned Edwina abruptly one evening. "If she's as bad as all that, maybe you should take her under your wing and—"

"And what!" Edwina glared at him. "I want this understood here and now. You will not see that tramp again, not here, not there, not anywhere! Do I make

83

myself clear?"

"Woman," he said, with the icy control of a gambler, "if you ever speak to me like that again, it'll be the last conversation we have. Do I make *myself* clear?"

She halted abruptly, realizing her mistake. Quickly, she tried to force tears to her eyes, pretending to be distraught. "Oh Tru, sweetheart, I'm so sorry. I don't know what has gotten into me." Her face burned crimson as she realized her vengeful act had backfired. "I guess I just care too much about you and those poor children—I mean when I think about how you're all being hoodooed by her, it just makes me so angry. I'm desperate for you to see her true colors!"

He set a chilly stare on the woman.

"But I understand what's expected of me. To whom much is given, much is required." Edwina struggled between her desire to see her cousin's reputation destroyed and a knowledge of the foolishness of seeming to be anything less than the kindhearted soul Tru thought she was.

Chapter 12

Sometimes the simplest actions in life can start a string of events which can cause a total shifting of our purpose and direction.

The wide, flat creek lapped with laziness against the sandy bank while a jon boat ponderously navigated a channel through new and freshly green marsh grass. Seabirds squawked overhead while the chant of morning cicadas rose from the maritime forest.

A blue haze hovered close to the surface of the water as the vessel slipped through the mist. The boat, once bright red, now faded and chipped, glided closer until it gently nudged against the warped dock.

A woman, old and bent with years, gathered her apron in her hand and held the dock post with the other. In one slow motion, she hoisted herself onto the pier. Bending over, she tied off the craft and eased up to straighten her body. Halfway down the uneven planks she stopped, patting her apron pocket before pulling a battered straw hat down to fit snug over her ears. The washed-out apron emphasized the smallness of her frame as the ties wrapped around and hung exhausted and limp from her thin waist. She wore a loose cotton shirt with sleeves rolled back to her rusty brown elbows.

Though it was still early in the dew-soaked morning, there was already a presence in the garden. The old woman smiled, as if knowing the importance of seeing about a garden at first light.

Leta Purviance was lost in her thoughts as she plopped down on a weathered bench in the garden, examining the stem in her hand. "Those kids are nobody's cast-offs," she said to herself and swallowed hard, knowing deep down that this would come. Ever since she'd arrived at Stone House, she'd been fooling herself. Nothing had changed. Her father had tried to warn her, but she hadn't listened. Lately it had seemed to Leta that even Grand Bess was dismissing her. Maybe she had only wanted her estranged granddaughter here as a kind of sport, a diversion from the mundane life of being a Purviance. Several times Leta had tried to see her grandmother, but each time she had been turned away. Even her phone calls had been ignored.

The sudden flight of a pair of mourning doves convinced her that someone was approaching. She heard a faint low hum on the air, the familiar sound she'd known since childhood. A cold shiver ran up her spine before she caught sight of an elderly woman making her way up the path from the creek. She was tawny in color. Her dark hair was frosted over with gray. As she came closer, Leta could see her face clearly. It was deeply lined and ancient, yet there was a spark of life in the soft brown eyes that age could not touch.

Leta stood, wet her parched lips with the tip of her tongue, and reached for her hoe as she waited for the woman, who was slow and unsteady on her feet. "Good morning," Leta called, her voice a little stronger, assuming the woman was hard of hearing.

The woman took her eyes off the path and looked up at Leta. "Mornin'."

Extending a hand, Leta helped the older woman up the small rise, then the woman leaned against the stone wall and fanned herself with her apron. "Lord 'ave mercy!"

"Here," Leta indicated the bench, "Sit down. Can I get you something to drink? Water? Juice?" Concern creased her brow.

"No, child, just let me catch my breath," she said, leaning back into the cool stones. She patted the low fence. "Mighty grateful for that Scotsman for hauling these stones in here. Came all the way over from Winnsboro, they say. Crushed up seashells make a nice lime chalk. Mix in a little sand and you got a fine mortar." Drawing a deep breath, her face grimaced. "Make sure to crush up the shells or they will scratch the fire outta you.

Leta's face mirrored her expression. She turned toward the dock and saw a jon boat bobbing on the surface of the creek. "Are you lost? It wouldn't be the first time someone got turned around in the maze of marsh grass." It looked like the sun had baked her. Leta sat down and was patiently silent as the woman shook her head.

"I've been tending this garden off and on for a while now." The woman's laugh was a high-pitched hoot, then it took on a more somber note. "I heard tell the folks here passed awhile back." She fanned the apron a few more times. "Can't abide to see a good garden go to seed."

The woman seemed to be more concerned about keeping up the order of the garden than the importance of not trespassing on land belonging to others; land that could be seen from the creek when she passed. Leta peered at her thoughtfully, wondering just what to believe about her mysterious guest. "Well, the mystery is solved then."

The brown eyes grew alarmed. "Maybe I shouldn't have, child. Just can't abide the abandonment of anything. Has a way of takin' the sweet innocence and beauty from God's plan."

"Oh no, I'm grateful! You just might have saved my life. You see, I've been harvesting the crops you've planted and selling them at market. I've been profiting from all of your hard work!"

The old woman bent over and let out a hoot, holding a hand over her heart. Straightening, she said, "What you got in your hand right there is lavender. 'Course, you generally harvest the buds right now when they're gray, before they burst open and flower on the stem." The woman puckered her lips. "Keeps the fullest fragrance that way. On hot mornings like this, if you drop them stems into buckets of cool water, you'll keep them from giving off their fragrance into the air and wasting it." She indicated the shed with a gnarled finger. "I've got plenty of buckets in there too." She pulled her head back and squinted her eyes. "What name may I attach to you?"

"Leta Purviance, ma'am. Maybe you know some of my family?"

"Leta," she stressed the name warmly while she looked her over a long moment. "I do." Without further comment she turned her attention to the garden. "Just seemed like a waste of a good garden to me. To see it sittin' here not used for its purpose. We all got a purpose, child. Don't never forget that."

"That's a matter of opinion," Leta said, brushing off

bits and pieces of leaves and stems from her jeans. She smiled slightly, taking the bite from her words. "What's your name?"

"August. The rest don't matter. You can just call me Gussie."

"Well, Miss Gussie, I think I owe you…since you've done all the work in this garden. All I've done is harvest what you planted." Leta faced her, wide-eyed gratefulness etched in every feature.

"Nonsense, child. Some plant, others water, and there are those who get to harvest." Gussie placed cool fingers against her throat and patted. "Just the way the good Lord intended. 'Sides, I get me a whole lotta joy puttering around this here garden. Can't put a price on that." Her thoughts were like a book being opened wide as she considered Leta. Keeping her eyes fixed on the girl, she dug around in her apron pocket, pulled out a pipe, and cradled it in her hand as she struck a match, puffing it to life. Squinting, she shook out the flame. "I like the thought of helping you out of a tight spot."

"Well, you've certainly done that." Leta rubbed a lavender bud between her fingers and sniffed the clean fragrance.

"Let me pray over this here garden, child. The house, too, and you. You live here alone?"

"No, I have two children with me, Abe and Journey. For at least a little while, anyway. Until someone comes to take them away from me."

Gussie snatched the pipe out of her mouth. "They tryin' to take ya children?"

"They're not mine." The whisper was like a pained admission. "I'm taking care of them because their parents left them."

The old woman grabbed Leta's hand and squeezed it tightly. She drew a deep breath of briny air into her lungs and forced out a prayer. Never in all her life had Leta heard a woman pray like that, like she was personally acquainted with the Almighty. *That prayer could draw the ghost right out of you,* Leta thought.

When the prayer was over, a summer breeze moved through the field of zinnias like fingers playing down the keys of a piano. Leta's hair lifted in the light wind, and she wondered about the sense of peace that came over her.

Gussie gave a firm squeeze to Leta's hand before letting it go. "I best be getting back before it gets too hot." She tapped her pipe against the stone wall and stuck it back in her apron pocket. "I like to start the day slow then taper off after that."

"Will you come back?" Leta asked. "Teach me what you know? I'll pay you. If you're interested, I mean. I could sure use your help."

"You offerin' me a job?"

"I am."

She cackled, and her laugh was like the squawk of a heron. "Well now, the truth of it is, I was lookin' for an excuse to come back." She winked and nodded once. "I'll sure 'nough be here when I can." Gussie looked around. "What you doin' with all these flowers, anyway?"

Leta tucked a fly-away strand of hair behind her ear. "I've always wanted to grow for market. Zinnia's, sunflowers, peony's, larkspur, and of course, lavender." The corners of her mouth lifted. "I've been known to mix in a little Queen Anne's lace on occasion."

"Not a thing wrong with that. What kinda numbers we

talkin' 'bout?"

Leta lifted her shoulders. "Thirty thousand per acre or so. Cut flowers are one of the best cash crops for small growers. I'm starting small, growing for local outlets like farmer's markets, florists, and restaurants. But my dream is to have a flower truck of my own one day so I can go to the surrounding coastal areas and sell my flowers...maybe even go to a few of the larger cities."

Reaching into her apron pocket, she pulled out a penny. "Here, read it."

"One cent."

"Keep readin'."

"In God we trust?"

"Exactly. Now, you keep that penny as a reminder to put your trust in Him...He'll direct your path. Ole' Gussie, she knows what she's talkin' 'bout."

Leta caught her grin before it spread across her entire face. Holding up the penny she said, "I'll treasure it."

Chapter 13

The heat of the summer sun bore down on the crisp straw hat covering the head of Bess Purviance. She strode out of the gated entrance of Tremont and leaned weakly against the mellowed Cotswold stone wall. Honeysuckle wafted on the thick air, and she breathed it in, relishing the scent.

Patiently she waited, knowing what she must do. Though she was tired from the long walk down the lane, she could not stay cooped up in the house any longer waiting for Leta to decide to visit. So, she took matters into her own hands. She'd watched Leta's comings and goings enough to know her routine. If the pattern held, her granddaughter would be coming along any time now.

Bess removed her hat and began fanning herself, then burst out into carefree laughter. Her eyes were bright with anticipation. She hadn't had so much joy in years. As age began to creep up on Bess, she'd been afraid of being doomed to a dreary, monotonous end. The thought of dull dinners and droning conversations about shoes and plastic surgeons congealed her blood. But since Leta had arrived at Stone House, her blood had started to flow again.

Leta rounded the corner of the narrow shady lane and

spotted a woman, hat in hand, waving her down in front of the entrance to Tremont. She slowed, then came to a stop, recognizing her grandmother.

She lowered the passenger-side window and smiled. "Need a ride?" She could plainly see Grand Bess was not in distress. The excitement on her face was evidence enough.

"I sure do!"

Leta reached over and opened the door. "Hop in. Where to?"

"Home," she laughed. Looking over her shoulder, she saw Journey sleeping in the back seat, then crossed her lips with her finger and whispered, "I was waiting for you. If I hadn't flagged you down, it might have been weeks before I'd see you."

This was not the complete truth, for Bess Purviance had been able to see Leta and the progress of her flower farm from the second floor of the old caretakers' quarters near the road. It was the highest point on Purviance land and afforded a birds-eye view of the entire property all the way to the creek.

Leta chewed her lips in bewilderment. "I've come by and called you repeatedly. Each time I was told that you were not to be disturbed."

"What!" She caught herself and lowered her voice. "Who told you that?"

"Is his name…Milton?"

Bess's eyebrows rose sharply, then she shook her head, staring at the jewels on her winkled hand. "Well, that explains it."

"Explains what?"

"Explains why I haven't heard from you—why my calls to you were never put through."

93

Leta drove through the dappled sunlight filtering through the trees toward the house called Tremont. "Sounds like you might need to fire Milton." She turned toward her grandmother. "I was beginning to think that you just didn't want to talk to me."

"Do you honestly think I'd let you get away from me again without putting up a fight? Child, you have a lot to learn about your grandmother. Milton has always been under the spell of Edwina. He follows behind her like a pulled wooden duck on a string. He'd do anything she asked of him."

"Is that so…must be nice to have your own personal assistant." She gave her grandmother a slow smile.

"He came to work for us as a young teenager, about the same age as Edwina. He's been smitten with her ever since. She doesn't give him the time of day, unless she wants something from him. Truth be told, I think Edwina is jealous of *you*!"

"Of me? That's laughable." She glanced across the meadow as they drove by slowly. "So, this Milton—he's a butler?"

Bess shook her head. "No, no, an assistant to my husband. He handles pretty much everything we ask of him, including our finances."

As they pulled under the canopy of a huge spreading oak near the front steps, Grand Bess said, "Come sit on the veranda with me and let's talk some nonsense." She turned and saw that Journey's lips were parted slightly and were vibrating with each breath. "We'll leave the windows down so she can catch a nice breeze. She'll be all right here. We'll keep an eye on her from the porch."

Grand Bess seemed so small, so defenseless to Leta. Yet somehow, she knew that there was a core of steel underneath her velvet exterior. She lowered the windows, checked on Journey, then followed her grandmother up the steps to a line of white wooden rockers spaced in front of three floor-to-ceiling shuttered windows.

Bess observed her granddaughter as she took a seat in the rocker beside hers. Her outward appearance pleased the old woman no small degree. *A woman of substance*, Bess thought. The underlying person fascinated her. Leta had a gentle hand with children and flowers, and strength when the situation demanded it.

"You seem to be enjoying Stone House and being home again," Bess half questioned almost hesitantly. "Are you?"

"I really am," she assured her with a warm and grateful smile. "Thank you for a place to call my own."

Rocking back in the chair, Bess stared out onto the grounds. "I believe you and I are a lot alike. I value the simpler ways and the freedoms they bring much more than all the showy frills and trappings. Simple pleasures, things that cannot be bought, things that bring lasting joy. Yes, every day we wake up and jump into a river of blessings. Most folks don't even realize they're wet...but I think you do."

A breeze blew across the veranda, and Leta smiled. The brief glimpses into Bess's character and personality surprised Leta. She was finding her grandmother to be a very likeable and pleasant person. Pushing her fly-away hair out of her tawny eyes, she watched as a car came down the lane and pulled to a stop in front of them. Edwina, Louisa, and their mother, Althea, all stepped out of the shiniest silver metallic Mercedes Benz coupe Leta had ever seen. She swallowed hard, ill at ease among them: a workhorse among thoroughbreds.

Leta had never wanted to be like them, just accepted by them as a part of the family, a common part certainly, but a part, nonetheless. But the fact was, she was liked even less now that she'd been given her spot of Purviance earth...looked upon like a wart on an otherwise smooth complexion.

Althea came toward the house, fingering her pearls as she glanced up at Leta. Her sleeveless linen A-line dress creased across her lap. "Hello! Are we interrupting?"

"Not at all, I was just leaving." Leta stood, turned to Bess, and took her hand, squeezing it. "I enjoyed our talk. Next time, call me yourself." She winked at her before leaving. Althea brushed past her on the steps, her eyes fixed on Bess.

Leta was wasting no time in making her exit and was about to get into the SUV when someone grabbed her from behind. She spun around, recognizing Louisa, red-lipped and wide-eyed, her dark wild mane of hair tumbling over her shoulders.

"Lou!" Leta said, smiling. Leta had given her the nickname in childhood and it fit the girl. Lou had always pulsed with life, looking alive and animated.

"Leta Purviance you little sneak!" Lou said, her voice high and excited. "Why am I just finding out that you've moved back home?"

"I didn't think—"

"Oh, never mind, silly, just give me a big hug." Lou squeezed her waist. "You're here now, that's all that matters."

If Edwina was the meanest, Lou was the kindest. And sometimes so dense that light could bend around her. It was impossible to stay in a bad mood whenever Lou was around.

She spoke so fast that Leta could only watch as the red lips rattled off rapid-fire questions, then she would answer them in her very next breath. Leta loved Lou, and she knew her cousin's feet had always been planted firmly three feet off the ground. Still, she was a caring soul, and Leta would take that any day over a mean spirit.

While Lou was talking, Leta noticed Edwina walking toward the rear of the house. She entered the side door of her grandfather's study and disappeared inside. She wondered what the woman was up to. It was still a mystery why a man like Tru Ransome would ever choose someone like Edwina. Sure, she was beautiful, classy, and no doubt wealthy—Leta heard Lou clearing her throat. She turned and found the wide, childlike, green eyes watching her. "I'm sorry, Lou, what were you saying?"

"I was saying that you really must visit me in Charleston. Daddy has the most wonderful little house on Lowndes Street. It just sits there empty most of the time. He uses it to entertain clients. We could have so much fun—I really shouldn't say that too loudly." She looked around and laughed to cover her embarrassment. "It might get back to Mother and I wouldn't want to hurt her feelings. I'm sure you know all about my daddy and what a fine businessman he is. Truth is, he said he'd rather have me there to help entertain his clients rather than Mother. She's not much of a conversationalist, according to Daddy. But he says I never meet a stranger. Wouldn't he just love it if you were to join me? He'd have two hostesses!"

Leta opened her mouth to correct her, but Lou continued with her chatter.

"While I'm here, I'm going to post myself inside the lobby of the hospital and *make* J.D. notice me," Lou said, flipping her glossy raven hair over her shoulder. "I tried asking for counsel just so I could speak with him, but he won't see me without that old busybody, Mrs. McCree, lurking in the shadows of his stuffy old office."

Leta looked at her wonderingly. "J.D. Redman? The pastor?"

"You know him?" For a moment Lou stood stunned. Almost hesitantly she asked, "You're not interested in him, are you?"

"What? No!" She saw that her words had ignited a spark of hope in Lou's eyes. "Are you?"

"Oh, yes! Yes!" She laughed and smiled so wide her pink gums showed.

Lou's exuberant face reminded Leta of the time her cousin had been left on the Tilt-A-Whirl too long. "From what I've heard of J.D., he would never avoid you on purpose. They say he's a really nice man." Leta's curiosity was aroused. "Does he know you're interested in him?"

Lou nodded. "He knows. But he thinks he's too old for me. He's firm in that belief. Said I needed a young man with a lot of energy. But," her green eyes smiled at Leta with mischief as her slender shoulder lifted in a brief shrug, "we'll see." She swung around and hurried off, leaving Leta staring for one dazed moment at her cousin's back.

***

Royce Purviance leaned back into his chair and made his fingers into a tent. "I don't see the problem here, Edwina. The girl doesn't bother anyone, stays to herself, minds her own flower farm business. What's the issue?"

98

"What's the issue? Try property value for one thing! She collects strays and riffraff and hauls them all home! One day, mark my word, we'll have to put up with the worst sort of people all hanging around out here on our land. We'll have to pass through a tent village of homeless shelters just to get home. Something must be done about it. That girl has no discernment. She's got those two kids—Flat Squirrel's kids! How do you like that for a name?"

Royce cleared his throat. "It's not my doing that she is here on Purviance land. You know very well that she's here because of your grandmother."

"Yes, but one day I'll have to deal with the consequences of your choice in allowing it."

"Yes," Royce replied. "It was a choice I had to make. You are my pride, Edwina, and Louisa, my joy, but you see, I have this overriding weakness—Bess. I cannot deny my Bess anything. If you want a change, then you'll have to appeal to her. The deed is done. My advice to you is to accept it and move on."

Edwina smiled stiffly. "You leave me no other choice. I'll have to handle this my way."

Leisurely Royce lifted his cup in a mock salute. "You always do, my dear, you always do."

Chapter 14

A melon pink sky deepened and began its gradual fade in the west while the rising hum of Katydid's filled the thick air. Coming from the flower fields, Leta trooped up the porch steps with Journey lagging behind, dragging a bucket, lengthening the day the same way she ate her striped candy, slowly.

Startled birds took flight overhead, and Leta reached back to clasp Journey's hand. Scanning the surroundings, she caught movement behind a patch of saltmeadow cordgrass. She eased Journey up the steps and through the screened door. "Go to your room and play. I'll call you when supper's ready."

As Journey traipsed off toward her room, Leta reached above the refrigerator and pulled down a rifle. Peering out the door, she spotted a man some distance away, half hidden in waist high grass. Leta eyed the stranger suspiciously, then stuck the barrel of the gun out the screened door, lined him up with her sight and aimed. A sound of heavy boots on the porch boards came from behind, making her whirl the gun around, aiming it at the belly of Tru Ransome.

"Good Lord, woman!" Tru said, incredulously. "Give me that gun!" He snatched the rifle from her hands, staring at her as if she'd lost her mind. "Abe!" he commanded. "Get in the house!"

The boy hurriedly obeyed, fairly flying through the door past Leta.

"How was I supposed to know it was you," Leta argued. "Besides, I know how to use a rifle."

"I'm sure you do," he mumbled, fumbling with the rifle until he slid the safety in place.

She tipped her head in the direction of the creek. "Someone's down there. A man."

Tru moved to where he could see past the trees. Narrowing his eyes, he spotted the man and watched his actions closely. The stranger appeared to be searching for something in the tall marsh grass.

"Stay where you are!" Tru called out to the trespasser. He held the rife suggestively in the crook of his arm.

The stranger's face jerked up, but the shadow from the bill of his cap hid his face. Scrambling, he ran toward the woods, then vanished in the dense brush.

Tru took off after him. But as he ran into the marsh, he scanned the area and was surprised to find no trace of the man, the edge of the marsh empty and quiet against the sky.

Leta rushed up behind him, out of breath from chasing him through the brush. "Where did he go?" She looked around, eyes narrowing as she inspected everything in sight. "What do you think he was up to?" She glanced up at Tru, waiting for a response.

They locked glances, and a certain respect grew in both pairs of eyes. She was the sweetest and most head-strong woman he'd ever met. She could fire up a little when something rattled her—and if that something happened to be you, you had better watch out. She had the spirit to buck when saddled. He cleared his throat and changed the subject in his mind.

Sweet pepperbush grew thick around them, and the fragrance wafted up, mingling with the masculine scent of Tru. She inched away from him, feeling uncomfortable. She kept her attention on his dark eyes. "Why are you looking at me like that?"

"I was just trying to figure out which side of you is the real Leta Purviance. The tough-minded survivalist or the soft Southern belle." He took in the golden-brown eyes, the defiant lift of her chin. Her words seemed to drip from her lips like molasses from a spoon as she gripped a spade in her white knuckled fist.

When Leta's senses were keen, her drawl became more pronounced, sort of low and lingering, a relic of her upbringing. "Like I told you before, I can take care of myself."

"I believe you." He broke the spell and moved past her to scan the area, looking for any sign that might give them a clue to the man's whereabouts.

Leta followed on his heels. "That guy is long gone."

"Has anything like this ever happened before? Trespassers on your property," he explained. Pushing back limbs and looking under brush, he set about searching the property for anything he thought someone might want to find.

Utilizing the spade, Leta poked around the ground, hoping to turn up something. "It's becoming a regular occurrence around here." She pushed the sweat-damp hair from her face with the back of her hand. "First it was Journey. She came in through a window. This morning an elderly woman came up in a jon boat. But that turned out to be a good thing…since I hired her."

"You what! You hired her!" He let go of the branch he was holding, and it swiped his face. "A woman you just met?" He turned away from her, swatting a mosquito and mumbling under his breath. "Of all the dumb ideas you—"

"To help with the flower farm!" Leta shot back. She straightened and leaned on a black gum tree, scanning the area one last time. She had long since learned to ignore Tru's little outbursts.

Tru shook his head at the ridiculous idea. "Come on, we might as well go back. He's long gone." They pushed through the dense brush, reaching the path that would take them back to the house.

In the last wash of day, the stone garden wall seemed to capture the light and absorb, then release it out again in soft amber tones.

"I can learn a lot from her you know," Leta said, not really knowing why she felt a need to explain herself to the man. "She's responsible for all that's here now. She's the reason this place is so filled with color and scent. Just breathe in those yellow roses—you can't bottle that fragrance. *I've* been able to make a living out here because *I've* been selling off all her hard work!"

The strong conviction in her voice caused Tru to stop what he was doing and look at her. He noticed a bench and paths of steppingstone winding through the gardens. "What are those shrubs with the deep blue flowers...next to the bench?"

"They're the star of the show—hydrangea! One of my favorite flowers." She smiled, enjoying his interest. "The place is covered with them. They're beautiful, aren't they? I like them dried too. They have a more subtle, muted color when dried, but they look perfect in just about any sort of vessel: vase, bowl, or pitcher. I keep them on my mantle all year long."

Tru looked around, enjoying how Leta's voice was smooth and sweet, like melted butter all mixed up with jam. "How did you get all this going so fast? It's so organized!"

Leta chewed her lip in contemplation. "At first, I tackled one area at a time, with no specific plan in mind. When I started seeing the garden develop, and how quickly it seemed to be coming together, I realized that someone else must've had a hand in its design. I could see the order in all of it."

Tru's quick glance about the garden allowed him some understanding of the woman's passion. It was beautiful, orderly, and in some places, wild and untamed, much like the gardener. There were mounds of creamy-white blossoms billowing over a stone wall like the train of a bridal gown. From some hidden place a faint tinkling of wind chimes sounded, then faded away with the mild wind.

A cricket landed on Leta's small boot, and she bent over to touch it, causing a chain necklace to swing loose from her white blouse. The necklace held three small keys.

A slow and subtle shift came over the face of Tru. He raised his eyes to Leta and smiled. "What's the meaning behind those keys?"

She fingered the metal. "I don't know, really. The original meaning, I mean. I found the necklace in the yard. The clasp was broken, so I fixed it." There was a thought in Leta's mind that she had tried to suppress but failed to. She blurted out, "I like to think they represent something good...like family, home, security.

Something good like that." She looked down at her boot again.

Tru reached over and gently lifted the chain away from her skin, rubbing each key with his thumb as he recited their meaning. "Forgiveness is *key* in the kingdom of God. Prayer is *key* to peace of mind, but love is the *master key* that opens every heart."

Leta stared at his work-rough hands and the tiny pewter keys he held so gently in his fingers. She raised her gaze and found his dark eyes burning into hers with an unspoken question. For a long moment she forgot to breathe. It was as if some strange force pulled her toward him and she leaned into him. The keys slid from his hands and fell against her skin. She was immediately aware of the manly feel of his lean and muscular chest pressed to hers. They stared at each other for a second of suspended time. Then slowly, almost haltingly, Tru lowered his mouth to hers. The shock was abrupt, and then the gentle kiss warmed her through and through, like honey melting over her whole body.

Tru straightened, regaining his composure. His ragged whisper came in form of an apology. "Not sure why I did that. I'm sorry. I hope you'll forgive me."

With a trembling hand, Leta gently lifted a key from the necklace. "I have the forgiveness key right here." Swallowing hard, she looked away.

A movement beside the house drew her attention. She was surprised to see Edwina stepping high through the grass toward them. A twinge of guilt rose up inside of her as she thought about the pleasure she'd just experienced in the arms of the woman's boyfriend.

Edwina was wearing a fitted Alice blue dress and was walking so gingerly Leta was sure she would topple forward with any misstep. Any meanness she may have felt toward the woman had suddenly been squelched out of her. Everything except a kind of stubborn pride. Edwina had never done one hard thing in her entire life. She had others to do it for her. So Leta was wondering what she could possibly want that would cause her to risk breaking a heel on her designer shoes.

"Tru?" Edwina's tone held a note of surprise. "What are you doing here? I didn't see your truck?" She continued to pick her way through the grass toward them, holding her hands in a praying mantis position as she watched the placement of each step of her Dolce & Gabbana sling-back pumps.

Tru moved toward her, reaching out a hand to help her cross the lawn and find firm footing. "I walked Abe home after work and came up on some trouble. We were just checking it out."

"Trouble? What kind of trouble?" Edwina latched on to his arm.

"Some guy came up…not sure what he was doing, but he's gone now." He squeezed Edwina's arm a little tighter than usual. "What are you doing out here?"

Edwina smoothed her hair behind her ear. "I came by to see Leta and the children—invite them to Vacation Bible School next week."

Leta crossed her arms and smiled. Covered in the early evening light, no one noticed the quick roll of her eyes.

Tru grinned, patting Edwina's hand. "Abe is a little past that, don't you think?"

"I do," Leta interjected, growing impatient suddenly. She remembered when she'd caught Abe rubbing spent firecrackers into his skin just so he could feel manly. The boy had confessed to her that he thought it made him smell like danger. He also liked the smell of cut grass, gasoline, and body odo

r and delayed taking a shower until Leta had to outsmart him. She threatened him by withholding his dinner until he came to the table freshly showered.

"But I think Journey will love it," Tru said, looking at Leta with something that looked too much like sympathy. "She'll make friends." Cocking his head, he waited for her response.

Leta squinted her eyes at Edwina and pointed her finger. "Are you teaching?"

"I wanted to," Edwina said, "but it seems I'm too late. All the spots are filled. Just my luck."

"Where do we sign up?" Leta said, fighting a private battle not to laugh at the expression on her cousin's face.

***

In the cool morning air of the flower field, Gussie waited for Leta. Across the creek the wispy clouds were softly changing their patterns and a little faded jon boat, tied to the dock, gently rocked in the current.

Leta spotted Gussie sitting on her garden stool, then looked at her watch. "How long have you been here?"

Gussie stabbed the ground around the zinnias, churning up weeds and raking them into a large pile next to the path. "Long enough to get this here pile of weeds." Straightening her back, she wiped her hands on her apron and frowned. "I try and get here early enough so I can see that trellis over yonder," she nodded her head, "it's just full of blue morning glories—so blue it's like drifting over a tropical sea." Gussie leaned forward and squinted her eyes. "Where'd you get that man watch?"

She glanced at the black leather watch Leta wore on her left hand. It had a large round face with gray slits for numbers and looked out of place on the graceful arm. "My grandfather, Patrick." She rubbed the face of the watch lovingly with her thumb. "He left it to me."

Gussie watched Leta's face. There was something rootless about the girl, as if she had not been planted into the fertile Purviance soil deeply enough. She sensed Leta knew this too. Like she was just living on the topsoil without putting down roots, waiting to be transplanted somewhere else at any whim.

"Where's them kids—still asleep this late in the mornin'?"

Leta lifted the latch on the wrought iron gate, pushing hard where the rosebushes had knitted the bars together with the stone wall. "All farmed out for the day. Abe's at work on Ransome Land and Journey's at Vacation Bible School in Quay."

Her eyebrows shot up. "At my church?"

"At Quay Community Church. Do you go there?"

She laughed with an ease of spirit. "Pastor J.D. used to come lookin' for me. I've known him and his sister, Molly, since way back when."

Leta had to smile at that, but she wasn't all that surprised. From what she'd heard about J.D. Redman, he wasn't the sort of man to play around when he saw a sheep that needed to be tended to.

"What about all them extra flowers you got back from that wedding? Them sick folks up at the hospital might like to have 'em. Pastor J.D.'s the chaplain up there. You should go see him."

"I may do that. He's the uncle of my neighbor I'm told," she said, a smile crossing her lips before she could catch it.

"I've seen the pastor's nephew. Even a blind woman on a galloping horse can see he's handsome. You like him, don't you?"

"What!" she cried, then thoughtfully lowered her voice. "What makes you think I like him? I mean, of course I like him, he's a good neighbor." She started to move down the row, then stopped. "I just feel sorry for him, that's all. I don't think he knows what he's gotten into with Edwina. If you ask me, he should've tugged on the buttons before he bought the shirt! You know, tested the quality of the fabric before he made a commitment." She swiped the hair out of her eyes. "That's all I'm saying."

Gussie turned aside with a grin. "I'll be lookin' to see how all that turns out. Could be they were made for each other. You know what they say about them opposites attractin'."

Leta narrowed her eyes. "Mismatched." She stressed the word, making her point as she snipped enough zinnias for a good-size bouquet.

They worked in the garden, side by side, for most of the morning. The sun was sweltering by eleven o'clock and the air thickened with salt and covered their skin like chalk.

Gussie sat up straight and fanned herself. "Hoo wee, but it sho 'nough got hot!"

"Come on, let's get out of this sun—call it a day and cool off a little." Leta propped her hoe against the bench. "Lemonade sounds about right. I'll come back and take these flowers to the garden shed and get them in some cooler water." She reached out and took Gussie's hand, leading her to the shady side of the porch and sat her down on the old weather-worn swing. The chains creaked slowly and rhythmically, a sound Leta knew in the deepest part of her heart. "Sit tight. I'll be right back."

Gussie looked over her shoulder, admiring the morning glory vines twining their way up a trellis. When the screen door snapped shut, she turned and saw Leta carrying a tray with a gleaming pitcher of lemonade, two glasses, and a small plate of cookies. She set it on the table with a soft *thunk.* "I found a few cookies." She winked. "I have to hide them from the kids. Those two can clean you out like a swarm of locusts!" Her voice softened a bit. "I wouldn't have it any other way."

A shaft of sunlight moved across Gussie as she gently rocked. "You're doin' good with them children, 'specially for somebody that never had any of their own."

"Sometimes I scare myself when I think of all I've signed up for. Especially someone like me." She took a seat in the rocker with a heavy exhale.

Gussie leaned back in the swing and looked into Leta's eyes. She was quiet for a moment, then gave her the strangest look before launching into a short sermon. "Goodness gracious, child, you got a whole lot of healin' to do. But you in the right place, yes child, you right where you ought to be." She leaned forward and patted Leta's knee reassuringly.

"How can you be so sure?" Something deep within Leta let loose and she poured out a gush of words before she could stop herself. "I'm over my head! I've got a flower farm and I don't even own a tractor! I've got two kids that are looking to me to take care of them and I've never even owned a pet! Who do I think I am, trying to raise kids?"

Gussie never said a word, just kind of grunted.

When Leta finally grabbed hold of herself, she saw those black eyes ready to spill over a torrent of truth. She pressed her lips together and willed them shut before she exposed the worst of her shame. *What kind of a person kills another person?*

"Life is full of change, child, and you sho 'nough have had your share. But listen to me—all that change—what happened to you—makes you the right person for them kids. The Good Lord knew them kids would need you. And, child, you need them too. It's how you gonna grow and learn what life is all about. Why the Lord made you in the first place. Them kids ain't the only ones around here needin' help."

Leta never blinked, never moved a muscle as Gussie put her finger so directly on the one thing that frightened Leta the most. With a single, nearly imperceptible nod, she acknowledged the truth.

Chapter 15

The wind around the town of Quay would vanish and return a moment later with the steady clanging of hardware of a dozen flagpoles. Each flapping flag that lined the boardwalk proudly displayed the colors of the town: green, blue, and white.

Pulling her eyes from the colorful display, Leta shifted her satchel higher upon her shoulder and began to make her way toward the steps of the hospital. Already dreading what she knew she must do; she approached the front desk to ask for directions.

"May I help you?" asked the woman in a crackling voice, wearing a shining silver halo of hair.

"Yes, please. I'm looking for the office of the hospital chaplain, J.D. Redman," Leta said. *Please say the ground floor.*

The woman pecked the name on the keyboard in slow, methodical taps. "His office is on the third floor…303," she said, squinting at the screen through her bifocals.

"Can you point me in the direction of the stairs?"

The elderly woman peered at Leta over the top of her glasses and smiled. "I'm sorry, but the stairs are only used in case of emergency. The fire alarm will sound if anyone opens the door. The elevators are around the corner to the right."

With a tight smile, she fought to control her sudden sense of panic. "Thank you." She walked toward the elevator, her heart thumping in her chest. Glancing behind her, she noticed a rather tall man with a cup of coffee in one hand and what appeared to be a Bible and a newspaper under his arm. He walked purposefully toward the elevator. As he was stepping near the doors, he was distracted by a man and stopped to chat with him.

Leta grew impatient at the slow progress of the man as several more people gathered around him. She tried to linger near the water fountain until he broke free from the conversations. Not wishing to enter the elevator alone, she made it a point to wait on the man.

Finally, he pulled away from the small gathering and with a departing wave of his hand, approached the doors and pressed the button. As the light above the door dinged, Leta rushed up behind him to enter the elevator. Upon entering, he came to a sudden and abrupt halt, causing Leta to bump into the back of him, sloshing his coffee onto the floor.

The man whirled to find the startled and widened eyes of a very pretty and obviously panic-stricken young woman. Mistaking the reason for her concern, he quickly reassured her, "No harm done, except possibly to the floor. This hospital coffee could peel the varnish right off the tile." He smiled, hoping to calm the woman's fears with his humor.

Leta's lips grew thin and white as she slid past him with a mumble. "I'm so sorry about that." Confused by the young woman's actions, he nevertheless stepped over the coffee spill and proceeded to press the floor button.

"Can you just push the button and back away from the controls?" she asked, her eyes pinched shut.

The man flung up his hand. "Gladly ma'am...which floor?"

"Third."

The elevator jerked once, then hummed as it climbed to the third floor where it slowly came to a stop. It hesitated for what seemed like an eternity before it opened. As the door slid back slightly, Leta bolted out, then stopped and released the breath she'd been holding.

An odd look came into the man's eyes as he followed her out, careful to keep his distance from the obviously disturbed woman.

Leta began making her way down the long, shiny tiled corridor toward the section where a sign indicated the direction of offices. Glancing over her shoulder, she noticed the man from the elevator following her apprehensively, it seemed. *Why won't he just go away?*

She rounded the corner and found the office door with the number *303* in block style white lettering underneath the word *Chaplain*. As she was about to knock, the man from the elevator appeared behind her, only this time with a set of keys in his hand.

He slid a key inside the lock and smiled down at Leta. "Leta Purviance, I presume?"

Like a stiff wind that blows up and hits you with full force in the face, she felt herself bracing for the words that would come next.

"I'm J.D. Redman, Chaplain. Please," he pushed the door open wide, "come in."

Before Leta stepped through the door, she winced slightly. Trying to explain her erratic behavior. "I don't care for elevators."

"Ah, that explains it," he said, with understanding. "Claustrophobic?"

Leta worried with the button on her cotton blouse, then smiled. "You could say that."

Conscious of the chaplain's stare, she stepped into his office and lifted a quick glance toward the bookshelves lining a wall. *He doesn't look like a chaplain. He looks more like Gregory Peck!*

J.D. gazed down upon Leta with more compassion than she was willing to accept from the man, chaplain or not. She could not find it in herself to give even the smallest explanation for her behavior. She preferred to change the subject and get about what she had come to see him about in the first place.

A smile tugged at the corners of J.D.'s mouth, but he suppressed it as quickly as it came. "Sit, please." He pulled a small leather chair away from the desk and removed a stack of books and papers from the seat. "I'm afraid I'm a bit messy," he said, giving her a reassuring smile. "Or at least that's what people have always said of me. I wouldn't want to disappoint them, so I keep up the charade."

Leta smiled and relaxed a little, easing back in the chair as she watched the chaplain walk around the desk and take his seat in the tall, tufted leather chair. It squeaked in protest as his weight shifted forward slightly.

"So, tell me…what has caused you to brave the elevator today and come all this way to see me?" He tapped his knuckles twice on the desk.

Leta fidgeted with her watch under the man's close inspection, then looked him in the eye. "I have an idea and I was told that you were the man I needed to see about implementing it."

J.D. responded with a low chuckle of amusement. "Well, it seems I have some power after all." He toyed with a stack of papers in front of him, fanning the sheets with his fingers. "Let's hear it. Maybe I can at least point you in the right direction. What's your idea?"

Leta ignored the polite lack of interest in his voice and came back to the reason she was here. "I have a flower farm just a little west of town. I sell to different people, local florists, restaurants, that sort of thing."

"Upriver?" he asked.

"Yes. I'm on Sweet Grass Creek."

"Near Tru Ransome's place?"

With a nod of her head, Leta said, "We're neighbors."

J.D. nodded his approval.

"I supplied flowers for a recent wedding and got a call from the mother of the bride asking if I wanted the flowers back. She said they were still so fresh and beautiful, she hated to waste them by throwing them away. So now I have tons of flowers on my hands. In fact, going forward, I'm making it a point ask my clients if they wish to donate their flowers after the event…to charitable causes, like this one. I have a truck full of flowers now, all going to a nursing home after I leave here."

White teeth gleamed in a charming smile. "I can't say I've had too much experience with flowers, Miss Purviance."

"I never assumed you did, chaplain. You don't strike me as the flower type." She put on a brighter smile, becoming more comfortable around the pastor.

"Well, that's a relief." He presented her another charming smile.

"What I'd like to do, with your permission, is accompany you on your rounds and give a small jar of flowers to the patients you visit. All I need is a rolling cart, like one from the cafeteria. I'll stand outside the room until you call for me, so I won't interrupt your private time with the patient."

"And you're willing to do this—even if it means riding the elevators?" J.D. pressed for his point.

All at once she felt mocked. She quietly came to her feet and squared her jaw. "I think it's worth it."

A silver chain caught his attention as it gleamed around Leta's neck. Dangling from it were three small keys, hung by a button on the front of her shirt. He slapped his desk and stood. "So do I," he stated firmly. "I'll take you downstairs so we can discuss this further. I'm thinking Thursday's at ten o'clock, just before lunch." He sauntered down the hall casually, then turned to her to ask a question that nagged him. "Tell me, did Tru Ransome send you to me?"

Leta shook her head. "No, Gussie did. She said you two know each other."

He stopped, stared at her in amazement. "Gussie?" He was more confused than ever. He racked his brain for some remembrance of the woman. "Oh well, I'm glad somebody out there appreciates me." He smiled. "What's her last name?"

"Don't know." Seeing the pastor's concern, she lowered her satchel to the floor and continued. "Her name is August, but she said to call her Gussie."

"August..." He whispered her name reverently and began remembering his long-buried history. "Ah, yes...I know August."

Throughout J.D.'s early childhood he and his sister

had floundered much of the time, being passed from one relative's house to another following the deaths of their parents in an accident. But after they came to the lowland of Quay to live with an aging aunt, their lives had taken an unexpected turn.

Leta was surprised by the soft, melodic timbre of his voice as he recalled Gussie. His face took on an expression of love and tenderness. "She told me plainly that her last name didn't matter." Leta shrugged. "I thought it odd but didn't really think too much of it at the time."

He glanced down at the floor and paused. "When I first came to Quay as a boy, I was in such a state that had anyone asked, I could not have said who I was or where my life might take me."

Growing intrigued, Leta motioned to a line of chairs in the corridor and they sat down, facing each other.

"Because of this…crisis, I guess you could call it, I was full of questions to which I had no answers. I had no solid boundaries physically or emotionally. I wanted desperately to feel secure and in control of my life. I used to surround myself with nature, I loved the steady patterns and rhythms of the sun, moon, and stars. The cycle of the seasons gave me a sense of order…security, when so much in my life was anything but. It was during one of my jaunts, when I was not buttoned up too tightly inside myself, that August found her way to me."

Leta's eyes grew larger. "What did she look like?"

"When she stood in front of me, she seemed six-foot-tall. She was the color of golden wheat and had the darkest eyes I'd ever seen. I wasn't in the least bit threatened by her." He pulled back his head. "You sure you want to hear all this?"

"Absolutely…go on." She brushed her hair behind her ear and fixed her eyes on him.

"Well, that's when my entire life began to shift, change, in profound ways. August was teaching me, and I wasn't even aware of it at the time. Showing me things I'd never once considered. I didn't know where any of this change was leading. I never would've thought in a million years that I would one day become a pastor. So, part of my long spiritual journey began when I first met August. One does not simply dismiss such a person, or ever forget them."

Leta grew quiet, thinking of the pastor's words. She'd thought she was going in the right direction but still had no idea what she was looking for. She felt a strong sense of awe and gratitude for the force, whatever it was, that brought people like Gussie into other people's lives. "No, you sure can't dismiss them."

Chapter 16

The slate roof of Stone House shimmered under the evening heat of the sun, and the scent of honeysuckle filled the air. Only in the cooler temperatures of the shady porch, where light breezes blew up from the creek, could even a small measure of comfort be found.

Leta rocked Journey easily on her lap as Abe, perched on the railing, told stories of his discoveries around the old houses and ruins of Ransome Land. Supper had long since passed and they were all wrapped in a kind of contentment as the voices of crickets and katydids sang to them the melodies of the marshlands.

Leta felt the porch boards vibrate beneath her feet and stopped rocking. Glancing over her shoulder, she saw Tru approach with Edwina lagging in the shadows. Even from that angle she could plainly see a smug look on the woman's face.

Tru wore a strange expression of resolve and dread. He cleared his throat and settled himself in a nearby chair, scraping it slightly on the boards as he turned it to face Leta. With elbows on his knees and hands clasped, he leaned forward. It was apparent he had something on his mind, but a long moment of silence passed. A look was exchanged between Tru and Edwina before he came to the point.

"May we talk in private?" Tru said, indicating the children with his eyes.

"Of course." Leta smiled at the children. "Abe, take your sister inside please."

Journey slid off Leta's lap and grabbed Abe by the hand as they reluctantly made their way to the door. The screened door creaked open, then Abe looked back at Leta warily before the door closed behind him with a snap.

Leta waited rigidly, watching as her cousin relaxed against the railing with arms crossed and a smirk on her perfectly glossed lips as if ready to enjoy a show. Leta knew that could only mean trouble for her.

Tru inhaled deeply. "Edwina has located Clyde and Cora Littleton, the paternal grandparents of the children." He continued calmly as if he had not seen the shock on Leta's face. "They live close by, on a pecan farm."

Leta gestured toward Edwina. "How did she get involved in all of this?"

"I'd mentioned to Edwina that Abe had talked about his papaw teaching him to drive a tractor. She took it upon herself to do some research, found them, even visited them...and they want Abe and Journey to live with them." Tru held up a hand to silence the words he could see were about to spew from Leta's lips. "The social worker, Mrs. Evans, is out front ready to transport the children. I asked that we have a chance to talk with you first."

"I see," Leta replied caustically, feeling more hurt and betrayed than she cared to admit. She shook her head and muttered a few unintelligible words.

Tru rushed on to explain and try to reason with her before she had a chance to argue. "Reunification with relatives is always ideal when possible, Leta. You know this. You even said so yourself. The Littleton's, I'm told, are good people, and the children will be cared for. They're older, but I'm sure they'll do their best for the kids."

"Their best!" Leta scoffed. "Where have these people been for the last few months?"

Edwina moved to stand behind Tru, placing a hand across his shoulder. "I know it's frustrating, but you must consider the children in this and not just yourself. The Littleton's had no idea what was going on with their son. And when they saw pictures of their grandchildren working on this flower farm, they were quite upset about it. To learn that the children were being used for cheap labor in that way, well, you can just imagine their outrage."

"What?" Tru turned on Edwina, more than a little stunned at what he was hearing. "What pictures? What's all this talk about child labor? These kids are happy here and well cared for! Is that what this is all about?"

Edwina took on a slight lecturing tone. "When you work children without pay, that's called child labor, and we have laws against that sort of thing in this country."

"That's the most ridiculous thing I've ever heard!" Tru shot to his feet. "I'll straighten this out with Mrs. Evans."

"You're wasting your time. A picture is worth a thousand words," Edwina mocked.

All the words washed over Leta like a rising tide, flooding her defenses. She stood up, and in a strong voice, conceded. "I'll pack the children's things and bring them out. Give me some time to explain it to them first."

Less than an hour later Leta stood where black-eyed Susan's and Queen Anne's lace bloomed beside the road all the way to town. She watched the vehicles leave, one by one, until there was nothing left of their passing but a cloud of dust hanging above the dirt road.

Walking back to the house, she couldn't make herself go inside. The dread was oppressing. Her mind reeled. The full comprehension of what had just happened was enough to make her grow heavy all over. She followed the narrow dirt path that led off to the garden. Some distance down the foot path she spied Gussie, leaning against the stone wall, waiting for her. The sight of sympathy in the old woman's eyes caused Leta to swallow hard. The strain of losing the children was mirrored in Gussie's face, as if she knew what had just happened.

Leta's shoulders slumped as she sat down on the low stone wall. Holding a hand over her face, she began to softly sob out her frustration and hurt. "They're gone, Gussie—gone!"

"Calm yourself, child. Hush now, everything's gonna be fine," Gussie said, her hand seemed to wave off the concern.

Leta opened her red-rimmed eyes, blinking back the tears. "But they're gone…gone to live with their grandparents…they're…just…gone." She spied a splotch of color on the wall beside her, Journey's ragdoll. "I feel so lost without them?"

"I know, child." She patted Leta's hand, her own eyes sparkling with tears. "But don't you say goodbye to them children just yet. No ma'am! You listen to old Gussie, you'll see them again. Them grandparents gonna need some help! And you's the best one to give it to 'em."

Leta's throat tightened as she swallowed down the lump of sorrow. She turned away from the sight of the ragdoll splayed on the wall. "They think I abused them! They'll never let me anywhere near those children ever again."

"That's nonsense and you know it. Them babies will tell their folks how much you loved 'em. Pretty soon this will all be just a bad dream. Go ahead and have yoself a good cry. Then after that, we got this here garden to see after." Gussie straightened and shuffled her feet around, looking out over the fields toward the shed. Cocking her head thoughtfully, she considered it before her shining eyes landed back on Leta. "That shed over there…sure would make a mighty fine workshop. Got power in it?"

Leta sniffed, blotting her nose on her sleeve. "I think so." She looked over her shoulder at the garden shed. "But it's a mess. Pop called himself a collector." Her nose twitched at the thought of the smell of decaying plants, dust, and stale air. "He collected old bottles, jars, cans…anything he could stick a root or a cutting in. I've added to the collection myself." Her grief changed momentarily to embarrassment as she confessed, "With about sixty Mason jars."

"Guess that apple didn't roll too far from the tree."

The shed itself was built of stone the color of wild rabbit fur. It had a large garden window that projected outward from the structure to create a shelf used to grow plants, flowers, and herbs, giving them the maximum amount of sunlight.

Gussie flapped her hand as if to dismiss the worry. "Well, we can put 'em to good use—'sides, we gonna need them for all them arrangements we're making for the hospital. We'll have that place spit and polished in no time. Just you wait and see."

Leta seemed overwhelmed by the idea. Her heart just wasn't in a place to get very excited about anything. Even so, Gussie saw a flickering light of hope burning deep within the girl. Saw what it was that pulled her, and knew when the moment was right, when her heart opened, Leta would drink in what her soul thirsted for most.

Leta nodded halfheartedly. Working herself into a good lather was about the only strategy for stress she knew of that worked. She rolled up her sleeves and set about finding the pace and rhythm she needed to steady her mind. "Okay, but you row on home before it gets dark. I don't like the idea of you floating around the marsh in daylight much less at night."

"Don't you worry none 'bout old Gussie. I was born to the water. 'Sides, I'm close by."

A fresh breeze stirred the blueberry bushes and brought with it the scent of rain. It embroidered in Leta's mind what would be a last sweet memory of Journey and Abe for a long time.

***

Tru wore faded jeans and a worn-out white shirt he hadn't bothered to button. Standing under a twisted oak on the edge of the salt marsh, he felt the sway of smooth cordgrass around him as leaded rain clouds began to pile up in the distance. A faint touch of a cool breeze stirred his hair and he closed his eyes, suddenly wishing he were a different kind of man.

There was always something at the back of Tru's mind telling him that he had failed somehow. That if he had just done things differently, paid more attention, things would have turned out another way. This day was one of *those* days. A day when he felt most keenly the absence of his father.

The face of Leta passed ghostlike through his mind. Slowly and without effort a vision of golden eyes, thickly fringed, crept into his mind as they widened in shock, then fell with the pain of betrayal. She had been living happily at Stone House with her makeshift family. But the last time he'd seen her, nothing was left of the joy and contentment he'd seen in her while the children were around. And what of Edwina. The thought nagged at him as he considered the possibility that he might not know her at all. He worried that he would make the same mistakes he had made in the past; that his life would be a running series of poor relationship choices. The problem was, how was he to know?

"Pray about it," he said out loud. That's what J.D. would tell him. In fact, that's what Tru had always advised as well. But J.D. didn't understand the life of an ordinary man. Or did he?

He glanced once more at the darkening sky, watching as lightning flashed within the clouds, then slid out his cell phone and made a call to his uncle.

***

As Tru stood in the open space of the hospital lobby, he paused to listen to the familiar footsteps coming down the corridor from the direction of the elevators. Then, those of a quicker, lighter, more feminine step joined the heavier step as J.D. and, to his surprise, Leta, rounded the corner and came into view.

Lifting his eyes from the polished floor, J.D. spotted

Tru. He spoke loud enough to be sure to reach the ears of his nephew. "Looks like the fun is over. Duty calls."

As they reached Tru, Leta stood regarding him with her head tilted a little to one side and a question in her golden eyes. Once more he was struck by the richness of her tawny skin, the wildness of her sun-kissed hair, and the carefree, almost gypsy quality about her. His eyes moved naturally to her lips—

Enough! Tru savagely attacked his rebellious thoughts until they fled back into a corner of his mind. But his pulse had picked up at the sight of her. "Leta," he said. "It's good to see you. What brings you to the hospital? Nothing serious, I hope."

"Flowers, actually," Leta said, forcing her best smile.

"Flowers, oh yeah—I've been meaning to stop by and buy some from you. Not for myself, of course," he said, half amused, "for Edwina. What do you recommend?"

"Wolfsbane," Leta stated, sounding as if she were struggling to keep her patience.

"Wolfsbane?" J.D. laughed. "Not unless you want her to froth at the mouth! That stuff is toxic! It's a beautiful flower, but poisonous."

Leta looked at her watch. "Well, I better get going."

"See you next Thursday?" J.D asked.

"Absolutely." She lifted her hand in a weak wave toward Tru, then adjusted her satchel on her shoulder.

Tru cleared his throat. "You're welcome to drop by my place any evening and visit Abe. He's there most days now."

"Thank you," Leta said politely, though she chafed at having to receive anything from the man. She wasn't sure what his role had been in taking away the children, but to her way of thinking, he was guilty by association.

Tru watched her make her way out of the hospital and through the glass doors. Glancing around, he saw the amusement in J.D.'s face as he fixed a stare on him.

"Are you in need of counsel?" J.D. questioned, barely containing the laughter he felt at his nephew's expression.

"Are you?" Tru responded suspiciously.

J.D. laughed. "No, I'm good. In fact, better than good. I'd say I'm doing just fine these days." He extended his hand toward the entrance to the hospital coffee shop. "How about some coffee?"

Tru's frown gradually faded into a look of resignation.

"Are you going to be difficult, Tru?" he questioned, recognizing the accusatory depths of those deep brown eyes.

"Aren't I always?"

They grabbed their coffee and settled into a booth near a window. J.D. fished in the pocket of his jacket, then tossed a Goo Goo Cluster candy bar across the table toward Tru. "This might sweeten you up a little bit. I keep a stash of them with me at all times for just such occasions."

A fat raindrop hit the window and was quickly followed by a steady pounding of rain. Tru relaxed back in the vinyl covered seat and indulged a hope that J.D. could help give him some perspective. He ripped open the wrapper on his candy bar and took a bite. Chewing, he said, "You know, most preachers try to win someone over with their good behavior. Most of the time you seem bent on the opposite." He tilted the candy bar toward him. "But this makes up for a lot."

J.D. swallowed down a sip of coffee with a grimace.

Looking over his shoulder at the hefty man behind the counter wiping his hands on his dirty apron. "I think Tegan strained this coffee through his apron."

"I went to school with that guy over in Charlotte," Tru said, watching the man pick up donuts with his fingers and lick each one after placing them under a glass dome. "He never needed a push to choose what would destroy him."

"Drugs?"

"Drugs, alcohol, tobacco…it's like he picked the most destructive thing he could find that said, 'Buy me, I can kill you!'"

"A little harsh, don't you think?" J.D. dipped his finger in the coffee and doodled on the table.

"Why do you do that?"

"Do what?"

"Write those watery crosses on the table?"

He shrugged. "To remind myself."

"Of what?"

"That Christ died for the Tegan's of this world too. I've been trying to help him for a while." He shrugged. "Guess I'd have to admit that I can't see how he's changed much, so far. But it's not important who does the planting or the watering. What's important is that God makes the seed grow. I'm in the business of seed planting. The cross reminds me of that. Of what we all need."

"What's that?"

"Hope." J.D. swiped away the wet crosses with a napkin and steepled his hands. "Now, what's on your mind? Leta Purviance?"

"What? No! What makes you think that!" Tru shifted in his seat, uncomfortably.

"It's all over you like a tattoo." He braved another sip of bitter coffee.

Tru shrugged, trying to appear casual. "I was just glad to see her out, that's all. I know losing the Littleton kids affected her." He folded the candy bar wrapper into tiny pleats. "I guess on some level I admire her. I always admire courage where I find it—even if it's in a bitter woman."

J.D. raised a single brow. "Bitter? I don't know that person. The person I know makes broken look beautiful. She stands and she deals with…whatever. But you're right, she is courageous. I witnessed her overcome one of her fears today just so she could help others."

"A fear? I don't believe it—that woman isn't afraid of anything. What fear?"

"It doesn't matter."

"Sounds like you're getting to know her pretty well."

J.D. stared at him blankly and gave a tight smile. "Most people are so fearful and guarded, they rarely show their true souls. I appreciate those who do. Now, back to you."

Tru got the message. "Okay." He let out a deep breath. "I…I guess I'm concerned about making the same mistake twice." He narrowed his eyes, rubbing his finger over the stubble on his chin as he waited on J.D.'s response.

No one knew Tru's situation better than J.D., so he proceeded with caution. "Are we talking about Edwina?"

Tru nodded. "She's different. I mean, there's this legend build-up about her. I guess I'm no different than most of the men of this town in my infatuation. People have wildly different opinions of her. Some say she's the worst kind of person, a fraud. Others think she's this mysterious heroine of the Purviance dynasty."

"What does your gut tell you?"

Tru braced both hands on the table and pushed back. "That she's both."

"No one is without faults, Tru. Do I really need to remind you that we live in a fallen world? My advice to you is to meditate on it and wait."

"Meditate? You mean like breathing deeply three times before going into a trance?" he joked, knowing the meaning, but unable to resist the comment.

"No. I mean like prayer. Pray about it. That's all I've got for you. And you know this. Just trust that what needs to be revealed to you will be revealed…in His time and in His way. Don't forget, God is always at work, even when we can't see it."

Chapter 17

A fine rain had fallen steadily all day, and a shroud of mist crept up from the creek and covered the fields like a smoothed-out blanket. The tall stems of hollyhocks and zinnias dripped with moisture and the hydrangea bushes bowed their rain-soaked heads in the last rays of the fading day.

Grand Bess's face was lined deeply by pride; pride of position and of birth—it was a face burdened by regret. She clutched her purse as she walked the path toward the flower fields, looking searchingly for her granddaughter. She paused often to scan the surroundings and thought she saw a form, strange and ghost-like in the mist, floating through the field toward the creek. But even as she looked it vanished among the haze and the wild heather.

The branch of an oak leaned over an odd assortment of rusted metal chairs and an old glider. Bess picked her way toward them. She stooped to brush away the standing water, leaves, and twigs from a seat, then carefully lowered her frame and sat down, clutching her small purse.

The sap of life was moving slowly through the veins of Bess Purviance, but her mind was still crackling with fire. She straightened against the back of the chair and waited, sure that Leta would soon be about her business in the garden in the cool of the evening. She rubbed at her elbow as if to soothe away the persistent ache that throbbed there. She wanted so much to better understand the girl, to know Leta. Her granddaughter had lost so many of the ones she loved. Bess could understand the girl's reluctance in getting too close. She smiled and patted the manila envelope in her hand. "Now, won't she be surprised," she said, smiling.

When Leta entered the garden, she pulled on her work gloves and reached for the hoe that was propped against a tree. It was then that her eyes fell on Grand Bess who sat haughtily erect in a rusted-out chair under the oak branch. She looked like a regal queen with her wide straw hat, each hand resting on the arms of the chair. She smiled at Leta and nodded her head in acknowledgment.

Leta's brows drew together in sudden worry. "Is something wrong?" she asked when she drew near.

"No, no." She lowered her hand to her lap and grasped the envelope. "I have something for you."

Leta sat down in a chair next to her, giving full attention to her grandmother.

The golden-brown eyes of her granddaughter had never been bashful but looked at you square on. She had a questioning, direct look that made Bess feel as if she were being absorbed somehow. She leaned forward and handed Leta the envelope, her lips twitched with the threat of a smile.

"What's this?" She opened the envelope and drew out a paper, scanning it quickly. "It looks like a title—to a 1965 Ford F100?"

"Yes, and it's all yours, such as it is." For a quick

moment Leta's mannerisms were so blatantly Heather's, the memory of the poor girl was brought fully to Grand Bess's mind.

"I don't understand. Whose truck is this, and why do I have the title?"

Grand Bess fumbled in her small purse and drew out a letter. She raised the paper and read, "Dear Mother, I would like to suggest that you give my old Ford truck to Leta, if it's still around and Dad hasn't scrapped it. She can make use of it any way she sees fit. I thought it might come in handy around her flower farm. I wish you luck in your attempts to convince her to take it, but as always, my money is on you. Love, Rod." Grand Bess folded the letter carefully and tucked it back into her purse.

Leta's face flushed as she stared down at her watch. "I don't know what to say…I'm beginning to feel like a charity case."

"Nonsense. You're a Purviance! And your father has every right to hand down that truck to you. It's not worth much in terms of money, but it means everything to your father. It was your mother's idea to paint it baby blue. Heather loved the truck. They used to ride the countryside in that old thing."

"My mother?" She straightened and, in a strong voice, conceded. "All right. I'll take it. Thank you."

"Good. Now, I have an idea on what you can do with your truck."

Leta let the words pass without verbal comment, but her eyes widened.

"You can convert it to a flower truck!" Her smile widened. "Like the ones you see on Pinterest! Have sturdy wooden platforms fitted to the truck bed so you can transport and display your flowers. I know someone from church who makes custom designed awnings. That would really make your flower truck stand out. Her name is Dewey Maude and she has a shop in town called Quaint of Quay."

Leta's brows rose sharply. She didn't know which surprised her most, that her grandmother followed Pinterest, or that she went to church. "You go to church?"

"Oh." She gave two quick shakes of her head. "I'm a member of Quay Community Church, certainly, but Edwina is the only one of us who actually works at it. She helps the women's ministry when she's here in town and some other things...I don't know what all."

Curious now, she leaned toward her grandmother. "Why don't you attend?"

"These days the church is mostly filled with common folks. It embarrasses me to outdress them every Sunday."

"Then why do you?" Leta responded.

Grand Bess half turned and lifted her brow at her grandchild. "You sure don't have any trouble expressing your thoughts. Do you, young lady."

"Not usually." She rubbed the top of her nose.

Grand Bess's brows arched in a half-frown, but before she could respond, she gave a short laugh. "You're so much like my son in that way. Tell me, do you enjoy the sport of business gambling like your father?"

The corner of her lip lifted in a sneer. "Not hardly. I can think of better ways to risk my money."

"Like on a flower farm?"

Leta's face grew thoughtful "Exactly."

The powdered and rouged face curved into a knowing smile. She glanced around. "This seems like too much work for one young woman. Let me hire someone to help you get started, dear. We have plenty of workers at Tremont."

Leta straightened herself in the chair and centered the hoe handle in her fists in front of her. "I'm not out here scratching in the dirt all by myself—Gussie helps me."

"Gussie?" Grand Bess looked at her curiously, amazed that she could tackle such a workload with only two people.

"She's older—been around this place for a while. Knows everything about flowers. And other important things."

Grand Bess looked at her granddaughter wonderingly. "Is she your friend?"

Leta nodded. "Yeah, I think the world of Gussie. As soon as she pulls up in her little red jon boat I start to relax. And when she speaks, I listen. I appreciate her. She seems to care."

Grand Bess's face softened. She looked down at her lap and picked at the material. A concerned, motherly smile beginning on her face. "What kinds of things do y'all talk about?"

Leta stared hard at the ground, twisting the blade of the hoe into the soil. "We talk about all kinds of things…flowers and…other things. She's lived here all her life and there's not much she doesn't know about this land. That helps me."

"What do you want to know about the land, dear? Maybe I can help answer some questions for you?" she remarked, resting a hand on her chest. She smiled indulgently, waiting on a reply.

Leta's eyes fixed on her grandmother, biting her lip she cautiously asked, "I'd like to know more about the hums I hear around this place from time to time. What makes them?"

The smile faded and was replaced by an expression of pity. Somewhat at a loss, Grand Bess narrowed her eyes and asked, "Hums, dear? What hums?"

"It's like a song in the trees or maybe it comes through the stones, I don't know. But whatever it is, it's a haunting melody."

Grand Bess drew her head back. "Hums? Dear one, I've lived on this place my whole married life and I've never heard a hum, except from that old air conditioner your grandfather keeps in the tool shed."

Leta glanced over her shoulder toward the flower fields, feeling uneasy, so she changed the subject. "Well, anyway, Gussie has been a blessing to me around here," she said softly. "I wouldn't have a flower field without her—or without you, for that matter. Thank you for Stone House and this beautiful land."

***

Bells clanged softly against the glass door of the Quaint of Quay shop as Leta slipped inside. Looking around, she saw an assortment of pillowcases stacked high against the wall in cubby holes, neat and colorful. There were soft colored prints in various shades of white, green, and blue on display. Large jars of potpourri sat on a highly polished mahogany table in the center of the room where small cloth bags with ribbon ties coordinated with the colorful pillowcase designs. The shop had bolts of fabric stacked everywhere in beauty and order. Fragrant linen water filled an antique breakfront and an old porcelain claw foot tub held a mound of sachets. Despite the abundance of fragrance, the scent of the shop was pleasant and fresh and not overpowering.

"Can I help ya?" called a voice from the back of the shop.

Leta smiled, remembering how long it had been since she'd heard a true Appalachian dialect. She looked up to find the woman staring at her from behind a counter. There was something in the face of Dewey Maude that commanded your attention. The intensity of her crystal blue eyes seemed to add strength to her tall, thin, and aging frame. Something in the way she looked at you, taking your measure by degrees, as her bird-of-prey eyes fixed on you.

"Bess Purviance sent me to you," Leta said, pulling back the hood of her raincoat. "I'm Leta Purviance. You make custom awnings?"

"What if I do?" She squinted her sharp eyes in suspicion.

Feeling ill at ease in the shop owner's presence, a thought began to form in Leta's mind as she watched the woman. *What a way to treat customers!* With slow deliberateness, she turned to the door, intending to make her escape from the peculiar woman.

"Where ya goin'? Thought ya wanted me to make ya an awnin'?"

Leta's hand was on the doorknob, a confused look played across her features before she turned around. "Uh, I do."

"Well, why didn't ya just come right out and ask for it, right plain like?"

She gave a quick glance around. "Will you make an awning for my truck?"

"Course I will. Pick a piece of cloth and show me whar you keep that truck." She reached into a low-slung cloth tool belt, strapped around her waist, and pulled out a tape measure.

Leta passed in front of the woman and pointed out the window. "There, under the tree next to the curb. It's the baby blue truck."

Leta watched in wonder as the woman puttered about her shop gathering supplies before she headed out the door. From the window, she marveled at how precise and detailed she was as she busily took measurements, collected information, and jotted down notes in a tiny flip spiral notebook. She'd dab the lead of the pencil on her tongue and scratched out a line, then began again, painstakingly drawing out a design before heading back inside.

"There 'ppears to be no problem with making ya that awnin'. What's it fer?" she asked, moving behind the counter.

"A flower truck...I intend to sell flowers from it," she said, trying to be as direct as possible with her answer.

"Were you get them flowers from?" Dewey Maude asked, turning her head slightly with an accusatory glare.

"I grow them." Leta stared at the woman for a long moment, then relaxed and tucked her hair behind her ears. "My place joins Tru Ransome's land up on Sweet Grass Creek," she said, regaining her composure. She had never liked being questioned, especially by someone she'd just met and was trying to give her money to. "Do you know him?"

"Any red-blooded woman who passes Tru Ransome on the street would usually turn fer a second look. I reckon men like that are in short supply in a day of soft men that take to comfort and ease." She pulled her head back sharply. "You live on that ghost land up from the Ransome place? I tell you it ain't livable! Gives me the heebie jeebies just thinkin' 'bout it."

Leta was not quite sure how to handle the comment. Whether the woman was serious or not, she couldn't tell. Hopefully it was only Dewey Maude's suspicious nature and mountain ways that made her seem at first unfriendly. "I live in Stone House, where I grew up."

She slapped her pencil on the counter. "You Mae's?"

Leta nodded.

"Well, why didn't you say so in the first place? I took you fer one of them uppity Purviance girls. Thought for a minute you lived up creek from Tru." She shook her head. "There's mighty strange things stirrin' up that creek. Did you ever see a haint 'round those parts? A ghost, some calls 'em."

"No ma'am," Leta reassured the woman, anxious to get back to the business at hand. "How much will the awning cost?" she asked, directly this time.

"Pick a fabric and give me a few days. Come back— with the truck and a check."

Leta paused a moment, her hand brushing lightly across a crisp white fabric with soft blue stripes. The cool hues of blue and white stripes provided an instant sense of tranquility. "I think this fabric will do. It has a fresh look to it."

"Right cheerful and happy," Dewey Maude said. "Where you settin' up your flower truck?"

"I'm not sure yet. Do you think they'll let me set-up here in town somewhere?"

"Law, yes! They'll let anybody down here."

Leta ignored the comment, fighting a smile.

"They had this one woman down here who sold her ex-husband's ghost. Called it 'Ghost in a Bottle'. I asked her how she knew he was in thar. She said she poured two fingers of Captain Morgan through the neck of that bottle, pushed in an old cigar butt, and his black spirit just sucked right in thar. That's how she trapped him. Sold him to Stella Novall. Course, if you be believin' all them rumors, Stella always had a thing for the man." With that said, Dewey Maude disappeared behind the counter like a deer in the brush.

Chapter 18

There is a bond of fellowship in sorrow that knows no predictability. Leta walked down the dirt road to where a clump of cedars showed dark and tall against the last purple glow in the sky. She was about to enter Ransome Land.

A movement down a well-worn path caught Leta's eye and she spied Tru, walking up from the creek, using the shovel in his hand as a walking stick. He spotted Leta, turned and whistled shrilly over his shoulder, then waved his hand forward before going inside an outbuilding.

Ambling up the path came Abe, moseying along like a man at the end of a long workday. The lingering light touched the unruly crop of hair sticking out from under his cap. She swallowed hard against the rising swell of emotions, then smiled at the grin on the young boy's face as he noticed her and came running into her outstretched arms. The boy seemed to have grown into a young man overnight.

She pushed him back to see into his eyes. "Look at you! You've grown so much and so fast! How are things going, Abe? Do you like living with your grandparents? Are they treating you both well?"

Abe shoved a hand up under his ball cap and scratched before he spoke. "It ain't like being home with you, but I reckon they're good to us."

"And Journey? Is she getting along okay?" She searched his face, taking in every inch of it.

"Durned if I know. You can't tell about her. She never talks." He seemed to be shaping his thoughts to say something else. As he spoke, anger grew dark in his face. "I told them you were good to us! That what that lady said was nothin' but lies!" Yanking off his cap, he slapped the side of his leg with it. "But they don't listen to kids."

"What lady?"

"That lady that comes around here. Mr. Ransome's girlfriend." His hands clenched and his frame grew tense. "She's always tryin' to talk to me, but I don't give her the time of day."

"Edwina?"

"Yeah, that's her."

Leta looked at the boy's face with quick sympathy. "Never mind about her." Her mother's heart was stirred at the sight of the boy taking up for her. "Do you think your grandparents might let you and your sister come for a visit sometime?"

The angry face left, and a hopeful smile replaced it. "I can ask! Maybe they'll listen to me this time."

"You do that and let me know what they say." She hugged the boy one more time before letting him go. "You best be getting back. I don't want Mr. Ransome mad at you for slacking on the job." After ruffling the boy's hair, she turned to go.

Tru leaned very still against a sawhorse as he looked out the shed door. He watched the two talk until Leta ruffled Abe's hair and walked away. An owl's call came from a nearby thicket followed by a faint drone. His curiosity was aroused by the musical quality to the hum. Turning to face the sound, he could see nothing but shifting lights and shadows in the purple depths of the nearby woods.

Then, from somewhere in the trees came the haunting melody of his childhood, "The Ashgrove." Pushing off the sawhorse, he walked toward the tree line, looking carefully in every direction. In that odd time of a long twilight, he suddenly felt as if he were not alone. A feeling of being observed caused the hair on the back of his neck to rise. The low tune came again and just as he was about to enter the woods, Abe came running through the field toward him.

The boy caught his breath from the run and raised his excited face. "I'm gonna ask my grandparents if we can visit Leta. She wants us to!"

"Calm down, son—what's this all about?"

"Leta! She wants me and Journey to come stay at Stone House again! To visit! Maybe she'll even let us spend the night!"

A sudden thought came to Tru. "Why don't I talk with your grandparents about it when I take you home. Maybe we can change the way they feel about her."

The boy nodded his head excitedly. "They'd believe *you* if you told them that we weren't never abused by Leta. We ain't never been treated so good by *anybody* as her!" Instantly the gloom was gone and Abe's face lit up again. "Maybe they'd even let us spend the night some! You could ask 'em, couldn't you!"

"Slow down, boy, first things first." He put his hand on Abe's shoulders and walked him back to the truck, the

144

tune forgotten as it faded into the trees. Abe went around to the passenger side of the truck, and Tru hesitated, his hand on the door handle. "When we get there, you stay quiet—let me do all the talking."

Tru turned off the rural road and pulled into the sand and dirt packed yard of the Littleton's. He rolled to a stop near a leaning concrete grotto that housed a statue of the Virgin Mary. Jumping out of the truck, Abe hurried up the brick and board steps, calling for his grandmother. Tru strode across the yard, scanning the abandoned pecan orchard that encroached on the house, seeming in places to almost swallow the modest plank structure. Low heavy limbs, some brown and full of dead leaves, obscured the roof and masked most of the windows on the side of the house.

As if to beckon him closer into the grove, an evening chorus of crickets and tree frogs began a slow song from the trees. Out in the orchard there was a tangle of green and dead branches choking the rows of pecan trees. Row after row of the finest pecan trees in the county. *An extravagant waste*, Tru thought to himself.

As if reading his mind, a cracked and shaky voice came from behind and echoed his musings.

"Eighty-four acres of mature pecan trees just sittin' there a wasting away."

He turned to find Cora Littleton gazing longingly across the pecan grove. "Must've been quite a farm at one time," he said, seeing the sadness in her eyes.

"It was a young orchard when we first set out, Clyde and me. Course, we were young ourselves." She smiled a little and shrugged. "We had our ups and downs like most farm folks, and there were times it seemed they were mostly downs. Right at first, anyway. Still, you got

145

to commit to care for an orchard for the long haul, I reckon. It pains me to see how neglected it is now."

"I'm sure your husband will get it in shape in no time, when he's back on his feet."

Mrs. Littleton smiled ruefully. "Clyde…well, he ain't been in no shape to do nothin' for the last couple of years. Not since his stroke. He's been in the hospital off and on most of the last two years. All he does is sit these days." She glanced back at the house, sadly. "Clyde always said, 'planting and maintaining a pecan orchard is like investing in the stock market. You gotta be willing to take a risk' and we did. Yes sir, we surely did that."

Tru rested his hands on his hips, taking in the sorry state of the grove. After a moment of studying the condition of the farm, he glanced over at the woman. "What about your son? I'm sure he would be more than glad to help you get this place up and running again."

"My son can't get his own life up and running again," she informed him bluntly, raising a brow as she looked Tru dead in the eye. "Abe does all he can, but he's still a boy. And I don't use children for farm labor like some folks do around here."

Tru narrowed his eyes and met the impertinent stare of the woman. For the first time since he'd arrived, he took a moment to take in Cora Littleton. The face was thin and wrinkled, leather like, and there was a hardness about her mouth. But her eyes told a different story. There was sorrow welling up in the faded blue eyes, replacing the harshness.

"If you're referring to Leta Purviance, I can tell you for a fact that you have the wrong impression of her. She's a kind and compassionate person and would never think of using the children in that way. She loves those kids. True, they had their chores to do, but what child is there that hasn't benefitted from a little responsibility?" He grinned charmingly as he teased. "My mother called a shovel a 'character building machine' and she was dead serious about building my character. But don't take my word for it," he nodded toward the house, "just ask your grandkids and then listen to them. Children rarely lie about whether someone is kind to them or not."

"I'm grateful to you for giving Abe a job. The saints of God know we need a little extra cash these days, but why should I take *your* word over the word of the social worker?"

"Well, the social worker knows only what my girlfriend, Edwina, told her. Edwina and Leta happen to be cousins with," he struggled for the right words, "not the best relationship."

For some reason that sounded reasonable to Cora. It was plain to see that Tru Ransome admired the woman. Maybe his girlfriend was jealous. Faced with a choice, Cora paused for a minute, then as if coming to a decision, turned and headed toward the house. "I'm gonna do just that. Just what you said," she called out loudly over her shoulder. "I'm gonna ask them kids how they were treated by that woman. I have no reason not to believe them. They've never lied to us before…as far as I know, anyway," she said, then stopped. "If you know somebody who wants a job helping me get this farm up a running, come see me before you leave. We'll talk some business."

Two hours later, Tru grinned as he pulled away from the Littleton's house. Feeling better than he had in a long while.

Chapter 19

Sunlight fell in long bars of colored gold across the wooden floors of Quay Community Church. Tru was like a prisoner, tugging at his straps. He sank back in the pew, his hand held out briefly as if to put a stop to the poisonous words spewing from the beautiful lips of his girlfriend. Edwina produced a paper where her accusations were all written out nice and smooth, just like her speech.

"I'm simply concerned for the safety and welfare of the children and anyone else whom Leta has had contact." Edwina glanced back and forth between Tru and J.D., trying to find some word with which to convince the men. "She says that she hears humming in the trees and talks to an old woman named Gussie who paddles up in a red canoe or something. A red canoe for heaven's sake!"

The peaceful minded minister placed his arm across the back of the pew and glanced back at Tru, trying to read his expression. He could not reconcile the woman he had come to know with this picture Edwina was painting of Leta. It was to him a ridiculous notion. At last J.D. spoke. "So, you're saying that Leta is a *danger* to everyone she meets? That she should be *institutionalized* for hearing the wind in the trees and talking to an old woman?"

"Not wind, a song being hummed. She said so herself! That's what she told Grand Bess. And now my grandmother is worried sick about Leta's *mental state*." She drew the last words out while she gave each man a searching look. "Someone overheard Grand Bess telling my grandfather all this. What I'm *saying* is that she shouldn't be allowed access to the rooms of helpless people in the hospital. And certainly not impressionable children! They're at her mercy, and she's not right in the head!" she exclaimed, stabbing a finger to her forehead. "Who knows what she'll do! We must think of the protection of others in this situation. If we don't, who will?" She stood erect, her proud chin lifting a notch. "And that's why I've petitioned the hospital board and they're taking the matter under review. They'll discuss it at their next board meeting. Leta should no longer be allowed to make rounds with you in the hospital. It's simply not safe, pastor. They'll contact her, so it will save you the embarrassment of having to tell her yourself."

Tru did not say a word during the exchange. He seemed not to hear, then all at once he murmured, "'The Ashgrove.'"

"The ashgrove?" Edwina said, her brow furrowed as she waited for an explanation.

"The song that's hummed in the trees...it's called, 'The Ashegrove.' Or it's a hymn to the same melody, there are several of them. It's an old Welsh tune. My mother used to hum it to me as a boy. I hear it at night sometimes, near the trees or at the edge of the woods down by the old church."

J.D. raised his eyes to the ceiling and smiled. "That doesn't surprise me…my sister was always rambling around those old stones near the church. She probably picked it up from there. In the winter we could cross the creek by a path of slick stones that led up to the old church yard." He released a sigh. "I hadn't thought about that in years."

A gasp of astonishment escaped from Edwina. "Do you hear yourself?"

Tru cocked his head and looked at her. She showed in her very posture the proud old southern blood. She had never struggled a day in her life. How would it be possible for her to show mercy to those without her advantages? What would this beautiful creature be had she Leta's heart? "Are you surprised to learn that I hear melodies coming from the woods, the same as Leta?"

"Yes, quite frankly, I am. Could it be you're taking up for her for some reason?" she accused.

J.D. cleared his throat. "You know, I think I know the woman in the boat too. Her name is August, but she goes by Gussie. If it's the same person I'm thinking of, as far as I know, she's not a ghost. Of course, I'll ask Leta to make sure she sees the woman's shadow the next time she comes around. Ghosts don't have shadows you know. They're insubstantial things."

Edwina straightened her blouse and mumbled under her breath. "I know when I'm being mocked." Cocking her eyebrow, she faced her pastor. "Where women are concerned, you two men aren't the most discerning, now are you?"

Tru appeared undismayed and nodded his head. "So, it would seem."

She glared at Tru. "One way or another, I'll see to it

150

that Leta will no longer have access to helpless hospital patients, even if it means going to the board myself! My family still carries a lot of weight in this town, in case you've forgotten."

Struggling to control a sudden urge to lash out, Tru responded carefully. "I've seen and heard some mighty strange things since I've been working on my property. The low country seems to hold its own secrets, particularly around that old church."

"You keep talking about a church—do you mean Shiloh? That's on Purviance land?" Edwina's full attention was on him now.

Tru leaned back and watched his girlfriend from beneath gathered brows. "Not anymore...it belongs to me. Your grandfather and I worked out an arrangement."

Before she could recover from her astonishment, J.D. cleared his throat, slapped his thigh, and stood. "Well, that's all settled then." He looked at Edwina. "There are many things in this old world that defy explanation. Mysteries, we call them. Seems to me that whatever is going on down there near the old church is one of them. I'll do my part to explain the situation to the board members. It's all been a big misunderstanding."

Edwina's face reddened, beginning at her throat, then rising to her brow. She snatched her purse from the pew seat and said, "I'll be in the car." All that was left of her was a faint trace of expensive French perfume in the air.

The men watched her out of sight until the clicking sound of her heels faded and a car door slammed. They turned toward each other.

"You know, it's rumored we're not very discerning where women are concerned," J.D. said. "Do you suppose they're right?"

Tru looked at his uncle hard before he answered. "Without a doubt."

At this, J.D.'s face and manner changed quickly, and he smiled, putting his hand on Tru's shoulder. "Leta has a sound mind and a kind heart. Something tells me God's at work in all this. We just have to trust Him."

Running a hand across his close-cut beard, he said, "I don't think Leta is too impressed with what passes for a Christian around here. I just hope we don't stand in the way of what God's doing."

Before J.D. could reply, Tru reluctantly stood and walked up the aisle in the direction of the church doors.

**

A flash of lightning lit the early afternoon sky as a light rain settled on the creek. Leta pressed against the high worktable, looking out the garden shed window, letting her eyes skim the lavender blue flower fields. They stretched along the land and down to the bank until they met with the dimpled surface of the water.

Once again, her mind wandered to Gussie. *What has happened to her?* It had been almost a week since her last visit. She could hardly deny a feeling of expectation whenever the old woman came to the garden shed. She hoped to find those shining black eyes watching her; ready to impart some truth or tale.

A strange sense of restlessness roved within Leta. The awareness that she was now completely alone weighed heavily on her mind. Earlier in the morning she had risen before dawn, after a night of tossing and turning, and made her way to the fields, working in the cool of the mists before the humidity began its steady climb.

A sudden gust of rain swept across the window, and

it struck full force with a spattering of raindrops against the tin roof. Her mood seemed much in accord with the elements. Looking up toward the house, she saw the trees swaying and being tossed in the wind. Under her feet she felt the vibrations of a rolling thunder.

Instinctively, she stepped away from the window, clutching her arms together as she watched the trees, flowers, and shrubs being tugged and twisted in their wild wrestle with the wind. Then, the storm was over as suddenly as it had started. The thunder now rumbled in the distance and a gentle rain began to fall. Rows of bent and defeated dahlias, sunflowers, and zinnias bowed their beaten heads.

Inhaling a deep breath, Leta leaned against the table and let it out slowly as her whole body began to relax.

The door flew open with a bang, causing Leta to jump and slam her knee into the leg of the table. And there stood Gussie, dripping wet in a yellow poncho.

"It's a mighty good thing I had this here rain cape tucked under my boat seat. Been caught out in squalls like this a time or two before," Gussie said, shaking the water from her hands.

"Good night, woman! You scared the life out of me!" As quickly as she could, Leta snatched up a few clean paper towels from the roll and began blotting the old woman's face. "You weren't out in your boat in all this I hope!" she fussed.

Gussie waved her away, "Quit your fussin', child, I be all right. Takes more than a little wind and water to do me in."

Leta looked out the door, and her voice faltered. "I wish I could say the same for our flowers. Looks like we've just lost some of our crop."

There was such a look of hopelessness on the face of Leta that Gussie fixed her eyes on the girl and spoke sternly. "Who makes them flowers, girl? Who sends the rain and controls the wind?" She pointed her crooked finger out the open door. Lightning still flashed in the distance, showing which way the storm had gone. But over the fields, sunlight began breaking through the clouds, dancing on the sparkling green of drenched flowers and wet grasses.

Leta turned to stare into the shining eyes of her friend. Gussie had always taught her to look for life that is more than what could be seen with the physical eye. She challenged her to see beyond what's there. Little by little, the old woman had been teaching Leta how to see with the eyes of faith.

"You get that worrying side of you natural, from your momma. She was a fretter too."

Leta widened her eyes. "You knew my mother?"

"Why course I did. Who do you think named you?" Gussie shuffled over to a cane-bottom chair and sat down with a moan. "Mercy. We used to spend afternoons over at the old church." She pointed toward the creek. "Shiloh's what they called it then. That's where we met for the very first time…where she told me about you and that you was comin'." The old woman's face was aglow with light. "You're sure like your momma. Yesum, you sure 'nough are."

Speechless, Leta could only stand and stare down in shock at the little crumpled woman. "Why haven't you said something before? I mean, we've worked together all summer—you could've at least told me!"

Gussie shrugged, "I didn't think nothin' of it. I meet all kinda special folks down there from time-to-time. But child, your momma was so happy to be havin' a little baby girl." With tender compassion, the old woman reached up to clasp Leta's hand. "She would be mighty proud of you, mighty proud."

Leta searched the face in front of her, remembering all the things she'd been told about her mother and trying so desperately to piece together a mental picture of her. "Was she kind, Gussie? Strong?"

Gussie squeezed her hand. "Heather was just bubblin' over with life. Had these sparklin' eyes that could just talk to you. Never saw her as happy as when she was with your daddy. They rambled around everywhere in that old truck you got." Gussie grew quiet and lowered her head. "They should've known."

"Who should've known? Known what?"

"Your momma and daddy. They should've gotten away from it all for a season, 'til you got here." Gussie let out a long sigh and eased herself back in the chair. "God's gonna teach that proud woman of culture and refinement a great lesson." She looked at Leta, knowingly. "That's why you here, child. You part of that lesson."

"Would it have made any difference? My mother died giving birth to me."

"She gave birth to you in secret, so as not to bring shame and embarrassment to the Purviance family by going to the hospital. See, some of them Purviance big shots ran that hospital. At least their money did. By the time Mae found your mother, she had lost too much blood."

A tear leaked from the corner of Leta's eye. She pressed her hands against her forehead trying to absorb the truth of the words. As she sat down, she heard the voice of Gussie, but it had something strange and new in it.

"I don't know how to say this so you can understand, but you bein' here, it's surely God's way, child, it's surely God's way."

***

All through the summer, until the day's work was done, Leta and Gussie were side-by-side. Gradually, the flower fields began to take on more muted shades and new meaning for Leta as Gussie led her along, slowly pointing out the wonders of God's creation. She taught her to pause in the hurried rush of the frantic world and listen to the sounds and rhythms of life that go unseen by most. The wind in the trees, the gentle lap of the creek waters against the bank, and all the musical voices of the day and night. All these were understood and answered by Gussie.

As evening neared, Leta straightened her back and glanced toward a copse of trees. "I've finally named our flower business."

"You have? What we callin' it?"

Leta brushed the hair from her eyes with the back of her hand. "Sweethums."

The corners of Gussie's mouth edged into a smile, and from her lips, her pearl white teeth gleamed. "That's a mighty fine name."

"I've even ordered business cards and a magnetic label to place on the side of the flower truck. I think you'll like the logo, it's blue and white with a wildflower in the center of the design."

"Yes ma'am, that's mighty fine indeed..."

"Gussie, have you ever heard the sounds of humming," she motioned toward the woods, "from the

156

tree line over there, near the old church?" She picked up the galvanized bucket full of water and moved it down the furrow closer to the woman.

With the slow deliberateness that was so marked in her character, Gussie placed a handful of flowers into the bucket of water, then straightened, wiping her hands on her apron. "Yes, child, many times. Many times, I've heard them hums. You know…flowers can hear hums too. The hummin' of bees. It's true. They hear them a buzzin' on the air around them and it makes their nectar so much sweeter. Maybe that's what the Good Lord is doin' to you. Makin' you sweeter."

Leta crossed her arms over her chest and stared at Gussie. She suspected that the woman's comment was deeper than her words, but she wasn't completely sure.

The wind picked up, and a low hum began to well up from the woods, sweet and honyed. Leta became fully aware of the music flowing around and through her. The air nearly vibrated with the tune. For the first time in her life, her heart surged in harmony with a tide of memory as the old hymn she'd heard so often before swelled within her. With the fullness of it, she hardly dared to breathe as the sound settled low around her.

Gussie's head swayed slowly with the music, but her eyes rolled upward. "We have churches, but not all worship God in them. Jesus said if we remain silent, the very stones will cry out. Maybe that's what we're hearin', child, somethin' you may have refused to consider. It might be *your* voice that's missin'. Maybe some rock out there is takin' your place in givin' God the glory He's due."

The humming quieted and faded like a ghost, gracefully, peacefully. The dying melody lingered for a few seconds, then disappeared.

Looking into the deep and shadowy woods for one quiet, unexpected moment, she began to sense something holy. "Walk with me to the old church, Gussie. I want to go there."

Grasping each other's arms, they walked through the sweetgrass to where the path branched off, making their way slowly down the old trail. Gussie had grown quiet when they entered the church yard. As they walked in silence through the sacred grounds near the cemetery, her face grew solemn. Rising clear, above the low sounds of evening crickets, came the plaintive call of a mourning dove. The coming of autumn's welcoming air could not be ignored as a touch of melancholy settled around them. Somberly they strolled through the grounds toward the church.

Leta thought back to the conversation they'd had earlier. When they'd reached the steps of the church, she stopped. "You said you and my mother met here. You said you named me. What made you pick the name Leta? Was it a family name?"

The woman appeared not to hear and began climbing slowly and steadily up the steps. She looked back over her shoulder to make sure Leta was following. Once inside the church, Gussie shuffled down the uneven plank floor and stopped in the middle of the aisle. Looking up, she pointed. "Up there, child."

Leta looked up, following the old woman's gaze. She saw the rough-hewn cross and the familiar words scrawled above it.

"There," Gussie said in a hushed and reverent tone.

Leta blinked her golden eyes and looked inquiringly at Gussie as if seeking her guidance. The old woman nodded toward the wall, assuring her that it held her answer.

Leta looked again, then her eyes grew enormous as she recognized her name spelled out in an acrostic of letters. She mouthed the words. "Love Even Through Anguish—LETA!"

Chapter 20

September was in the air around Sweet Grass Creek and the leaves of an occasional tree deepened into wine from the sun. The cool autumn wind was exhilaratingly fresh, and all the colors of the woods were washed in pale shades of gold and persimmon.

Tru walked along the path, dragging his thoughts through the dirt behind him. His heart ached like an old bruise when, on days like these, his thoughts turned to Marbella, his ex-wife.

At the first hint of autumn his mind would often wander back to when he'd first met his wife. Life had been good then, and full of promise. Until it wasn't.

The inner upheaval had begun eight years into their marriage when he had been confronted by Marbella with the news that she was in love with Hawk, Tru's closest friend.

Mystified by the revelation, his emotions ran the gamut. His first reaction was sheer disbelief. But one look at his wife's contorted face convinced him of the truth of her words. Deeply wounded by the unfaithfulness and more than a little stunned that the two people he had loved and trusted most in the world had betrayed him.

The news of the affair had caused complete turmoil in the church where Tru had pastored for those same eight years. After his wife left and filed for divorce, he'd tried to shove all his troubles away and get on with his life as if it had never happened. But he couldn't. For a myriad of reasons, he could not go on as before. As the pain rolled in on dark nights, hate began welling up inside the man and the direction of his mind began to scare him. He'd thought about running, used to dream about leaving it all behind. One black night he did.

He angled toward a path leading down to a swimming hole—the only deep pool in Sweet Grass Creek—with stinging cold water as clear as crystal, fed by a spring. It looked blue-gray until you waded into it, then you could see your toes on the sandy bottom.

Tru had discovered the pool one hot August day after working in the merciless heat. Since then, he'd made it a practice to visit the place on days when he needed to cool his blood.

Stepping into the shade of a huge eastern pine, the sound of his approach was muffled as he walked across a deep carpet of needles toward the pool. The area was clear of undergrowth where the shade and the thick pine needles had all but smothered out the weeds. The clean scent of pine hung in the air, and Tru drew a heady breath of it, filling his lungs, hoping to clear his mind.

A swooshing sound in the distance caught his attention. He took a half-step back to scan the area. It was as if someone trudged through the marsh, just out-of-sight around the bend. He stared into the grasses where the spring-fed water permeated the creek. He waited to see what would emerge from the reeds. He caught sight of a woman, wading through the water toward the pool.

Rounding the reeds, she touched her forehead, shading her eyes from the brilliant sun as she glanced around.

"You prefer a water path over a clear trail?" Tru asked, recognizing Leta as she came into view from behind the manna grass. His deep voice seemed to come as a shock in the whispering quiet of the clearing.

Spotting Tru, Leta regained her composure. "Absolutely. This way if anyone tries to track me with a pack of wild dogs, they'll lose the trail." She entered the shallow water in a pair of hip-boot waders, carefully maneuvering around the deep center of the pool as though she knew it was there.

Tru caught his smile. "Happen to you often...being chased by a pack of wild dogs, I mean?"

"Well, no...but if I'm ever hunted, I'll be ready for them." She swaggered a bit. "You've got to stay in practice for that sort of thing."

"Aren't you afraid of what might *really* come after you out here?"

"Like what?"

"Gators, water moccasins, cottonmouths..."

"No, it's too cool for snakes, and I can spot a gator a mile away. Besides, Pop taught me what to do with fear a long time ago." She waded her way through the pool and up to the bank.

He walked to the edge of the water, leaned down, and grasped her hand, pulling her to a patch of level ground. "Yeah, what's that?"

"He told me to bury my fears in the dirt, then plant flowers over them. Only now I sell the flowers, then repeat the process." She grinned and looked around, admiring the little secluded glade. "I'd forgotten how nice it is here. The pool seems smaller than I remember—of course *I* was smaller too. I guess I still see it just the way it was," she touched her forehead, "up here."

"I forgot about you growing up here." He reached down and picked up a smooth stone, skipping it across the surface of the water. "My mother and J.D. lived across the creek," he pointed toward a bank of trees in the distance, "with their great aunt."

"That's right—J.D. is your uncle...I keep forgetting that. You two seem more like friends."

"We are."

Leta removed a small pack from her back, sat down with her back against a tree on the needle-blanketed ground, and pulled up her knees. "That was a long time ago...when I lived here. I feel like I was somebody else back then." Reaching into her pack, she pulled out a chicken wing. "Want one? I have plenty."

Tru shook his head and lowered himself onto a root beside her. "I know what you mean. I feel like I've lived several lifetimes already." He picked up a piece of pine straw and rolled it between his fingers. "Nice waders."

"Pop's," she said, chewing on a mouthful of chicken. She ran a hand down the front of the boot. "I found them in the garden shed—wanted to try them out." She hugged her knees and ate her chicken and sat like that for a time without saying anything. Then she raised her head and looked at him. "What are you doing?"

"I'm watching you denude a chicken wing with your teeth...to a point just beyond normal."

"No, I mean out here." She wiped her mouth with a napkin before wrapping the bone and stuffing it back in the pack. "Tell me about yourself."

"Not much to tell. What do you want to know?" His

mouth softened into a lazy smile as the woman carefully avoided meeting his eyes.

"How about start with one of those lifetimes you've lived." Blowing the hair out of her eyes, she waited for his response. She took a quick glance at him, but only saw reluctance. The hesitation in his face told Leta that Tru's past was obviously not something he cared to talk about. She rephrased the question. "So how did you end up here…building a place of retreat for men?"

He looked at her musingly with a tight smile. "How does anybody end up anywhere? And it's not a place *of* retreat, it's just a retreat."

She turned her face away from him and stared ahead, watching as a blue heron glided smoothly over the surface of the water, coming to a graceful landing in the reeds. "Same thing—I can't tell the difference." She pulled off her boots with vigor and sat cross legged. "Why did you retreat here?"

"I was tired," he said, with some exasperation.

"No better place to hide from life than way out here, that's for sure," she stated the obvious directly.

Tru considered the girl. Her features, despite her best efforts to seem tomboyish, were not. Even with oversized boots and a two-sizes-too-big flannel shirt, it hardly worked at all. Her small, pert nose with its sun-touched color and a far too soft looking pink mouth were certainly not boyish. Far from it. But the eyes! The sparkling golden eyes fringed in silky black lashes were a hazard that could wreck a man, to Tru's way of thinking. "Is that Pop's shirt too? And what makes you think I'm hiding?"

"When I'm tired or mentally troubled, I hide in my work. I keep my hands busy so my mind can rest." She shrugged. "Maybe I'm the only one that does that."

Tru tossed the pine needle down and said, "Well, you've grown quite a few flowers in that field of yours. From the looks of it, I'd say you've been *mighty* troubled."

Leta smiled, unable to resist the humor of it. "And yes, this is Pop's shirt." She pulled at the fabric. "I wear his watch too. Makes me feel closer to him when I miss him. But it's okay, I don't expect you to understand."

He studied her for a minute, very still, absorbing her. "That's why I order candy bars from Nashville…they remind me of my dad. He was from Tennessee and swore there was no better candy in the world than a Goo Goo Cluster."

"What? I've got to disagree. The Butterfinger is hands down the greatest candy bar, ever! Gussie and I argue about it all the time."

"Gussie still around?"

"Been with me nearly every day. Except when she disappears for a while to who knows where. For an older person, she's sure not afraid of work."

Tru silently agreed with Leta, then asked, "Does she live around here?"

The golden eyes narrowed. "I'm not really sure. She comes from that direction." She pointed up the creek passed the old church. "She lives alone, I do know that." She collected a little pile of pine needles with her fingers. "I pay her, but she seems more interested in just having somebody to talk to."

"Sounds like most elderly people I know," Tru stated, remembering his former flock. "She sounds lonely. It's an epidemic these days."

Leta shrugged noncommittally. "I don't think so.

She's the most positive person I've ever met. So full of joy, even on the worst of days."

Raising his eyebrows, he said, "She sounds like a woman who has a close relationship with her creator."

"If *any* woman does, *she* does."

"What about you?" He noticed the sunlight reflecting off the three small keys which hung on a long silver chain about her neck. She fingered them nervously.

"Not really." She pulled her hand from the necklace and looked away. "Gussie said she named me. Can you believe that? She got the name from the old church wall." She looked back at Tru timidly and rubbed the tip of her nose with a slim finger. "LETA: Love Even Through Anguish."

Tru was silent.

She glanced at the round face of her watch, noted the time, and began pulling on her boots. "Guess I better get back before it gets dark. Wouldn't want some gator to mistake me for a muskrat."

Tru stood to his feet. "Are you going back the way you came?"

Shading her eyes against the lowering sun, Leta tried to see his face. "I was planning to. Why?"

"I was wondering if—" He found it hard to admit to Leta that he still wanted to talk with her. "I've been meaning to talk to you about a job opportunity I've stumbled on. See if you'd be interested in helping me get the Littleton's pecan grove up and running again. Could be worth a small fortune to all of us. It's a massive grove, and they'll split the profits in exchange for labor and selling the produce."

She got to her feet, but in the process felt herself become unsteady and wobbly in the oversized boots. She reached out to brace her hand against the trunk of the pine, but Tru grabbed her arm to steady her. "You're asking the wrong girl about that job."

"Thought you might need another source of income in a few weeks—that'll be just about time for the pecan harvest." He reluctantly let go of her arm. "Seems like a perfect fit to me. You already have a sizable customer base, from what I've been told."

"Yeah, well, I don't think the Littleton's will care too much for your plan. They don't like me. They'll probably shoot me on sight."

"That was all just a misunderstanding. It's been straightened out. I spoke to Cora Littleton myself. So did Abe and Journey."

Leta carefully avoided meeting his eyes. "I'll partner up with you when I get a personal invitation from Mrs. Littleton telling me that she has revised her opinion of me…and not before."

"Shake on it?"

With a start of surprise, Leta grasped the broad hand. "If you don't pay closer attention to the people you want to partner up with, Tru Ransome, we'll *both* end up being run out of town on a rail."

***

Leta Purviance was left speechless. She'd ended the call from Cora Littleton, placed the cell phone on the little wicker table beside her, and sat back in the porch rocker, more than a little stunned. Grace began to dawn upon the shadows and doubts of her mind, and Leta could only smile.

"What you grinin' 'bout, child? You look like the kitty that swallowed the canary. Who was on that phone?" Gussie tapped out the last words with her hand on the arm of the rocker.

"Cora Littleton. Looks like I'm partnering up with Tru Ransome after all."

Gussie rocked forward and stopped. "That handsome devil? You better watch yoself or Miss Edwina gonna stir up a lot of mischief around here…and it won't be pretty."

Having Edwina stirred up about anything was like looking down the wrong end of a rifle—Leta would just as soon not be on the receiving end when it went off. Still, the prospect of earning enough money in a few short months to get ahead of next year's growing season excited her.

"I'll take my chances. Besides, I know what a pain Edwina can be, but I can handle her. Tru's no picnic either when he sets his mind on something. He's a man, completely and totally. I've watched him command that crew of his all summer long. When his frustration is at an all-time high, he runs his hand through his hair. That's how you know to back off. Then, you just think smarter. Try and sugar him up."

"Just how you figurin' on doin' that?" Gussie eyed the girl suspiciously.

Leta knew something about men. Even the most ornery, sour-faced men in the community turned into grinning idiots at a bake sale table. She would make a mental note that if she ever needed extra help from Tru, she would make a pie. And not just any pie, but a Goo Goo Cluster pie. That would be sure to sweeten the man's disposition.

Leta was about to allay the woman's fears with her plan when Gussie interrupted.

"I'll tell you how you do that—with respect! It's what

every man wants. Now you listen to ole' Gussie—you show that man respect and you're in for a good partnership. Same's true if you're wantin' a good marriage. Same thing. Trust and respect."

The golden eyes narrowed. "You sure don't need to worry about that! A husband is the last thing I'm looking for. I came close enough once to know what I don't want—a man! Of course..." she drew the last word out while she considered Tru Ransome. Had she been of such a mind, she might have admired the handsome swarthy features, the dark eyes that seemed capable of piercing Leta's innermost secrets. "He's not too hard on the eyes, either." She winked at Gussie. "You can come along and help if you want. We'll cut you in. How about it?"

Gussie laughed aloud at the woman's grit. She had already concluded that Leta was single-minded in her pursuits. She also knew that sometimes our best laid plans had a way of cutting their own course. "No thank you. You just leave ole' Gussie outta your plans for now."

The bond between the two women had been forged during the difficult days of farming the flower fields. They'd shared triumphs and defeats, survived storms and dry spells and, at the end of the day, they would each go their own way, one toward the creek, the other toward the yellow lights of home, satisfied with their day's work.

Chapter 21

On the first day of work at Littleton Pecan Orchard, Leta got out of the SUV and started toward an old, faded barn. She plodded through the grove in her boots, stepping over fallen branches and high grass. A thick layer of debris had accumulated beneath the trees, and old, discolored trash was strewn around the grounds.

Though it was early in the morning when Leta arrived, there was already activity near the barn. She could guess the reason. Tru Ransome.

Cora Littleton emerged from the barn and upon seeing Leta's approach, called out. "I can't even tell what the harvest is gonna look like beneath all that trash 'round them trees. Briars, weeds, and debris make finding these little camouflaged rascals even harder. Once we get all that cleaned up, we can better tell what we're lookin' at."

"Sounds like a plan," Leta commented, realizing there would be little chit chat from the woman, which suited her just fine. She'd worried it might take a while for Cora to warm up to her. "Point me in a direction and I'll get started."

Cora reached back and grabbed a rake and handed it to Leta. She tossed an apron to her and led her through the grove, pausing at each tree to give brief, pertinent instructions as to what would be expected. "Old timers like my husband used to use their shirt-tails for an apron to hold their pecans. But I find this suits me just fine." She reached down and picked up two pecans and began to shake them in her hand.

Mimicking her instructor, Leta did the same.

Cora caught her smile, pleased to be imitated. "This might seem strange to you but pecans, when they're rattled together, can tell you about themselves. If they sound hollow, they're not filled out. If they sound full and solid, well that's just what you're lookin' for. Crack a few suspicious ones open and it won't be long before you get an ear for the sound of a good pecan. The good ones feel weighty and a good picker will know by the feel of a pecan if it's good quality just by the weight."

Leta held the pecans to her ear, rattled them, smiled, and dropped them into her apron pouch.

"I got a feelin' we're lookin' at a good crop this year. Had some good soakin' summer rains." Cora pointed to her little house. "See those trees closest to the old homestead? They're larger than the others 'cause I water my garden over there. My pa did the same, years back. Pecan trees love water."

"So, you grew up here?" Leta asked, picking through the weeds, searching for pecans.

"Sure did. All this used to be way out in the country, surrounded by fields and meadows. But Quay has sprawled and now this place, and everything it seems, has grown too close to my way of thinking. Used to be just us, and a few families original to the countryside of Quay, like your folks."

Leta caught a movement and looked over her shoulder toward the barn. She watched as Tru emptied a bag into

171

a container and fastened it to the back of a mower. He glanced up, and as he took note of them, grinned. Sometimes the man could be so completely exasperating, yet there was something about him that was likable too. She just had the usual difficulty figuring out exactly what to believe about the man.

Cora followed Leta's eyes to the barn and saw Tru yanking on his gloves. "Guess that's our cue to get started. Rake away as many of the fallen limbs as you can." She pointed to a peculiarly shaped tree out of order with the symmetrical lines of the grove. "Start with that big tree closest to the house. That way Tru can mow around it first. It's the hardest to reach 'cause it clings to the house." She laughed. "The way the tree grips that old house, you'd think it's very life depended on it. Guess it ain't never figured out that life comes from another source, one it can't rightly see."

Leta felt a pang of pity for the tree. "I guess some people would want to cut it down in order to preserve the uniformity of the pecan grove. It just seems so out-of-place with the other trees," Leta remarked. There was something about the tree that bothered her sense of harmony.

Cora smiled. "I'm more interested in the fruit than the form. That tree has yielded more pecans than any of those other trees that conform to a more regular pattern. The fruit of a tree tells the story of a tree." She winked. "Same goes for people."

When Cora left her, she did not waste any time. With the heavy rake she reached into the weeds beneath the tree, raking out piles of debris. All through the morning her labors were ignored for the most part by the other workers more engrossed in their tasks. At one point she looked up and noticed Abe and Journey, not far from her, tossing sticks into a pile. They stole glances at her every so often and waved timidly. Leta knew they'd been warned not to bother the others while they were working. Still, they seemed happy to have her here.

A slim figure with a shaggy mop of dirty blond hair slowly stepped from behind Abe. As if with a common habit, the boy swiped back his unruly hair with a quick hand and with the same hand, threw it up at Leta.

She waved back and smiled. The boy seemed friendly and not much younger than Abe. Under closer inspection, Leta thought there was something familiar in his face. But it was a face that spoke of need and that seemed to speak the loudest. Watching him, he yawned until his jaws had to have cracked.

Cora chuckled as she walked up, seeing what held Leta's attention. "No one understands those boys as well as each other. They speak the same language, so to speak. Why, I've seen them talk to each other with only their eyes."

"Who is that boy? I've never seen him around."

"Name's Justice Box, but we all call him Juice. Juice Box."

Leta lifted her eyebrows. "Juice Box? Is he related to Jim Bo Box, the shrimper?" She remembered the man from her growing up years in Quay. He had been a stocky man, broad-shouldered and thick-chested and in a rough and rugged way, rather handsome.

Cora gave a quick sideways glance at Leta and, without giving an answer, drew in a deep breath.

Cora Littleton seemed a contradiction. She was tough, but you could sense compassion in her that came from a natural flow deep within. Then, all at once a barrier of pride seemed to fall into place while you were not paying attention.

"Yeah, they live down the road," Cora offered without any further comment. "Come on to the barn and eat dinner. We got it all spread-out. Cornbread, field peas, fried chicken, and mashed potatoes. Clyde loves company, but he can't get out in all this—makes him antsy, so I'm fixin' us a couple of plates. I'll eat with him back at the house."

"That sounds good. Let me wrap this up and I'll head that way." Turning back to the work at hand, she glanced up and saw Tru walking toward her with a question in his expression.

"Hold up," Tru said as he approached.

"Is there something I'm doing that's not good with you?"

"No, no, you're good, you just might want to leave some of the pecans behind, though. The harvest machine works better if it has something to harvest," he said, controlling his smirk only slightly.

"It might be helpful to have a clear picture of what's expected of me from the get-go. I was told to rake it, so, I raked it!" She leaned on her rake and blew the hair out of her eyes. "Seems to me like you're the one with the problem if you can't find pecans in a pecan orchard— under a pecan tree."

Her eyes were direct and, he thought, just a little challenging. "Well, you sure did rake it, that's a fact. You could plant corn in those furrows." Tru's mouth relaxed into his signature smile as she glared at him. He enjoyed riling the woman. Sometimes she could get so exasperated her eyes sparked and her lips puckered. His amusement was cut short by the sound of gears shifting on a clanging truck, drawing his attention away from her and onto the road.

Shading her eyes against the noon day sun, she tried to see who was pulling into the yard. "Oh, that's the guy who's going to fix my roof," she said, stepping back to prop the rake against a tree. "I told him to meet me here." With Tru's back turned to her, she reached down and snatched up a pecan, pelting him in the back of the head with it.

He turned around sharply, rubbing the spot on his head. "What was that?"

Leta pointed up into a tree. "A pecan?" Undismayed she began walking toward the truck, watching as the driver slid from behind the wheel, planting his boots on the ground.

Tru observed the woman suspiciously from a distance. He was about to turn away when he heard the stranger laugh. There seemed something familiar about him. The straight black hair, the long curve to his lanky build. Despite himself, Tru felt pulled toward the man. He crossed the grove and approached them, smiling as he extended his hand toward the stranger. "Tru Ransome." Sudden recognition hit him. "Injun?"

A slow, spreading smile transformed the ruddy face. "None other, preacher!"

"Preacher?" Leta gestured with her finger. "Tru?" She looked at Tru skeptically. "Are you really a preacher?"

"Well, it's been argued both ways," Tru stated.

Shaking his head, Injun paused for a moment, then threw a thumb over his shoulder and explained gruffly, "He's the reason I'm not dead or rotting in some jail cell." His eyes filled with pride. "He pastored one of the largest churches in Charlotte and still found time to get out to the reservation and hold services for a bunch of renegade Indians. If it wasn't for Pastor Tru, my buddies and I would still be wasting our lives gaming on the reservation and getting drunk most nights."

Leta leaned forward, her golden eyes glowing with expectant curiosity. She swallowed with difficulty and managed to ask Tru innocently, "What happened?"

"Life." Tru searched for more words to clarify the answer but couldn't find them. "Good to see you, Injun. Tell the boys I said hello." With that said, he slapped his work gloves against his thigh, turned, and walked back to the barn.

Leta opened her mouth to respond, but before she could utter a word, Injun had hopped back into the pick-up and waved, disappearing in a cloud of white dust.

***

At the end of the day a smothering heat had set in with not a breath of wind. Such days were rare in autumn, but not unheard of. Cora Littleton sat on the front porch in the shade, sipping sweet, iced tea.

Tru walked up, wiping his face with his sleeve. "Got everything locked up." He glanced around. "Have you seen Leta?"

Cora rocked steadily, head back, fanning her face with a magazine, her expression unreadable. "She's gone," she drawled reflectively. "You were right about that girl. She's a hard worker. Reminds me of myself at that age."

Tru smiled. Coming from Cora Littleton, that was the highest form of praise.

***

It was no surprise to Leta that with the unusual heat, there was bound to be a storm. Heat in the low country could suck the moisture right out of the earth and make steam from it as it fueled into an afternoon thunderstorm. Driving the rural roads back home, she steadied the basket of leftovers Cora had given her on the seat beside her and glanced skyward as thunder rumbled to the west. Rain thickened to a downpour. The drum beat on the roof of the SUV grew to a roar as the wipers slapped furiously back and forth.

Leta was more curious than ever about Tru Ransome. *A preacher! He could have told me. He didn't say diddly squat about it.* She felt herself tense, gripping the steering wheel until her knuckles grew white. She'd watched a blue shadow pass over Tru's face, and a certain sadness filled his eyes as Injun spoke about their past. Something had dredged up a long-buried memory.

The SUV bumped off the county road and onto the overgrown ruts as Leta drove slowly through the gate and back to Stone House.

***

It was a fresh, soft day, filled with a peaceful radiance as though Sunday morning were somehow a quality in the air. Leta ducked her head under the vine-covered trellis, her arms filled with blooms. She ambled toward the garden shed, intent on the task of hanging up bundles of apricot and silvery rose strawflowers to dry.

From the corner of her eye she caught sight of Gussie, perched at her favorite spot on the warm stones of the wall. "I didn't expect to see you today." She shifted the flowers to one arm, stepping near the woman. "Thought you'd be in church by now, praying for me," she teased.

"Most days I wake up prayin'—sayin' my prayers in whisper. But on Sundays—I shout them out! I sing all day long 'bout how God's been good to me. How He saved me!" She crooked her gnarled finger and put it under Leta's chin. "Lift your chin, child, so I can see them eyes."

Leta smiled and titled her head back, heaving an exaggerated sigh of submission.

"Don't never forget this. *All* who call on the name of the Lord, shall be saved!" She held Leta's chin for a silent, tense moment, peering into her eyes. She let her hand drop. "Do *you* pray?"

Leta's throat thickened. She swallowed hard. "No—I mean, I guess I pray, but all my words seem to catch on the wind and get blown away somewhere." She shrugged. "They don't stand a chance of reaching Him."

The old woman wagged her finger. "Let me ease your mind…ain't no such thing as a place where God ain't. He's everywhere, even somewhere."

Leta nodded once, conceding, then turned away from the piercing berry-black eyes. "Maybe you're right."

"Course I'm right. Now, why ain't you at church?"

With her free hand, Leta leisurely examined and adjusted the soft leather tool belt draped around her waist. "I'm not about all that." She jerked her head up. "Wait—why aren't *you* in church?"

"'Cause I've come here to remind *you* that *you* gotta whole lot to be thankin' the good Lord for. Ain't no better place to do that than down there at that church." Gussie rested her hands on the warm stone wall. "Go on up to the house now…get yoself ready. You can make it if you hurry."

The idea was not to Leta's liking. It had been a long time since she'd darkened the doors of a church. A half-frown, half-smile crossed her face. "A wise woman once told me that God is everywhere, even right here in this garden. So, there's no reason for me to leave here to worship God there. I'm out here surrounded by His creation!" The dark eyes that found hers were so intense that Leta had to fight the urge not to cower away.

"God places a higher value and a greater priority on human beings…'cause they're made in His image. He don't want us to quit comin' together…that's what the Good Book says, now—"

Leta raised a hand to halt Gussie's sermon. "Okay, okay…I hear you." She ducked her head under the confederate jasmine vines and made her way back down the path toward the house. She called over her shoulder. "If I decide to go, and that's a big *if,* I have only one nice dress—better pray it fits!"

A hush fell over the house as Leta stepped into her bedroom. She fell back on the bed, arms flung out, staring at the ceiling. The faint scent of lavender linen water floated up from the bed linens. Since purchasing the scented water from Dewey Maude, she had made a habit of sprinkling her sheets with the water as she ironed them. The aroma took her back in memory to a time in her life when she was innocent. The time she had lived at Stone House with her grandparents, spending her days simply and honestly with goodness all around her.

"God help me!" A low moan started from deep within her chest. "I know how bad I've been; my sins are staring me down right now." She grabbed the coverlet and clinched her fist. "You have all the facts before you; whatever you decide about me is fair. I've been out of step with you for a long time—I wouldn't blame you if you struck me dead! But if you don't, I'm about to get up and get dressed and go to church."

***

The day cleared as the sea mists vanished with the warmth of the sun. Sea birds cried overhead as light glinted on the ripples of the ocean. Leta stood motionless outside Quay Community Church. It was a beautiful structure, with a stately steeple rising to the heavens. The dark thoughts and reluctance she had experienced so strongly only moments before, seemed to be lifting along with the fog. A surge of unexpected hope replaced the hesitancy, and she made her way up the steps and through the church doors.

"Leta?" Tru questioned uncertainly. He'd spotted the woman in the foyer of the church, lingering near the doorway. His eyes took in the soft, cream-colored dress, the sun-lightened brown hair hanging loose down her back. Tilting his head, he chuckled as he surveyed her. "I almost didn't recognize you without your tool belt and jeans."

Leta smiled, clearing her throat. "I started to wear my boots—then, decided against it at the last minute. Didn't want to scuff up the floors."

"We appreciate that." Tru laughed and pulled open the interior door to the sanctuary. "Glad you're here."

"Thank you." Her eyes flitted over the rows of pews and came to rest on a vacant seat near the back of the church. Much to her relief, the entire pew was empty. As she made her way toward the seat, a man appeared almost immediately at her side. He was a tall, lanky man, thin as a sapling with a wide grin and an Adam's apple that bobbed up and down as he swallowed.

The man made no pretense as he searched Leta's hand for evidence of a ring. He stared dumbly at her, as if considering a course of action that might be open to him.

"Oh, excuse me. Is this your seat?" She stepped aside for the man, allowing him to pass.

The lumbering man was in no rush to answer. He stood grinning with a mouth full of little bleached "chicklet" teeth. "No ma'am…if it was, I'd gladly give it up for *you*." He waved toward the pew. "After you."

Observing the scene from the doorway, Tru shook his head and passed a hand reflectively over his close-cut beard. Slowly he walked down the aisle toward Leta. Putting a hand underneath her elbow he whispered, "Your seat is up there," he motioned toward the front of the church, "next to your cousin." He glanced back at the man and nodded. "Emmett, how are you?"

Emmett hitched up his pants. "I was doing pretty good 'til you came along."

Leta looked at the eager man, then glanced at the back of Edwina's head a few rows ahead. She was undecided which course to take until Tru took the decision from her and began walking her forward.

"Won't Edwina be thrilled to see you here!" A smile flashed rakishly across his swarthy face.

Leta fixed him with an intensified glare. The boldness and obvious enjoyment the man was having with the situation was beginning to wear on her nerves. She tried to pull free of him but found her arm firmly grasped. Not wishing to cause a scene, she smiled and spoke through clenched teeth. "I'm sure all her prayers have now been answered."

"You really should thank me for the rescue," Tru whispered under his breath. "Emmett is…well, let's just say, starved for affection."

The low, velvet smooth voice answered, "If the

choice is between one starved for affection or one completely devoid of it, I think I would prefer the former."

Tru dropped his hand and looked at her, his brows coming together in bafflement. After a prolonged moment, he turned his attention to Edwina. "Look who's joining us today. Isn't this a pleasant surprise?"

The stiff blonde head indicated an almost imperceptible nod. "Of course."

As Leta slid into the seat, she looked up at Tru, eyeing him with annoyance. He stood before her, his face unreadable, but his eyes held a challenge. She was beginning to have doubts about ever being rid of the man and his snooty girlfriend. Everywhere she turned, he seemed to be there. She ran a hand through her loose hair and said, "Thank you. I can hardly wait to repay you for the favor someday."

"Don't mention it—I would do the same for any damsel in distress." He winked at her. But before he stepped away, he saw her cheeks flex with irritation and her tongue come out in a quick, mocking gesture. His brow rose sharply, then a soft, lazy smile spread across his face.

The trembling warmth that ran through Leta completely disrupted her composure. She turned her face away and betrayed the sudden flush that did not go unnoticed by Edwina.

The older cousin cut her cold eyes at Leta. "You embarrass us all with your childish gestures. How dare you. And in church in front of God and everybody."

"When you speak to me," Leta whispered, "use a more respectful tone." She smoothed her dress over her legs. "We wouldn't want anyone to get the wrong impression of you, now would we?" The gleam in her eyes did not disguise a threatening smile.

Edwina shrugged insolently. "I'm not the one who should be worried about making a bad impression. You know who you are and so does God."

Leta inclined her head to Edwina, who held herself aloof by staring at the pulpit. Leta spoke low, as if imparting a deep secret. "I met someone the other day. For some reason he reminds me of you. A young boy...Jim Bo Box's son. Do you know him?"

Edwina snapped her head toward Leta, then snatched a bulletin from the back of the seat and busily scanned it.

Tru slid into the seat next to Edwina, missing the exchange between the cousins. "J.D. will be surprised to see who's here today," he said. "Won't he, Edwina?"

The icy eyes considered Leta without a hint of expression, then with slow deliberation, she folded the bulletin and tucked it into her Bible. "I'm sure he will."

Leta saw the uncertainty that crossed her cousin's face, cutting through the chilly demeanor. Whether it was humiliation or irritation, she couldn't tell. But she saw the muscles in Edwina's cheek tighten as she stared ahead.

J.D. Redman casually walked to the pulpit and, tapping the top of his Bible, leaned back to scan the crowd. Spotting Leta, a smile swept across his face briefly before he turned his attention to the order of service.

Chapter 22

Stone House sat dismally beneath a chilly autumn haze.
Nearby, the garden shed with its door ajar, creaked and
popped like old bones with the slightest stirring of the
air. A thin growth of zinnias fought vainly for the
attention of the waning light, but the drifting leaves of
dried gold told the true story, that the end of the growing
season was upon them.

Inside the house, Leta was warm and comfortable in
her chair. A soft blanket covered her lap and a cup of
mint tea sat steaming beside her. Her toes, no longer
chilled from the cool dampness of the cottage, lay tucked
beneath the covers. She was content to stay curled in the
soft folds of the chair.

The room was now cast in shadows and indistinct
shapes. She caught a whiff of a scent reminiscent of shoe
polish as it drifted past her. Was it her imagination that
made her think she was not entirely alone or was it her
need? Distractedly, Leta reached for the teacup and took
a long smooth sip, trying to sort out her own feelings.
Earlier in the day she'd received a call from a very blunt
and calloused woman, a representative of the hospital. A
cold, tight feeling began to form in the pit of Leta's
stomach as she recalled the words. *A situation has been*

brought to our attention. We regret to inform you that your services will no longer be needed at the hospital.

"It's just the same as always," Leta half snarled, half cried. "Edwina is behind this—I am certain of that."

Edwina's life had been a whole series of charades and false pretenses. Leta knew she'd struck a nerve when she'd mentioned Jim Bo Box and his son to her cousin. She'd not been certain of her suspicions until she'd seen the reaction, for a fleeting second, chiseled on the face of the ice princess.

Her cousin had always been attracted to the manly shrimper, Jim Bo. During her teen years, Edwina would often go to the wharf late in the day as the fishermen were returning from their labors. When reports began to surface implying that Edwina and Jim Bo had been seen together at all hours of the night, Edwina had repeatedly lied to her family about it. But when confronted directly by her mother, Althea, she had only shrugged indifferently, sneering that she knew what she was doing and that she would see whomever she wanted. Not long after that conversation, she'd been sent away, returning home only after a full year had passed.

Some say Edwina's father, Randall Purviance, had had the final say on the matter. Randall was a man rarely seen and seldom heard, preferring to run his business affairs from his Mount Pleasant office near Charleston, safely away from all the drama his household of women kept stirred.

Leta breathed deeply, trying to fight the frustration of living in a place where the shallow brook of conformity flowed on its nervous way, thinking all else unaffected by its passing. *And what of the boy, Justice Box,* she thought. *Could he truly belong to Edwina?*

A knock on the door echoed through the house, and Leta jumped, sloshing tea from her cup. Uncertain of what lay beyond the door, she slipped from the chair and grabbed the rifle propped against the fireplace.

"Who is it?" Leta called through the door.

"It's Grand Bess, dear!"

In the next moment Leta snatched open the door. Grand Bess stood stock still in the entrance. She wore a silk robe of teal, tied loosely over matching silk pajamas. Jewel encrusted silver house shoes peeked out from underneath the hem of her pajama pants.

Leta's eyes widened with concern. "Grand Bess—are you okay?"

The older woman smiled indulgently. "I can't be certain until I'm safely out of the crosshairs."

Leta lowered the rifle and propped it behind the door. "Come in." She carefully averted her grandmother away from the kitchen with its sink full of dirty dishes that she'd abandoned in favor of a cup of tea. Directing her toward the living room, she asked, "I was just having a cup of mint tea. Would you like one?"

"No dear, thank you, but no." She took a seat on the overstuffed couch and sank backward, her feet rising off the floor. "Dear me, it seems your sofa wishes to swallow me."

"Here, I'll prop a pillow behind you." Leta lifted a pillow from the end of the couch and tucked it securely behind her grandmother. "There, that's much better."

"Yes indeed, thank you. This must be what is referred to as overstuffed."

Lowering her gaze, Leta caught her laugh, remembering her grandmother's objection to unladylike ways.

"Not me, the couch."

Unable to think of anything to say, Leta simply sat down in a chair across from Grand Bess and smiled.

"It has come to my attention, my dear, that you may have accidentally stumbled upon a bit of information concerning a rather unfortunate and delicate situation." She adjusted her back against the pillow and gently pressed into it.

She raised a brow. "I have?"

"Indeed. If the full story comes to light." She smiled graciously. "No need to concern yourself too much, dear. I'm sure you wouldn't want it spread about any more than we do. All families have their secrets."

"Secrets?" Her voice and smile were mildly questioning.

"Good, then we understand each other," Grand Bess said, decisively. "I told them you would listen to reason. We must all do what we can to protect the reputation of the Purviance name. We have a certain standing in the community, you understand. People look to us as an example, a standard, so to speak...have for generations."

Leta drummed her fingers against the arm of the chair. It was a full minute before she spoke. "Oh, I think I understand—perfectly. It was for the reputation of the Purviance name that my mother lost her life. At a tragically young age. It was for that same reputation that I was left without a mother and kept out of the way most of my life so as not to be an embarrassment to the Purviance name. So, you see, I do understand. In fact, you could say I have first-hand knowledge! Forgive me if I choose to see things differently." A shudder of revulsion passed through her. The anger she was feeling was so powerful that her hands shook. "I have a different perspective—entirely."

Grand Bess was quiet, and completely still. Like a shimmer of dew reflecting off the petals of a pale pink rose, tears smudged her cheeks. She gently blotted them with a touch from the back of her hand. Unaccustomed to having the truth of her life so blatantly displayed, Grand Bess was at a loss for knowing how to respond. She lowered her head. "I'm so very sorry for my part in your mother's untimely death." She pressed her lips together and sniffled. "I have many regrets in this life. Nothing haunts me…nothing…so much…as that."

Leta never blinked, never moved a muscle. She knew it had been her mother's choice to give birth in secret. Still, the pressure Heather must've felt from the Purviance family had to have been overwhelming. The storm she'd felt raging within her was beginning to subside, vanishing as suddenly as it had come as she looked into the tearful face of her grandmother. With a single, nearly imperceptible nod, she accepted the apology.

"Many in our family are not going to be pleased should it ever come out about Edwina," Grand Bess said in a broken voice. "It could mean trouble for you, and I certainly wouldn't want that, dear. It would upset me, terribly."

"Don't let my minority status bother you too much. I can take care of myself."

"Why, your dear Ma Mae would come back to haunt me if I allowed anything to happen to you." The woman patted her eyes again and sniffed. "Do you have some plan of your own for Edwina's child? I know how you like to take in those with…disadvantages."

Leta bristled at the comment and the implication.

"No, but if I can make a difference in his life or in the lives of other misfits like myself, you had better believe I'm going to do it. And I don't care *what* the Purviance family thinks about it either."

The way the girl boldly spoke told Grand Bess that Leta had convictions, and the rigid set of her jaw said she was ready to fight for them. She could not help but wonder at the grit of the young woman. She certainly had sand. Since she saw the lack of those same tendencies in herself, Grand Bess could only respect her granddaughter even more for having what she so desperately wanted. "I see." She considered the irate young girl for a long moment. "Well, you have made your intentions very clear. Tell me about the boy—this Justice Box?" She folded her hands together in her lap resolutely, as if settling the fact in her mind of the boy's existence by attaching a name to the child.

Leta pursed her lips. "I don't know much, but when I find out more, it'll be best for you not to get involved. I wouldn't want to cause trouble for you with *your* family."

Grand Bess burst into relaxed laughter, and when she leaned forward from the couch, the blue eyes were lively with excitement. "I want you to know something, young lady. I haven't felt so free and alive in decades. Positively purged! Why, since you came back to Quay, my blood has started pumping through my veins again. I was afraid I was doomed to a passive, fading end, but now I'm certain I can change! If I have breath left in me, there is hope yet!"

Leta's eyebrows rose sharply, but Grand Bess was up and off the couch, making her way to the door.

Grand Bess could hardly contain her bubbling

189

excitement. "Maybe there are better things waiting for me down the path than anything I've experienced so far? I want to see that boy—it's time I met my great grandson. It's time I went back to church too! Thank you, dear, for reminding me that I was once like you. Once, long, long ago—I had courage too."

***

Across the sleeping countryside eerie mists hung low to the ground. The only faint sound to break the silence of the morning was the tires of Tru Ransome's truck rolling over the packed pavement like a silent ghost. Noiselessly he passed a few lamp-lit houses at the edge of town where barking dogs threatened to rouse the households. A few yards farther on, he came to the entrance of Stone House. He peered into the grayness where the house sat shrouded in the autumn haze.

He had traveled only a short distance when, through the fog, a dark gray shape flitted across the road and disappeared behind a large cedar. Drawing near, he scanned the area but could see no other movement. He stopped the truck and reached into the glove compartment where he drew out his handgun. Tru stepped out and stealthily crept toward the tree.

"You, behind the tree!" He commanded. "Step out where I can see you."

Nothing moved. Tru raised the pistol, and the double click of the hammer being drawn back echoed in the shrouded mist. He was about to call out again when a small, thin form stepped out from behind the cedar. Recognizing the boy by his crooked front teeth, he lowered the weapon.

"Juice! What on earth are you doing out this early. Does your dad know where you are?"

The boy stared at Tru. Isolation radiated from him like an aura, but there was this desolation in his eyes, made up of fear and suspicion. The shaggy blond head gave a negative reply.

"Hop in, I'll take you home." Tru said, his voice stern. He was fair, but he was tough.

Juice reluctantly met Tru's eyes. They seemed to burn a hole through him. With another shake of the boy's head, he waited for the man's response with trepidation.

At the current rate of exchange, Tru would do better making the decision for the boy. He walked to the truck, reached over, and stuck the gun back into the compartment. "I can't leave you here alone. You'll have to come with me, son. When your dad wakes up and finds you gone, he'll be worried sick."

The boy swaggered a bit. "My daddy ain't home. Down at the wharf, same as always. 'sides, I been taking care of myself since I was little."

Tru chuckled lightly, then turned his head to consider the boy more closely. "Okay. Who watches you while your dad is away?"

"Nobody. Don't need nobody watchin' me. I been taking care of myself—"

"I know, I know, since you were little." The sarcasm was bold in the man's tone. "I'm not leaving you until I'm sure of your safety. What about your mother?"

Juice shrugged. "I ain't got no momma. Least—no mommas got me."

Tru slid his hand into the pocket of his jacket for a stick of gum and handed it to Juice. "That's Purviance land over there you were about to trespass on."

Juice stuffed the gum in his mouth, then swiped the hair out of his eyes. "I know that."

Inwardly, Tru groaned his frustration and reached into his pocket for another stick of gum. He eyed the boy, folded the gum in half, and stood patiently in the road. He was sticking the gum in his mouth when his attention was arrested by the boy's face. His brow rose sharply as the grimy cheeks flexed with irritation. He'd seen that look before. Clamping down firmly on the gum, he began to chew slowly, staring into Juice's eyes. Mouthing a startled oath, he questioned, "Who *is* your mother?"

"Don't know. Dad won't say. Some say she's a no-account from the marsh—a swap rat." He shrugged.

"Who told you that?" Tru felt a pang of pity for the ragged boy.

Juice squirmed uneasily and glanced around. "Kids at school, mostly. They've got a few names for me…none of them good. Mostly say I'm trash and come from trash and smell like trash."

After a long moment, Tru rested a booted foot on the step rail of the truck. "Where were you headed? Stone House?"

"No. I go down to the dock sometimes. He chewed his lip. "You gonna tell my dad?" He wiped his nose on the back of a dirty sleeve, mindful of the intensity of those dark eyes as they focused on him, and he looked away.

Tru's frown softened into a bittersweet smile. "No." He dropped his boot to the ground and let out a long, steadying breath.

Juice's eyes darted to Tru. "He don't like me roamin' around too far from the house. But he don't mind if I go fishin'. Got me a pole down there, tucked up under the dock. I don't bother nobody. I see Miss Leta, but I reckon she ain't never seen me."

"What about your friend Abe? Do you ever meet him down there?" Tru secretly wondered if Abe ever found his way back to visit Leta.

"Nope. Saw that man who comes to see my dad down there once. He was taking pictures with a camera, but mostly I just see fishermen. Course, me and Abe been all over them woods. We stay away from your place. 'Ceptin' the church. Ghosts won't go near there. Has special powers to help and protect folks, from what I hear."

Tru's eyes skimmed over the boy casually, not sure if he was glad or not that Juice seemed to have found his voice. "Ghosts? What makes you think my place is haunted?"

"'Cause of them voices, them hums. Even my daddy says your place is haunted. Told me to stay away from there. Found a picture of that old church taped to the ceilin' below the deck of his shrimp boat. Says it brings him good luck. Has a charm of a white-haired mermaid danglin' on a chain next to it. It just swings there next to the picture. Told me Shiloh church was a special place with special powers. Guess you know that for yourself."

Before Tru could wrap his mind around the boy's words, Juice turned, ducked his head under, a cedar branch and was gone from sight into the mist.

Tru stared dumbly after the boy, considering all the courses of action open to him. He passed a hand reflectively over his beard. The more he thought about it, the more he wanted to confront the boy's father outright. Why would a father fill his child's head with so many superstitions? In his mind he imagined the life of a shrimper. Maybe all seamen had tall tales and fanciful stories to tell their children. He glanced about in frustration. The boy would have no reason to doubt his father. He yanked open the door to his truck, making a mental note to inform his neighbor about the young visitor. He laughed and whispered under his breath. "Better stay out of sight, son, or Miss Leta will sure take care of you."

Chapter 23

The weeks drew out, the days passing like beads dropping from a broken string, one after the other and all much the same. The end of the growing season was upon them and now, more than ever, Leta felt the confinement of it.

The pecan crop harvested from the Littleton grove had yielded a good income for all parties involved. Now, Leta had the funds to complete the conversion of her truck into a mobile roadside stand. The extra influx of money had given her some financial relief, allowing her to increase her inventory to include fall mums, pecans, and colorful pumpkins she could sell on the seaside streets of Quay. From time-to-time her path had crossed with Tru's and she had been forced to accept the company of his girlfriend. Blood kin or not, Leta found every encounter with the woman challenging. To stay long in her cousin's presence was to alter her mood considerably.

The spire of Quay Community Church caught Leta's attention, pulling her in as the bell tolled the afternoon hour. The steeple reached high above the treetops, ramrod straight, impervious to the thrashing winds of the approaching storm. Potent scents of salty waters blew in from the sea as commercial fishermen, no less salty, ponderously plowed their way toward the harbor. These weathered men, which made their living from the sea, also plied the estuarial waters near the mouth of the river, hauling in boatloads of fish, shrimp, and oysters. Their squat boats, heavily laden with the day's catch, wallowed toward the dock with deceptive laziness where Leta knew, from days past, that Tru would be waiting for them.

For several weeks now, fishermen had been met on shore by a bevy of men from Quay Community Church. Leta had noticed Tru with the other men, waiting on the docks to greet the seamen with steaming cups of hot coffee. After exchanging a few back slaps and boisterous greetings, the men all worked together to help bring in the load. She'd heard comments by several of her customers and began piecing things together. A woman had informed her that it was a ministry, a way to give back to the community. The lady told that when she had asked one of the men from church why they were doing such a thing, he'd only winked and said, "Jesus was partial to fishermen too."

The lump in Leta's throat grew tight as she thought about each man and how they were serving these roughneck fishermen. In the next instant, Edwina's low and mocking laughter drew her attention away from the harbor and toward the last person in the world she ever wanted to see standing in front of her truck.

"For a minute there I thought you were praying. Then I remembered—wait, this is Leta." Edwina shook her glossy blond hair, smirking.

Leta wisely turned her back and continued with her duties, straightening pots of mums and filling in gaps where pumpkins had been sold. "I hear it's nice over in Mount Pleasant this time of year. I bet they'd throw you a party if you go back."

"You'd like that, wouldn't you?" Not getting the reaction she anticipated, she looked around. "Have you seen Tru? I'm sure if he were anywhere around, you'd know it." She took a casual sip from her water bottle.

Leta ignored the sarcastic inflection in her voice, having grown accustomed to it. She raised her eyes and her chin. "He's at the dock. Helping Jim Bo Box unload his catch."

Edwina choked and had to cough to clear her throat. "What! Why would he do such a thing without telling me?"

Sighing impatiently, Leta looked at her cousin. "I would assume it's because he's a Christian and doesn't need your permission to do for others. He's a real one. You know, the kind that actually tries to live what they believe and not just put on a show of it in front of others."

Edwina controlled her glare only slightly. "Be careful with your words, Leta, or I'll see to it that your life is miserable here." She smoothed her sleek hair with a heavily jeweled hand. "Let me assure you, I have the means to do it. I know things. Things that might make you *rethink* your devotion to your closest neighbor."

"I doubt that." Leta looked away with an unlikely eye.

Edwina managed to smile dazzlingly. "You know, just the other day Milton said something interesting to me. It seems he came across some papers showing the transference of a small piece of Purviance land to Tru Ransome...payment for services rendered."

"So?" She began stacking jars of honey on the sideboard of the truck. She couldn't be still when Edwina

197

was around.

"So, the most interesting thing I learned from his little discovery is that *you* were listed as the service rendered!"

Leta turned sharply and met the haughty stare. "I don't believe you *or* that dog on a leash you call an assistant."

This time Edwina's reply took longer, as if drawing out the response so she could get more enjoyment out of it. "I don't want to ruin the image you have of your knight in shining armor, but truth is truth. And the truth of the matter is, Tru wanted the land the old Shiloh church sits on and was willing to trade out for it. All he had to do was help Grand Bess's illegitimate grandchild by plowing her fields. Oh sure, some money was exchanged, but you were part of the bargain. Mission accomplished. So, have a care with the way you speak to me or else I'll make known to everyone that little Miss Entrepreneur is, in fact, just as dependent on Purviance money as everyone else in this pitiful little town."

In the face of the threat, Leta leaned forward, a feral gleam in her eye. "You have no power or control over me." Her face was flint like, but her voice was soft and slow. "I'm not threatened by you or anyone else in this town. Money, position, *and* reputation mean nothing to me."

"That remains to be seen, doesn't it?" Edwina walked back to her sand-white Bentley convertible and sped off, leaving a trail of dead leaves swirling in her wake.

With some mental effort, Leta began sorting and stacking pumpkins, anxious to keep her hands busy so she wouldn't have to think on the words of her cousin. Tootsie Morgan, a common sight around town, came into view, leisurely strolling up the sidewalk. Pausing in front of Leta's flower truck, she fingered a bright orange pumpkin, brushed back her hair, and cast her eyes toward the dark, steel-gray sky that hovered close about the rooftops.

It was clear to Leta that Tootsie Morgan was no stranger to the dark side of things. She'd heard of the woman's reputation as having a rather promiscuous past. She watched as Tootsie swept a piece of the unnatural shade of burgundy hair from her eyes and just stood there looking up at the sky. The stench of the night before was still on her and from the smell, it must have been a smoky, stale beer stinking, rat hole.

Two loud and rowdy women crossed the street, coming up to join Tootsie. One shouldered a large, shiny golden tote bag bulging at the seams. They glanced around expectantly, as if awaiting someone to appear and rescue them from their sordid lives.

"Hi ladies. Need a pumpkin?" Leta asked, a little at odds as how to proceed. The women clearly meant to hang around in front of her flower truck with no intention of buying a thing.

"Ladies! Ha! Did you hear that Tootsie? She called us ladies. We ain't never been accused of bein' no ladies." The woman with the golden tote smiled, revealing a shiny golden tooth to match her bag.

"Shut up!" Tootsie said. There was no need for others to tell what she plainly knew for herself.

"We's told to meet Tru Ransome here. Got a little business to tend to with the man."

As if he'd materialized from their thoughts, Tru pulled up at the curb and got out, signaling the women to join him.

"And there he is now—right on time as always!"

Tootsie gave the girls a sly smile and they began to shriek with laughter.

Tru shook his head at their carrying on and motioned again for them to join him. Taking little, short steps with their high wedged heels, they hobbled over to him.

"I brought it. The least you can do is come and get it," Tru reprimanded, smiling.

Engrossed in the scene, Leta thought the women looked out of place next to Tru, like bumper stickers plastered across the rear end of a Lincoln Navigator. Even tired, dirty, and wet, Tru Ransome was in a league of his own. By his clothes, the man seemed every bit the weatherworn seaman. But he carried himself with the unconscious air of one long used to a position of command and influence. The dark eyes snapped with fire in a face marked by life's storms and grief, but there was compassion in them too; a kind of understanding Leta could not quite grasp.

As he talked, he doled out cash, looking searchingly and compassionately into the faces surrounding him. Faces not elegantly formed or proportioned but fixed with attention to his every word. But in all the time she'd known Tru, she'd never once seen him look at another person in such a way. Disturbed by the strange sight and by what she had learned from Edwina, she turned away and watched a leaf fall to the ground. A shudder ran through her, and she rubbed her arms with her hands methodically, wishing she were anywhere but here.

The passenger side of Tru's truck creaked open and J.D. Redman got out. Ambling over, he came to stand beside the flower truck, resting his arms on the railing. "Hello stranger." He motioned with his head toward Tru and the women. "This might be a while. Mind some company?"

"Not at all. Want some hot cider? Or do you need something a little stronger?" She smiled and reached up to loosen a Styrofoam cup from a short stack, motioning toward the carafe. "Help yourself."

"He took my advice for once," J.D. said, smiling as he took a short sip of the cider. "Told him to go around town and get to know people. Find out who needs work and hire them. There are plenty of people in need, even in a quaint little sea town like Quay. You just have to look for them."

"Hire them. For what?" An anxious moment passed as her thoughts went wild.

"Besides Ransome Land, Tru runs two private cigar clubs—has one just outside of town and another in Charlotte. Those particular women work for him locally."

"Cigar clubs? I thought he was a former pastor. Seems like an odd thing for a pastor to get involved in. Don't you preach against smoking?" she asked, surveying the scene with more than a little interest.

He flashed her a broad grin. "The best relationships don't restrict lives; they expand and enrich them so that we're free to be who God designed us to be. Being in a relationship with Jesus brings obedience. Then the Word of God and the Holy Spirit help us to do what we can't do for ourselves. He gives us grace to get it right. We've learned that when men talk...I mean really get honest with each other, there's usually a cigar involved. So, in these cigar clubs we have men available, guys we trust with something as important as the Gospel and men's lives and, well, you get the picture." He winked at her. "You should know better than to question a preacher. It will always lead to a sermon."

Leta stepped back and shifted a bucket of sunflowers near the tailgate of the truck. "So, you trick them."

"What? No!" he assured her. "It's important to identify as closely as possible with those you wish to reach. Jesus was even called a friend of prostitutes and tax collectors. The purpose is to lead them to salvation, not trick them into believing." He looked at her more closely. "We don't compromise the truth in any way to satisfy anyone. We just become all things to all men, that we might by all means save some."

Leta smirked. "So, what do *those* women do for him?" She glanced over her shoulder again trying to imagine where they fit in to the plan.

"They clean, restock, and report to Tru when supplies are low. Basically, they keep things running smoothly. Most of their work is done after hours—that's on purpose too." He felt a pang of pity for the women. "Keeps them occupied at night."

An easy autumn breeze played through the trees, scattering leaves, then quieted as Leta turned her attention toward Tru. Her hand trembled as his eyes caught hers. She felt weak, shaky, as if she were caught in the cross hairs of a Remington. In some powerful way, those eyes seemed capable of stripping the false from whatever passed before them. It was all she could do to face him and not retreat too quickly from his gaze.

Looking away casually, she asked, "Why can't he just mail their checks? Call them or text. Why does he have to meet with them in person?" She wouldn't admit it, but she found the attention the women were showing Tru annoying.

"Sometimes presence is what is most needed. Words

only will not do. You must be present," J.D. said, half smiling into her searching eyes. "My guess is he's planting a few seeds of his own."

A warmness grew within Leta. Her voice was tiny and hesitant as she questioned, "Why would he do that...for people who can do nothing for him? For people like those women and the fishermen down there. What kind of a person is he?"

J.D. laughed in amazement. "Why, he's a Blue Saint."

"He's a *what*?" Leta said, staring at J.D. like she hadn't heard him.

He shrugged. "No great mystery. A Blue Saint is someone who trusts God to use his past, his failures, hurts, and wounds to help someone else. A Blue Saint once explained that to me a long time ago. Saved me from throwing away my life." He flashed a smile. "And just look at me now."

"So, you're telling me that a Blue Saint rescued you?"

"Only God rescues...but He allows His children to play a crucial role in that rescue."

"I wish there was a way for you to just *breathe* your wisdom over me so I could understand you," Leta said. "Sometimes it's like you're speaking a foreign language."

"You should be asking God to do that for you—not me."

As Leta listened, an ache grew within her chest. For the most part, she felt unfit to ask anything of a God who speaks worlds into existence.

"Go someplace where you can hear His word and read it for yourself. Truth never goes out of style. It's as fresh as the morning. And remember, He never gives up on us. Ask any Blue Saint."

Leta thought back to the words Gussie had repeated over and over to her when times had been difficult. *God is good; whatever He allows He has His reasons; you've got to trust Him.* At the time, she hadn't understood the meaning behind those words, yet as she had looked at the shining face of J.D., she could not help but wonder at the root cause—some underlying mystery to it all. Glancing over her shoulder, she noticed the same shine on the face of Tru Ransome.

Chapter 24

Leta awakened with the first streaks of gray dawn. For a long, drawn-out moment, she snuggled deep into her warm quilt. Each November morning, she dreaded the moment her toes hit the cold floor. Tossing aside the covers, she gave in to the inevitable and quickly ran across the pine floor. She slipped her feet into the fuzzy house shoes she'd regretted kicking off near the bedroom door.

For all its stone and wood and sturdy construction, Stone House was cold and drafty. Childhood memories of waking up to a fully stoked fire now came flooding back. If this were a sampling of what could be expected from winter, something had to be done to see that firewood was split and stacked, ready to use.

Making her way downstairs, she reached the hearth and raised the lid on the wood storage bin. Splinters of kindling and three half-logs filled the space, just enough for a little warmth to chase off the morning chill. Arranging the pile into the fireplace, she lit the kindling and worked until tiny flames leaped upward around the sticks. The logs caught fire and soon the cracking heat drove her back. Warmed now, she went to the kitchen for coffee. Filling the coffee pot under a cold stream of water from the sink, her eyes widened at the beauty of the landscape outside the kitchen window. A smoky mist drifted over the surface of Sweet Grass Creek, and the trees stood washed in gold in the rising light.

Pulling herself away from the window, she waited as the coffee brewed. Then, sipping her coffee, went back to the fire. It took an effort, but she managed to slide into the chair closest to the fire and pull a thick blanket from a basket to cover her legs. Staring at the stone hearth, she thought of Gussie. She missed her friend. It had been a month since she'd last seen her. All attempts to find her were unsuccessful. It was as if she'd vanished into thin air.

The voice of Gussie, rich like mocha, played in Leta's head. Because of her, she'd begun to see things in a new light. Things like stones. *If we don't praise God, the very stones will cry out! Do you want a rock to take your place in the choir?* Leta smiled, remembering. She couldn't explain it, but she had sensed in Gussie an aura of wisdom, the spiritual kind, as if she were one of the few people in this old world who knew true North.

Feeling a strong desire to work outside with her hands, Leta got up, aching to throw herself into a task, some activity that would spend her energy in a meaningful way. By the time she had dressed and tugged on her work gloves, the sun had grown higher in the sky, but the cool temperatures remained.

Digging around in the garden shed, she found an ax propped in the corner, a silvery web encasing the handle. Lifting the ax, she freed it from its spider threads and headed in the direction of the woods.

After some searching, she came to a place where a tree had fallen across the path. Planting her feet squarely, she gripped the ax handle, swinging hard until she struck the center of the fallen tree. She worked it out of the wood with more than a little effort and struck it again, and again. This time a few chips flew out, but without much progress. Out of frustration, she raised the ax high above her head, ready to strike again, but the handle was seized from behind, mid strike.

"Mind if I help?" Tru whispered deep and throaty near her ear.

Leta jumped, then shivered. Recovering herself, she quickly let go of the ax handle and surrendered it to the man. Pressing her thumb into her raw hands, she said, "Have at it—unless I'm hindering you from church."

He looked at her confused. "Why would you say that?"

"This path takes you to the old church...just didn't want to be the one to keep a preacher from his prayers."

"Prayers can be said anywhere." He gripped the ax handle in his hand, his well-muscled arm flexing with the movement. "I've got a load of wood coming for the camp." Checking his watch, he said, "Should be rolling up any time. Plenty to share."

"How long have you been watching me?"

He held his amusement and answered the question. "Just long enough to know that *you* need help."

Leta bristled but didn't glance away. She met his words with rich golden eyes that never wavered. With a stiff back, standing straight and undaunted, she said, "I'll ask for your help when—"

"Watch it, Leta. Remember you're a lady." He caught his grin just before it spread across his face. He handed her the ax handle then bent down to lift the dead tree, tossing it away from the path. "And not just *any* lady, but a Purviance lady. What *will* people think?"

He said it so kindly, with a flash of white teeth, that it was not until he stressed the last words that Leta felt the sting of his rebuke. Something in her snapped, like a dry twig under a heavy boot.

"And if I ever need *your* help in the future, *I'll* ask for it!" She'd had about enough of the man and his lopsided grin.

He raised a dark brow in wonder as he saw the line of her jaw set with the same stubbornness he had witnessed before. For a moment he could only admire the way her anger brought out a wild, and slightly dangerous, beauty from within her.

Leta walked past him with her fists clenched and her head down. Spying a hickory nut, she grabbed it and hurled it in his direction, not seeing where it landed.

"Oooooh!" Tru made a sound like a wounded dog.

She turned to find him sprawled on the ground, the breath gushing out of him as he gasped.

She couldn't think; she couldn't breathe; she was terrified. *I killed him. A man that belongs to God.*

Just then a deep, vibrating sound rose out of the man as he rolled over holding his side, laughing uncontrollably.

The whole thing had only lasted about thirty seconds, but to Leta, it had seemed a lifetime. She kicked the ground, spraying him with dirt, turned and stomped off.

He caught up with her as she stalked along. Her lips were tightly clenched, her eyes fixed straight ahead. "Leta." His voice was tense. "I'm sorry. I didn't mean to scare you. I was aiming for humor. I haven't laughed in so long, I thought I forgot how."

She stopped dead in her tracks, turned, and fastened a

stare on him. "Yeah? Well you missed what you were aiming for!" She blew the hair out of her eyes. "Just so we understand each other, I couldn't care *less* about protecting the so *highly* revered Purviance name! Not now—not ever!"

"So...what *are* you interested in, Leta?" He searched her face, hoping he could pump the truth from her lips in her fit of anger. A tactic that had worked before.

"Ground of my own where I can live and breathe! I want to plant flowers and watch them grow, harvest them, and maybe, *just* maybe, make a dreary day a little bit brighter for someone else out there. Is that so wrong?"

"No...that's not so wrong." Tru said, trying hard to mask the growing admiration he had for the girl. He brushed a hand over the sleeve of his shirt, removing the dirt.

She looked across the landscape, hopelessness leaking into her speech. "Now look at it. My fields are dying. Dying of cold and darkness."

"No way...your fields are just settling down for a good long nap." He picked a leaf off his shirt, rubbing the stem between his fingers. "They'll wake again, come spring." He watched in fascination as the fire snapped in her golden-brown eyes. "Every flower returns to sleep in the ground. Of all the performing arts, gardening takes the longest time, but the rewards make it worth the wait." He stopped for a moment, then laughed. "Guess that could be said for a lot of things."

"Why are you out here?"

He grinned casually and shrugged. "I heard you hitting something...thought whatever it was had to be dead by now."

Leta could feel his smile in every fiber of her being.

She brushed the hair from her eyes to focus on him. "No, I mean why did you choose to live here. To make this place your home?"

"Wanted to escape my old complex life, I guess." He tried not to meet her eyes.

She studied his face. "Sometimes you act like you're out here licking your wounds."

"My wife ran off with my best friend and I miss him."

She rolled her eyes. "Stop with the jokes."

"I'm dead serious," he said, slowly, awkwardly. He hadn't had much practice revealing his past.

For the first time since she'd known him, she saw a smidgen of real pain in Tru's eyes. Anxious to remove it, she changed the subject. "Well, do you like it here?"

"It's kind of primitive and peaceful here." He threw the leaf to the ground. "I can almost rest."

Leta agreed silently, then plopped herself down on the carpet of dried leaves and looked up at him. Something in his voice, his face, caused her to feel sympathy for him. She lost a lot of the aggravation she had felt earlier. "I didn't think anything bothered you...certainly not anything you'd want to escape from. But I know what you mean." The words of J.D. Redman came flooding back to her. "There's something comforting about the repetition of nature—the moon and stars following the same path. Knowing that the sun will come up over there," she pointed toward the marsh.

Tru's eyes grew hazy and dark, as if remembering. When his words came, they were soft and slow. "Do you still hear the hums?"

She looked down, brushing leaves into a small pile. "I don't really want to say...besides, nobody believes me, anyway."

"I do."

She looked up, narrowing her eyes, searching for the sincerity of his words.

"It's true. I sometimes sit at the edge of the woods, near the tree line, motionless. It starts low, really low, then I begin to make out a tune. It's usually one I remember from childhood...'The Ashgrove.' My mother used to hum it to me."

"'The Ashgrove'? I don't think I know it." Leta studied the man; he seemed humbled somehow. "Maybe your mother heard the hums in her childhood."

"Could be...she lived not too far away."

Leta frowned and thoughtfully considered the pile of leaves, then swished it slowly from side to side. "Have you ever taken Edwina to the tree line with you?"

"No. I go alone. Out there." He nodded toward the trees. "I remember it all. The woods do that to you. They pull out all the long-forgotten past, the loss, the heartbreak, all the stuff that's gone on in your life. Maybe it's the feeling you get when it all comes out of you, a feeling of release or something. No...if you've ever gone to the woods with me, I must love you very much."

"What are you running from?" she asked, bluntly.

"Who says I'm running?" Scowling, he stuffed his hands in the pockets of his jeans. "I'm not here to talk about myself. I'm here to see if I can—"

"What? Save me? Recue me from myself? What? What do you want with me this time?" Tension and aggravation had been building since the day Leta had learned of Tru taking a bribe from her family. Land in exchange for help, or so Edwina had informed her. "Or is it more Purviance land you're after? I know all about the little exchange program you had going on with my grandfather."

His face was tense and unsmiling. He leaned against a tree and looked at her. "It's not what you think. It was simply an offer."

"That's not an offer, that's called a deal!" she shot back. "How did the deal go down? Help the love child—get land in exchange for it!"

"There was an offer. Grand Bess wanted you to stay here, period. She convinced your grandfather to contact me to arrange a job for you, hoping that would secure you to the place. I said no. It was only after I shot down the idea of you working for me that I suggested helping you with your venture. I'd just learned from you that you were planning on growing flowers. At the time, it seemed the right thing to do, with or without the land offer."

"Oh yeah, it was the right thing to do for you! So now you expect me to believe that you want to give me a load of wood out of the kindness of your heart?" She stood up, brushing the dirt from her jeans. "What will my grandfather offer you for one load of wood—a place next to Edwina at the Heart Ball!"

"Don't be ridiculous. I helped you because I think you're a pitiful little love child that desperately needs direction in life," he shot back. "Look, I don't really care what you think my motives are in helping you. *I* know my motives, and more importantly, *God* knows my motives. You'll just have to trust me…or not. It's your decision."

Confused by the directness of his words, Leta could find no comment. It was hard to determine if he mocked her or spoke the truth. He was not like any man she had ever met. She had seen many sides to Tru Ransome since she'd known him, but none of them had ever been untruthful. Without a word, she got up, brushed off, and followed the path toward home.

Slipping through a break in the underbrush to the back of the house, she rounded the structure. Hearing voices near the edge of the porch, she stopped and stepped back a few paces, recognizing one of the voices as that of her cousin, Edwina. Boxwoods grew thick alongside the house, and she quietly crouched behind their cover where she would not miss the exchange. Slipping her cell phone out of her back pocket, she pressed the record button.

Edwina was pointing her finger and demanding some action from the man standing next to her. "Burn this place down! Nobody is inside I tell you! If you won't do it, I will!" she declared, withdrawing a lighter from her coat pocket. "See that smoke, Milton?" she pointed to the chimney. "Now's our chance! A faulty fireplace will be the cause, and no one will be the wiser. Once and for all we'll be rid of her. Burned out! That's how you rid yourself of vermin."

The nervous and shaky deliberations of the assistant seemed to infuriate Edwina.

"Oh, get out of the way, Milton, and let me do it." She shoved him away, fumbling with the lighter.

Reluctantly, Milton stepped forward to where the woman stood. "I'll have no further involvement with you *or* your schemes." He paused for effect. "I took pictures of those innocent children helping out on this farm so you could snatch them out of your cousin's care. I've spent the past decade being the liaison between you, Jim Bo Box, and the son you gave up without a second thought. I've done your dirty work for the final time. I won't stand by and watch you destroy what Grand Bess so desperately wants, a granddaughter she can be proud of. Not some mean-spirited, spiteful, arrogant, spoiled brat like you!"

"Oh, the things you rave about. Let's not forget that *you* did those things, not me. Now get out of my sight and off this land—you are done here!"

His face went red and his hands began to shake as he struggled to spit out his words. "I-I don't want you or anything to do with you—you are an evil woman. I only wish I'd realized it sooner."

His words were cut short by the approach of a truck loaded down with firewood. As the truck came toward them, Leta press the stop button on the recording and slid the phone back into her pocket.

"What's going on here?" Leta asked, taking in the scene as she stepped from the side of the house.

Edwina, undismayed, spoke smoothly. "We've lost a peacock. One of the white ones. Milton and I have been searching for hours but haven't found even a feather," she said in dry amusement. She turned, noticing the truck. "Looks like you're getting a load of wood...we'll get out of your way."

Leta nodded innocently. "If I see your peacock, I'll let you know." For the moment, at least, she'd let the situation simmer in her mind. She waved the truck forward and pointed to the woodpile, knowing that accepting the wood would be the quickest way to see Tru again. She knew he'd stop by to speak with his friend and, after seeing wood stacked in a pile, would try to pay for it if he hadn't already.

Faced with a choice, Edwina paused a moment, then

as if coming to a decision, said, "Thank you. Come on, Milton." She turned to the red-faced man and handed him the car keys. "You don't mind driving me home, do you?"

After the car pulled off, Leta saw Tru walking across the yard. He whistled sharply, trying to stop the car, but it kept going, faster, it seemed.

"Was that Edwina?" Tru asked, walking up beside Leta.

Slowly it began to dawn on her what had almost happened. She glanced up at Tru. "Yes, it was."

"What did she want?"

A subtle and intense change had come over her. "To burn my house down."

The smile faded and was replaced by an expression of confusion.

"You may know who my cousin *appears* to be, Tru, but you've got a lot to learn about the real person inside those designer clothes." Her voice was low and oddly strained. She pulled the phone out of her back pocket, swiped, and pressed until the recording came into view. She handed him the phone, turned, and went into the house, leaving him to stare at the phone in his hand.

In the silence that followed, she picked up her keys from the counter and headed out the door. It was past time she did something about Edwina Purviance.

Chapter 25

By the time Leta reached Tremont, the place was a frenzy of activity. Milton had stationed himself by the front door and shook his head at what seemed to be the repeated attempts of Royce Purviance to convince the assistant to stay. Without a hint of recognition, Royce's eyes passed briefly over Leta as she walked by, went to Milton, then returned to Leta with an abrupt accusation.

"Leta! Milton is leaving! Did you have anything to do with this!" Royce looked first to Milton, then to Leta. "Is there something going on I should know about? If you're behind any of this—"

"I sure am." Leta slipped into the calloused role of the street wise. "That arsonists you call a granddaughter tried to burn my house down. And all right under your almighty nose too!"

Before Royce could reply, there was a heavy tread of boots on the front steps, and a stone-faced Tru Ransome stomped past them, Mumford following closely on his heels. They crossed the foyer as bold as brass.

For a moment none of them moved. Royce was struck speechless with the audacity of the man who just strode by him, intruding on his house! Leta followed the heavy footsteps as they echoed through the entrance hall. She never removed her eyes from Tru as he crossed to the staircase. Wonderingly, and without a word, she looked up to find Edwina gazing down from the upstairs railing, a frosty stare on her porcelain face. Leta clasped the balustrade, but before she could move, Tru seized her hand.

"Stay where you are." Tru's gaze fixed on the girl, and Leta dropped her hand.

Beginning to understand what was going on, Leta stood still with one foot on the step as she watched a series of mystifying actions. Tru took the stairs deliberately, one at a time, and upon reaching Edwina, grabbed her hand and pulled her toward the study. Edwina shouted something in a high-pitched voice that faded in the air as the door slammed with a solid bang.

"Now see here! I will not be disrespected in my own house!" Royce railed.

Leta's eyes narrowed dangerously. "You created that monster. Now, step back and let a real man handle it."

Royce's face reddened, and his eyes seemed to protrude forth as he glared at Leta. Taking several steps toward her, he spoke through grinding teeth. "You're nothing but filthy white trash! How dare you speak to me that way!"

Oblivious to the horrified looks he drew from the room, he raised his hands to push her out the door.

"Royce!" The sound of quick footsteps echoed in the room, and he was seized by two very firm hands. He spun around to face the blazing blue eyes of Bess that bore into him mercilessly.

"Be careful that you never raise your voice or your hand to my granddaughter again," Bess spelled out the warning. "You slander what I hold most precious and value more than perhaps you realize. Edwina tried to burn down Leta's house, without thought or care for her cousin's welfare. Milton told me everything." She pointed a direct finger toward Milton. "And if you'd listened to him instead of bellowing your outrage, he would have told you all of this! He's fed-up with her lies and God knows, so am I! It was Edwina who bore a child out of wedlock and gave him away without a second thought. That poor, pitiful Justice Box. He doesn't deserve to live like a vagrant!" A single tear trickled down her soft white cheek. "Edwina's only concern is for the sham and pretense she's made of her life. I for one, am *done* with it! And hear me good—I'm done with *all* of it! Even if it means you too! I will tolerate no more!" She was furious as she stepped around the foyer table to face Leta. Tears suddenly blurred her vision, and she drew a ragged breath. "As for you, dear child, I'm so sorry. If I hadn't been so passive all these years, it might not have come to this."

Royce sagged into an empty seat near the stairs, his face crumpling, his anger dwindling into remorse.

Witnessing the whole scene was Mumford and Milton. Mumford stood tall and proud. He was a giant of a man, white from head to toe from his seventy years of living. He had the look, and right now the demeanor, of some Old Testament prophet who had just been handed a set of stone tablets.

Leta grappled in her mind for an explanation as to what she had just witnessed. She glanced up at the closed door again, hearing only muffled voices with snatches of words. Then the door opened abruptly and Tru walked out. He took the stairs in the same deliberate manner as before, only this time in a trancelike silence. Passing

Leta, he handed over her cell phone without a word, then gave a quick nod to Mumford and left through the front door.

Mumford stared at Leta for a moment. "Well, I guess that's that."

As if on cue, both turned to glance up the stairs at the study door when, in one quick movement, it slammed shut, rattling the crystals in the chandelier above their heads.

In spite of himself, Mumford gave a short laugh, shook his head, and wandered out the door to catch up with his boss.

***

A gentle rain had descended upon the boarding house with the calm quiet of relief. Tru stepped out onto the porch and sat down to think, staring into the drizzle. A situation, to say the least. The full weight of what he had learned pressed upon him. As they'd left Tremont, hardly a second had passed before Mumford had filled him in on the happenings and the revelations in the foyer. Now that he was coming out of the spell of Edwina Purviance, he saw things crystal clear. Whatever the outcome, he told himself, he would not allow that woman within ten feet of him ever again.

A desire, like a strong thirst, came over him. He needed to see Leta, to know she was okay. She was the true victim in all this scheming. But he wavered in his thinking when he thought of what her reaction might be. The last time he had spoken to her she wasn't exactly cordial. Clearly not in the mood to contend with another draining conversation, especially with the recent events so fresh on his mind, he thought it better to cool his heels for a while. Let the Purviance family handle their own

affairs. His part in the family had just ended—
permanently!

He gazed up at the massive live oak whose branches
could be seen from nearly every home in the marshland,
like a mother whose presence is reassuring. The limbs
rocked on the air, keeping time to the slight wind. The
sight of that old tree settled him somehow. Settled him
from the pain that had knocked the wind out of him. His
thoughts gave him an edge like anger, though mostly he
was angry with himself; disappointed that he had been
fooled so easily—again! How could he have ignored the
same feeling—that something wasn't right? He knew
how. He believed what he wanted to believe. He saw
what he wanted to see. He trusted when there was no
support for that trust. It had been the trouble all along.
The one woman he should have been able to trust had
betrayed him. His wife had fixed his morning coffee,
cleaned and pressed a week's worth of shirts, then
walked away and never looked back.

A marriage, a home, a family of his own—did he want
these things? He'd spent so many years convincing
himself that he didn't, he no longer knew if it was true.

Chapter 26

The sounds of reveling radiated from the streets as darkness fell over New Orleans. An eerie gray mist began to snake its way through the French Quarter as Leta hurried down the wet brick sidewalk. Flickering lights of gas lanterns threw their shadows across the familiar green door. She reached for the doorknob. Mixed with the lingering scents of fresh beignets and coffee, she caught the faint smell of warm pipe tobacco. Top notes of anise seeds and cherry left little doubt as to who would be waiting for her behind the door.

Rod Purviance stood in the courtyard as the door opened. In a low voice he said, "Welcome home, sweetheart." Removing the pipe from his mouth, he stepped toward his daughter and wrapped her in his arms. He turned his head slightly and spoke over his shoulder, a gruff pride in his voice. "See, I told you my little girl would be back home for Christmas."

A slim, well-dressed man moved from the shadows of an old crepe myrtle and smiled to himself. His eyes roamed over her. "Hello, Leta."

Rod pointed with his pipe to the staircase which led up to a set of French doors. "Your room is ready. I'll take your bags up while you two get reacquainted." He nodded toward the dark water of the saltwater pool where a bar had been set-up under a magnolia tree. The shimmer of candles and white twinkling lights reflected from the old silver worn mirror behind the bar. "As always, complimentary cocktails are served daily," he said, winking. "Hot buttered rum?"

"None for me, Dad," Leta said, already feeling awkward and not sure why. "Spiced tea sounds good, though…if you have some."

"Anything for my girl."

As Leta watched her dad climb the steps to the gallery, the red embers of his pipe flared, and a cloud of dense white smoke mingled in the air and twirled with the mist. He disappeared inside her room and a moment later, a yellow light shone in the window.

The trickling sound of the fountain drew her attention and she turned, knowing Gordon would be there.

"I've missed seeing you appear on that balcony," Gordon said. "I never realized how much until you went away."

Leta ignored his words and spoke in kindness, falling naturally into the role of hostess. "Would you like to sit down?" She pointed to a wrought-iron table tucked in a corner near the fountain.

Gordon pulled out a chair for Leta, then settled his weight in the chair and leaned back, looking around. "I've always loved this place. And the name too: The Hideaway. Tried to buy it off Rod a dozen times…he won't budge. Says it traces back 200 years to when it was a hideaway for a profitable pirate."

Leta nodded once. "Ah…that explains the appeal." She tried to relax in the man's presence but was finding it hard to calm herself. He got up and stepped away toward the sideboard and poured a glass of brandy.

"Here, drink this," he said, handing her the sparking glass with its burgundy liquid. "You seem tense. It'll relax you." He watched as she took the glass and sat it away from her on the table. A long silence passed between them before he sat down again and reached for her hand, casually caressing it with his thumb, he asked, "You all right? You seem...different—distracted."

"I'm good." She was struck by the numbness she felt at the touch of his hand and, finding an excuse, slid her hand away to pick up the drink. Placing it before him she said, "Here, you need this more than I do." Beneath his intense stare, she brushed her hair behind her ear and smiled. Turning her attention toward the fountain. "I'd forgotten how beautiful this place is at Christmas."

Gordon cleared his throat. "Your dad invited me to stay the night. I'm in the room adjoining yours." He waited to continue until her eyes came back to him. "There are no other guests." A lazy smile played across his face as his finger slowly circled the rim of the glass. Her eyes dropped, then returned to his with a steadiness and resolve he had never witnessed before.

"Gordon, you have such a way about you. I'm sure there are still plenty of women here in New Orleans who are unable to resist your charm. Whatever happened to your assistant...Noel, isn't it?"

It took an effort, but he tried to look surprised. It baffled him that she would make such a bold statement. It mystified him even more that she had tried to pull away from him all because of a temporary fling with his assistant. "I've told you before, Noel is nothing more than an employee. I can't believe you are so insecure! Where's the woman I used to know?"

223

Leta smiled sweetly. "Dead."

He drew his head back in confusion at the single word. "Dead? Are you serious? What does that even mean? You look plenty alive to me. In fact, better than I remember."

"I am serious," she stated, resolutely. As the idea took deeper root, she smiled and took a breath, beginning to feel a completeness she'd never felt before.

Gordon looked at her with an air of skepticism. "Whatever has happened to you in Quay, it's all behind you now. It's over. You're home. All you need is some time and rest. You'll be back to normal soon. Trust me. I know whatever *this* is, it won't last."

It was a rare day when Gordon White appeared in need of anyone. Rather, it was said of him that he was something of an opportunist who had gained his wealth through the misfortune of others. Gordon had set his sights on Leta Purviance and was eager to seize whatever opportunity he could to have her, completely.

No one was aware of the effort it took Gordon to divert attention away from his involvement in the murder of Wade DeClan. By casting guilt for the unfortunate shooting entirely on Leta, he thought the situation effectively handled.

Leta faced him, wide-eyed, joy etched in every delicate feature. "I've never felt more normal or more at peace in my life."

"Clearly you are not yourself." He lowered his voice and slipped into a persuasive tone. "It's simply a matter of logic, Leta. You've been away too long, isolated in the backwaters of nowhere South Carolina. Around all those rural people with their backward ways…it was bound to have had an influence on you. Your attempt to run from the past has only led you squarely back here, where you belong. With my help, you'll be safe and back to normal, soon. I promise."

She regarded him with some amazement that quickly turned to amusement. "I think you've underestimated me. Not to mention the people of Quay."

He smiled at her indulgently. "We'll see." He took a slow sip of the brandy, his eyes fixed on her over the top of the glass.

As she looked at him, she marveled at the lack of attraction she felt toward the man. Gordon had always been like a strong magnet, pulling her into his orbit. Once there, she would feel completely within his control. Now, nothing. Not even the barest sense of allure. There seemed to be a stronger force at work within her heart. An unceasing current of love and compassion. Leta wondered at this unexpected gift of grace. The fire that had once burned so strongly within her, and had so effectively consumed her, seemed to be nothing more than a pile of sour ashes. Still, the wisest choice would be to keep her distance from this man who had once ruled her heart. And that was what she intended to do.

A familiar pair of worn brown hands slid a plate of brownies before her.

"Reck!" Her shriek of joy pierced the stillness of the courtyard, and in the next moment, Leta jumped up to throw herself into his lean frame. She brushed away a tear of relief as he clumsily patted her back. "I can't tell you how good it is to see you!"

"I've been keeping an eye out for you ever since your daddy said you were coming home for Christmas. I figured you'd come back sooner or later." He tilted his head as she stood back, getting a good look at her. "You look good—real good."

"I feel good, Reck." She brushed away the tears and gestured to the sideboard next to the bar. "You always make this place shine at Christmas."

Reck wiped his eyes with his sleeve and swallowed his tears. "Your daddy just won't fire me. I've been telling him to let me go so I can run my restaurant the way it's supposed to be run, but he won't listen." He winked. "Course my wife likes the run of the place when I ain't around. Says I mess up her doin's."

The idea that a world-renowned chef would choose to work part-time for her dad still baffled Leta. The strange trio began their relationship when Rod and Leta had first arrived in New Orleans. They'd walked into the restaurant, Reck's Last Resort, after being drawn in by the spell of a saxophone player. His tones seemed to be an outward extension of the player's soul. He'd pulled them into his spell with his ability to float them between crying the blues and infusing them with hope as he effortlessly shifted into a smokey version of "Amazing Grace." Now, it all came upon her with a staggering truth that made her weak inside. Reck Johnson was a man of God, saved by grace.

She sat down and reached over, lifting a brownie from the plate. "You remembered."

Reck pursed his lips. "Now, what makes you so surprised at that? Course I remembered." He lifted a glass of chilled milk from the sideboard and handed it to her. "Your daddy is on a call. You know how long-winded he can be. I told him to forget about that spiced tea—you'd want milk to go with your brownies."

Gordon picked up a brownie, sat back, and thoughtfully chewed. His eyes slowly narrowed, and the mocking gleam that came in them began to annoy Leta. "I've never realized how your tastes run to the simple." He gave her a reproving look. "Milk? Interesting."

Biting his tongue, Reck scratched his cheek and turned back to the sideboard and began arranging dishes for their meal. He listened for the exchange he knew would follow. The young woman could put people in their place, and Reck wasn't about to miss it.

Leta picked up a brownie and dunked the crusty end of it into her milk and smiled. Then, with one slow and drawn-out slurp, she sucked the milk from it before taking a bite. "Um." She licked her fingers and popped the rest into her mouth, saying as she chewed, "Nothing comes close to the pleasure I get out of one of your brownies."

"Who you bake for makes all the difference," Reck said with a smile, watching as she wiped her mouth with the sleeve of her shirt.

Gordon's mouth softened into a lazy smile. "Lovely. I take it the traditions in the boondocks are a little more relaxed than what you were used to. Places where slurping is an art form."

Ignoring his comment, she reached for another brownie at the same moment Gordon extended his hand. Their fingers touched.

Gordon spoke first. "I want it. It's mine." His green eyes said volumes, leaving no doubt as to his meaning.

Reck shook his head as he wiped around the chafing dishes, waiting for Leta's response. He'd always made it his habit to watch over the girl and this night was no different.

The reply from Leta was barely heard. "You're laying claim to something that belongs to another."

227

"Now we're getting somewhere," Gordon said, smugly. "That explains it. Who is he? Some white trash from South Carolina?"

Leta choked and had to clear her throat. "Hardly."

"That's a relief. I was afraid you'd slipped into the gutter since leaving me. From what I've seen so far, I'd say you're well on your way."

Silence answered him as her thin face turned to the sideboard and golden-brown eyes brimmed with tears as she stared into the dark eyes of Reck. "No, I was pulled from the gutter and embraced with a love so deep, so intimate, and so strong that it is, even now, in the process of restoring me. I have a long way to go, but by the grace of God, I intend to get there."

Reck's heart squeezed so tight he couldn't speak. Weakly he raised his hand to the air and mouthed, "Thank you, Jesus!"

Leta slipped from the table and moved toward Reck. Standing on tiptoes, she kissed his cheek. "Thank you for praying for me all those years and never giving up on me."

Over Leta's shoulder, Reck watched as the door to the courtyard opened. Two men came in and walked toward Rod who had appeared from the house. The men were armed detectives, and Reck and Rod had been expecting them.

Since the shooting of Wade DeClan, an investigation had been ongoing with very few leads. It was only when witnesses had affirmed and proved Gordon's text messages to Wade that the authorities gained the leverage they needed to make an arrest on the grounds of assault with a deadly weapon. The truth finally came to light. Gordon had hired Wade to attack Leta. The plan was all set for Gordon to arrive on the scene and rescue her from her assailant. Providence, however, decreed otherwise, and Reck Johnson came on the scene ahead of Gordon. Wade DeClan was shot and killed by Leta as she tried to protect Reck from being stabbed.

Seeing nothing to be gained by watching the detectives lead Gordon away, Rod took Leta by the hand and walked her inside, speaking in low tones as he explained the recent events and their part in the arrest.

Chapter 27

What passed for rush hour in Quay, South Carolina was little more than a few trucks pulling boats and the occasional car. The early morning regularly scheduled school bus would, from time-to-time, get held up by Mr. Porter's tractor. But for the most part, traffic was a non-issue for the citizens of Quay. But this bright morning, traffic in the sleepy coastal town seemed to be experiencing an uptick.

Tru pulled up to the curb and stared at the glass door that led into Quaytown. For several long moments he just sat, gazing at the coffee shop. This was where he and Edwina had first met. He still had a blood rush when he thought of all he had wasted trying to convince himself that he loved the woman. Shaking his head as if to clear his mind, he got out and entered the shop.

"Join me," said the old familiar voice of J.D. Redman. "You know I hate to drink alone."

Tru glanced briefly at his uncle, unable to defeat the scowl that creased his brow. "Why are you hiding over here in the corner?"

"You've got to keep well hidden when the Purviance girls are on the prowl." He threw a thumb over his shoulder toward the waitress. "Rosetta warned me when

I came in. Said Louisa stuck her head in the door asking if anybody had seen me."

Before he sat down, Tru looked around with all the intensity of an animal with no intention of being caged again. He began second-guessing his decision, realizing maybe he'd made a mistake in coming here. "The last thing I want to deal with today is a Purviance."

J.D. managed to comment with a quieter dignity. "Louisa is a sweet soul. She's like a pair of children's scissors; bright and colorful, and not too sharp. She won't come back this way."

Rosetta paused in her work, snatched up the coffee pot, and crossed the room. "Who y'all hidin' from way over here in the corner?" Her face betrayed no emotion as she stood in front of them, the coffee pot raised high in her hand. "Y'all got women afta ya?" The stout owner of the place let out a belly laugh. "Won't surprise me none. Not with the two of you!" She turned over their cups and filled them to the brim. "Coffee, just the way you like it." She looked at Tru. "Who's your one and only?"

Tru slid into the seat and picked up his coffee cup, savoring its aroma. "No one but you. Thank you, my love."

Rosetta threw her chin out. "That's right, baby, and don't you be forgettin'."

"Was Lou by herself, Rosetta?" Tru pulled his cap off and slid it into the seat beside him.

"No, that highfalutin Althea was with her." She snarled her nose. "And that's all." She ground the words out in a slow drawl and slapped the table twice before leaving.

"Speaking of Purviance women, have you heard from

Leta?" J.D. reached across the table for a sugar packet, shook it, then tore it open. "She's been gone for a while now. That's one Purviance I wouldn't mind seeing."

"Not since before Christmas—what's that, a few months now? Heard she went to visit her dad in New Orleans...spent Christmas with him." Tru straightened slightly, his dark eyes burned with an unspoken question.

"Yeah, Bess told me. Did you know the old matriarch has been attending services? Can you believe it?"

With a start of surprise, Tru questioned, "You mean with us? Why haven't I seen her?"

"She comes to the early service...with Justice Box in tow. At first the sight was so odd. A gangly young coyote keeping company with an old, pampered poodle. If cleanliness is next to godliness, then Justice Box got baptized somewhere along the way." He tapped the sugar packet over his coffee and stirred. "Even suggested she would be making a rather large contribution at the church fund raiser tonight. Said she needed to make up for lost time. Two other non-profits are on the short list for donations as well."

Word had filtered down to the pastor that Bess Purviance had experienced a radical change of heart. She was rarely seen without Justice Box these days and proudly introduced him as her great-grandson to anyone she happened to meet. The boy's appearance wasn't all that had changed. There was a warmer light in his eyes, a spark of life that had never been there before.

White teeth gleamed in a reckless smile as Tru responded. "Better make sure her donation doesn't come with a...stipulation. You'll sure pay for it." He took a long pull of his coffee.

"Stipulation?" J.D. narrowed his eyes. "Like what?"

"Like a pair of children's scissors. Purviance women don't usually give something for nothing." He casually glanced out the window as he swallowed his coffee, narrowing his eyes as a familiar SUV swept into a parking space behind his truck. He would have known it anywhere, just as he would have recognized the form of the woman who owned it. Leta Purviance was in town. The thought raced through his mind and his pulse quickened a beat or two. His eyes locked on her. She looked good, he decided. Real good. But there was something different about her too.

A flare of jealousy sparked as Tru observed a man getting out of the SUV. A man in the presence of Leta had been the one thing he'd not been used to seeing. The surge of emotions he felt surprised him. The two stood together a moment as it seemed questions were asked and answered, then the man looked at his watch and noted the time. Miserably Tru watched as Leta stood on tiptoes and kissed the guy on the cheek. Lowering his head, he spoke to Leta in an intimate way and squeezed her hand as she pulled away. The guy smiled and watched her as she left, and it was a long moment before the man pulled his eyes away, walked toward a black Lincoln, got in, and drove off. But not before Tru noticed the Louisiana license plate.

The coffee shop door was open to the spring weather and Leta stepped inside and up to the counter. Looking up at the list of options chalked on the blackboard, she considered them a moment, then placed her order. "I'll have a caramel macchiato."

"Sure thing, honey—large?" Rosetta said, already mixing the concoction.

"Please."

With coffee in hand, Leta turned toward the door when she heard her name spoken from across the room. She turned with a start to see Tru and J.D. raising their cups in a mock salute. Surprised at seeing them, she was unable to speak for a moment as she made her way toward them.

"Well, if it isn't long lost Leta returning home from the Paris of the South," J.D. said, smiling as he stood. He took her hand into his. "Sit down! I was beginning to think we'd never see you again."

"I don't want to interrupt all the plotting and scheming going on over here," she teased. She slid in next to J.D., sipping her coffee to cover her growing smile. It was good to see them.

Tru smiled, but it never reached his eyes. "You've interrupted a major plot. We've decided to take on the entire fishing industry, one fisherman at a time."

"Oh? So, what are you planning on doing with them after you catch them?" she asked, drawing out the vowels in a smooth-as-honey voice. Relaxing back in the seat, she stirred her coffee leisurely with a plastic spoon.

"We're going to make them fishers of men—of course." J.D. laughed, throaty and low. "I mean why waste precious time going after little fish when you can haul in the big ones. The mean and nasty ones make the best converts. Just look at us!"

"No better proof than that," she said directly, enjoying the light banner as they sat there with all their history hanging between them. It felt good to be known and have connections again. She glanced up at the ledge encircling the room where white coffee cups were on display; all the same and perfectly spaced and even. The whole shelf was like a shrine to Rosetta's OCD.

"How was your trip to New Orleans?" Tru asked, not too sure he wanted to hear the response.

She swallowed down a sip and said, "Good—in fact, better than expected."

Tru nodded almost agreeably. "Good. Well, I'm glad to see you're home again."

J.D. cleared his throat and spoke up. "Tru's been keeping an eye on your place while you've been gone."

She looked up, lifting her brows. "Oh? I really appreciate that. Everything okay?"

Tru shot J.D. an annoyed look before turning his attention to Leta. "Just walked around, made sure nothing was out-of-the ordinary. Everything's fine."

"More coffee?" Rosetta said, sashaying up to the table holding a pot level with her shoulder. The bell on the counter tinkled and she turned. A young couple stood at the counter. "Tourists."

"Now, just how do you know that?" J.D. chided.

"'Cause you only get that kind of crumpled look from riding in a car all day, that's how I know." She filled up Tru's coffee cup, her mouth curving into a wide smile. "You want some steamed milk in that, baby?"

Tru grinned. "Yeah, it might help it go down." He took a long, searing gulp. "This stuff is so thick it's practically tar. I don't think you've put nearly enough whiskey in it either."

"My coffee is as smooth as a widow's kiss. Whatchyou expect with a double shot. As for the whiskey, I ain't runnin' no saloon here. You'll just have to settle with the same two shots of opium as always." She winked. "Now, don't you be flirting with this here pretty girl, none. You know I'm the jealous type."

Tru gripped her forearm. "You're the only girl for

me."

"That's right, baby!" Rosetta said, whirling toward the front counter.

"Kinda early in the season for tourists, isn't it?" Leta said, glancing out the window. "Seems like the foot traffic has picked up some too."

J.D. turned his cup around and around, his movements measured and precise. "They're having the Heart Ball tonight to raise funds for the new wing at the hospital."

Leta took another sip, then looked up at him from under her lashes. "You'll enjoy it."

He shook his head. "Oh, I'm not going."

"Why not?" She smiled. "I bet you're a good ballroom dancer. Besides, it's a worthy cause and you're an essential part of the hospital staff. Everyone loves you."

He didn't smile back. "Unfortunately, I have very little influence in the hospital these days."

"Why don't you tell her the real reason you resigned your post at the hospital." Tru leaned forward, bracing his elbows on the table as he clasped his hands. He looked at Leta. "I tried to warn them, but they wouldn't listen. People always mistake the Redman good nature for passivity when it's anything but."

Leta turned toward J.D. "You resigned?"

"I did. I was seen consorting with the enemy, so to speak. Or at least that's what Edwina said in front of the hospital board after I'd given my speech."

Tru piped up. "I wasn't in the best frame of mind myself that day. We came close to being arrested. I'll never forget the look on Bernese Jackson's face when J.D. told them all off. He shamed them to the roots of their silver hair—then resigned."

"Wait a minute." She snapped to attention. "What could Edwina possibly have against you? You're her pastor, for heaven's sake!"

Tru answered, "In a word—you."

Heat crept up her neck, and her mouth dropped open. "Me?" She was close to laughing. "What did I do? I wasn't even here. When did all this happen?"

"Sometime before she tried to burn your house down," Tru commented dryly. "She's back in Mount Pleasant, trying to reconcile with her family. But your grandmother is not having it…supposedly cut her out of the will. It's been said that she's taken Edwina's portion and put it in a trust fund for Justice Box."

Leta gaped at them, unable to process it all.

J.D. held his hand up to explain. "I have some recent news along those lines. Bess is taking the sizeable donation she usually gives to the hospital's Heart Ball and she's giving it to other charities this year, namely, Quay Community Church, Ransome Land, and the Fishermen's Ministry. She'd gotten word about the hospital banning you from giving out flowers to patients, and she was as mad as a hornet about it."

"Wait, what?" Tru said, holding up both hands.

"You heard me…it'll be a game changer, no doubt about it."

There was a long silence as everyone tried to sort out the news. Leta looked from Tru to J.D. and back again and then said, "It couldn't happen to two nicer guys."

Chapter 28

A chilly spring thunderstorm had washed the pollen from the air and left the day with erratic squalls chasing themselves across the low country. The wheels of Tru Ransome's truck splashed through mud holes and jolted its way toward the dock, making a careening turn as it swept down a narrow waterfront street. He pulled up next to the loading dock where a small sign rattled and clapped above a door, identifying the building: *Fishermen's Quarters*.

Tru stepped from the truck and turned toward the sea, the wind ruffling his close-cropped hair. The *Flaxen Maid* stood out in the open harbor several hundred yards from the dock awaiting her turn at unloading. Just coming into view, a sailboat skimmed toward shore coming in from the open sea, two deckhands straining at the sails as a circle of sea birds glided over the vessel.

Closer around him, the dock was alive with the sounds and scents of the waterfront. Idle men and a few desperate boys, scruffy and drab, loafed about hoping to make the noon meal and land a job provided each day at *Fishermen's Quarters*. He ran a hand across his beard, still finding it hard to believe how the men's ministry had taken off. Linking the *Fishermen's Ministry* and

Ransome Land into one entity had been the right move. *Fishermen's Quarters* was already impacting the lives of many in the low country around Quay.

This was the life of a minister—this scene around him and people desperately looking for purpose, a reason to keep on breathing. What part he would play in their lives, he did not know, but one thing he did understand, he would give it his all. But as he faced the wind that brought with it the scent of the sea, so he knew he must face life head on, taking whatever opportunities God allowed him, and being content with it. In time, hopefully, he wouldn't care that love and family had passed him by.

There was a light chop rolling before the breeze, and he watched as the small sailboat navigated toward the harbor. When the craft first touched the dock, the man leaped up on the boards, secured it to the cleats, then turned to grasp the woman's hand, pulling her up next to him. Tru adjusted his cap and was about to turn away when he realized with a start that he recognized the young woman. The man reached for Leta's hand and tucked it in the crook of his arm as they began making their way down the pier.

His eyes were drawn reluctantly to Leta, and he watched her, remembering the Lincoln that had been parked at Stone House for the past few weeks. He tried to convince himself he didn't care. That it was none of his concern, but his heart wouldn't go there. He could not forget the girl. No matter how hard he had tried, memories came flooding back to him at the worse possible times, reminding him of the things they'd shared, things that haunted him in the middle of the night. Shoving his hand into his pocket, he fished out his keys and headed toward the warehouse.

A startled gasp escaped from Leta as she spotted Tru. Hurrying down the pier, she pulled the man along behind her. "Tru! Wait! I have someone I want you to meet!"

A small frown touched Tru's brow, but he quickly lost it as he turned around to face them. The man had hair streaked golden blond with the sun and lively blue eyes. His skin was toasted butternut brown. He walked with a rakish air as he tried to button up his shirt with one hand, Leta dragging him forward by the arm. *Is this really happening to me*, Tru thought miserably. They stopped in front of him, and he looked down into the sparkling golden eyes of Leta.

"Tru Ransome," she said proudly. "I want you to meet my father, Rod Purviance."

Tru glanced back at her, eyes wide. A subtle but intense change had come over him when he realized she was serious. He stuck out his hand. "Pleasure meeting you, Mr. Purviance." He won a private battle to not laugh. "You, uh…look too young to be Leta's father. I thought you might be her boyfriend."

Rod laughed as he grasped the proffered hand. "Leta wouldn't put up with a man like me for two seconds!"

Leta prodded her dad's shoulder. "Certainly not the man he used to be."

"It's true," Rod admitted. "But like I always say, it's not how you start, it's how you finish."

"That'll preach," Tru said, feeling suddenly cheerful. He swung off his hat, ran a hand through his hair, and flashed a winning smile.

"I was hoping for a tour of Fishermen's Quarters," Leta said. "Dad is headed home today, and I didn't want him to leave without seeing what you're doing down here on the waterfront. Something tells me he's going to like it." She looked up at her dad. "Maybe it's something you might want to implement back in New Orleans."

The two followed Tru into the warehouse where tables were being set by a staff of chattery men and women of all ages and, seemingly, from all walks of life. Tru leaned against the wall and folded his arms as if he were about to share some vital wisdom to the pair. "This ministry does a lot of good for the people of these waterfront streets. I'm thankful for a pastor that shares the vision. Down here you have people falling all around you. We try and help everyone; some will let us, some won't." He spoke low as he looked around. "One thing is certain, there's always more where these come from."

"Where did all the volunteers come from—the church?" Leta asked.

Tru nodded. 'Some. And some are people that we've helped in the past who want to give back."

About that time an elderly woman in a floral apron pushed through the wide doors from the kitchen, carrying a tray in her hands. She began unloading drinks from the tray, lining them up on a table in neat little rows.

Rod approached the table, then paused, turning his head slightly and chuckled. "Mother?"

The woman looked up. "Rod! How nice to see you here—now, be a dear and help your mother get this tea out. I need to finish cutting up the lemons." She dried her hands on her apron, then waved toward Leta and Tru.

Leta nearly choked. "Is *that* who I think it is?"

"None other." A tiny smile crooked one corner of Tru's lip. "She flits around all day long. I passed through here the other day and she was on all fours mopping up a spill."

"I don't believe it."

"It's true. If there's any part of her I could recognize, it's her hind end. She scrubs the floors in the kitchen after lunch—says it makes up for the fact that she doesn't cook." He shook his head. "It's probably not the most refined descent she has ever made in her life, but it might be the worthiest."

"Grand Bess, you do surprise me," Leta whispered, her heart nearly bursting with pride.

***

On the day of the take-over, as it had come to be known, Leta was kneeling between wet garden rows, her fingers in the dirt. She pinched the offending weed close to the base of the plant and gently, but firmly, plucked it out of the ground and tossed it aside.

She looked back on the garden, fretfully wondering if her mind was playing tricks on her. The heat simmering off the fields fooled her into thinking that Gussie was approaching, walking toward her down a dirt path. She had the impression the image was not quite belonging to earth, yet not quite free of it either. Glancing toward the dock, she scanned the waters for the little faded jon boat. Dismissing the illusion as wishful thinking, she turned her attention back to the task at hand for a moment, then leaned her back against the stone wall.

"When you were a baby child, you played your mornings away right here on this very spot," Gussie said with some dignity.

Leta turned sharply at the voice and stared into Gussie's shining berry-black eyes. "Gussie! Where have you been? I was beginning to wonder if I'd ever see you again!" Her words seemed a prayer of thanksgiving.

Spying a large flat stone covered with a blanket of green moss, Gussie bent to sit, stroking the surface with her wrinkled hand. "You used to build little houses with pebbles, then roof them with moss. You'd take a stick like this," she picked up a dead branch from the ground and began scratching the dirt, "and make roads in the dirt."

Leta grew serious as she reached out to pluck a wild violet from between the stones. "You're a mystery to me, Gussie. How do you know all the things you do?"

The old woman pointed to the sky with the stick. "Sea hawk."

Looking up at the sky, Leta watched as a sea hawk flew low, making a plaintive cry as it passed overhead.

"I've been around these parts for a while, child. Don't much happen I don't know about. Take that bird, for instance. Now, I don't know what that bird said, exactly, but I know that everything else in these woods listened to what that bird had to say. See how quiet it is. That means someone is coming."

Leta swatted a gnat with the back of her hand, then looked around. "I don't see anyone."

"Maybe it's love that comes seeking you. Coming out here to take over your heart."

Inwardly Leta cringed. "My heart's full of love. I just doubt that it's reciprocated."

"Oh, don't you doubt, child. Don't you *never* doubt!"

Leta paused in indecision, then got to her feet, slapping off the grass and dirt from her backside. She stepped toward the clearing, following the line of trees with her eyes until they stopped on a figure. Emerging from the shadows of the woods, a person walked straight up between the motionless trees and into the open field.

She fingered the keys of her necklace, stepped back, and turned to question Gussie, but she was gone. Glancing around, Leta rushed toward the stone wall. Her mind, like her body, had time only to register the sense of being caught in a drama that was meant to unfold. The ground had given way under her feet, and she had a feeling like something was being torn from her hand. A shout rang out across the field, and the sound of Tru's voice echoed in the air. Her body lunged forward as she plummeted headfirst into the stone wall. The next thing that registered was a feeling of pressure, as if being in the grip of a great force, a feeling of utter helplessness. Then, blackness.

Leta woke to the earth-sharp smell of damp grass and mud and felt what seemed like a bag of frozen peas covering her forehead. She realized she was stretched out on a bed with the words of an unknown masculine voice going in and out as she tried in vain to wake fully. The words: seizures, confusion, hydrated, rest, Tylenol, swirled around in her brain.

The next time she woke the air smelled of spice, sweet and tangy, like simmering apples. She touched her forehead; the peas were gone. So was the earthy smell. She peered out the window with heavily lidded eyes. Without moving her head, she watched the moon climb on its lengthy path into the night sky. Low hanging silvery clouds drifted across its face. She blinked slowly before sinking back down into the depths of oblivion.

Lying still in the comfort of a bed, a small sound from somewhere nearby convinced Leta that she was awake. It was daylight, and from the light behind her closed eyelids, she guessed it was well into the day. Her head still ached with a dull, throbbing pain, and when her fingers moved to her forehead, she found a large, tender lump right between her eyes. Slowly she opened her eyes and stared dumbly around the unfamiliar room. A soft, denim-like comforter covered the bed, plain and without frills. The room was equally plain with nothing more than a dresser, nightstand, and one lamp to fill the space. The only attractive feature was the view from the window in front of her. It looked out across the lush marshland and over the slow-moving creek she knew instinctively to be Sweet Grass Creek.

A voice in the next room caught her attention, and though it was low and muffled, like the creek, she'd have known it anywhere. She tried to wet her dry lips with her tongue and call out to him.

"Tru?" Her voice cracked, and she cleared it. "Tru!" She heard a quick pounding of steps before the door came open.

He hurried to the bedside, his eyes moving with concern over her face as they examined the bluish bruise on her forehead. "Hey...feel like you've been hit?"

"Yeah, by a truck. Can I have a little water?" Her voice was barely a whisper.

"You got it."

She gave a faint smile, closing her eyes against the pain as she listened to his footsteps move from the room. Then another, lighter, set of steps came into the space along with a whiff of perfume, something light and spicy, like the simmering apples she'd smelled in the night. Opening her eyes, she found a woman watching her closely. Every part of Leta's face ached as the pain throbbed through her head. Raising her head off the pillow slightly, she said, "Hello."

"Would you like something to eat?" the woman

asked. "We're having lunch. I can fix a plate for you if you're hungry."

Leta searched the face as she leaned back into the pillow, trying to place her. She was a pretty woman, with long wavy chestnut hair and green eyes, but there was an aloofness about her. Despite the kind words, her eyes and mouth held a type of harshness. "That would be nice. Thank you."

The tray holding a small plate of grilled chicken, salad, and a sweet potato was accepted with gratitude. The woman helped Leta sit up and, lifting a pillow from the bed, placed it behind her for support.

Leta grimaced as she adjusted her weight. "Thank you...have we met?"

"I'm Marbella—Tru's wife."

Surprise etched her wounded face. "Where am I?"

"At the moment, you're in *his* bed."

Embarrassed by the blunt revelation, she swallowed hard. "I'm sorry I've taken his bed, but I thank you just the same."

Tru stood in the doorway. "What I'm wondering is why you left out the *ex* part of wife," he smiled leisurely. "I was sure you'd never forget."

"No fear of that—you seem to remind me of it often enough," Marbella retorted, uneasy beneath his stare. She stepped away from the bed, not giving him opportunity for further comment.

"What happened to me?" Leta questioned, her eyes flicked over to him.

"A stone wall flew up and hit you right between the eyes; knocked you out cold." He peered at her thoughtfully and shook his head. "You must admit that's a turnabout," he smiled leisurely. "I was sure it would end up the other way around. You've thrown enough things at me—I really should be the one wearing the goose egg."

"Divine justice I suppose."

"No," he drawled as he rubbed his chin reflectively. "I was out in the field and saw you trip and fall." He pointed to her head. "You've got quite a lump. But that's a good sign—according to the doctor."

"Doctor?" Leta questioned. "Seems like I remember him. Was he asking a lot of questions?"

Tru nodded. "Agreed to turn you over to my care for observation—instead of going to the hospital. Said someone should stay with you for at least twenty-four hours to ensure that your symptoms aren't worsening. We kept a check on you off and on last night." He placed a glass of water in her hand, picked up a bottle of Tylenol from the nightstand, and shook two out in the palm of his hand. "Here, swallow these down."

She did as she was directed, then frowned in bewilderment as a thought struck her. "Where are my clothes?" The smell of dirt and grass was gone and, in its place, the fresh scent of Dove soap. "Who bathed me?"

"Marbella. I removed your shirt so she could get the mud and grass off you." He had been far more concerned with her injury than with her modesty. "Your grandfather's shirt and your jeans are clean and folded," he pointed to the dresser, "complements of Marbella."

Chewing her lip, she turned to Marbella. "Thank you."

Marbella hunched her shoulders indifferently. "It was nothing." Then, the green eyes took on a firmness. "That's certainly one ugly knot on your face. You'll be lucky if you're not permanently disfigured."

Leta looked down at the covers a long moment, holding tightly to the fabric. "I'm just grateful to be alive." She loosened her fingers from the quilt and looked up at Tru. "I'm glad you found me before the buzzards did."

"I was nearby." He placed the Tylenol bottle back down on the nightstand. "We'll let you eat your lunch in peace. I'll be in the next room if you need anything."

As the door closed behind them, Leta began to think about all that had happened to her in the past few months. Making the decision to winter in New Orleans with her father had been reactionary. At the time, her blood had boiled over with the havoc Edwina had brought into her life. She wanted nothing more than to escape. She'd worked at the feelings of bitterness, trying to form them into a good solid hatred for her cousin; she would have felt more comfortable with those emotions than any that she had been experiencing lately. Absently, her hand went to her chest, searching for the necklace that held the small keys, but it wasn't there.

She'd worn the necklace for almost a year. Strange that after so much time she could still recall Tru's words as he had touched each key: forgiveness is key in the kingdom of God. Prayer is key to peace of mind, but love is the master key that opens every heart. The unimpressive necklace had become a constant reminder, a continual wash of words through her mind. That, coupled with the life-giving wisdom of Gussie's words, had brought spring to her soul. And on a black highway, headed for New Orleans, she had surrendered her life to Christ.

The time spent away had been valuable. She'd found out quickly that somehow along the way she was beginning to change. Even her father had noticed. The day Leta was to leave The Hideaway, she'd stood at the door, suitcases at her feet, when Rod's deep baritone voice, husky with emotion said, "Leta, you've changed. I'm not sure how I know, but I know. There's something that comes from the inside of you now. Something I can't really put into words." He bent down to kiss her cheek. "I may just have to come home myself...one of these days."

The words had held a more sacred meaning for Leta. "Come home with me now," she'd pleaded. And he did just that.

***

In the next room, Marbella's mind thrashed itself in confusion as she watched Tru from the corner of her eye. He seemed like a stranger. The man she observed was not the man she had left. There was a calmness about him now, a strength, a certain power under control.

Tru stepped out of the house and onto the back porch, leaving the door ajar. The unexpected visit from Marbella had come as a shock, and he knew that whenever such a visit had come before, he had been met with bad news. He wondered what cataclysmic event would confront him this time. When she followed him to the porch, he pulled a chair around for her and moved to the rocker and sat down, bracing for the worst. He leaned back, lit his cigar, and puffed it to life. Squinting through the smoke he asked, "Is this a friendly visit, or is there something on your mind."

She looked down at her suddenly clumsy hands and clasped them tightly together. She heaved a deep sigh, fighting back tears. "Hawk is having an affair," she said, choking on the words. "Oh, Tru—I am so sorry for what

249

happened to our marriage."

Holding himself in check while he watched the pain and suffering spill out in tears down the face of his ex-wife was one of the hardest things he'd ever had to do. He put down the cigar with complete control, as if he had all the time in the world, then got up from his chair and went over to her. For a moment he stood looking down at her. She seemed to shrink back into the chair. He leaned over and pulled her up and into a hug. In a half-whisper, he spoke into her ear the words she'd longed to hear, "I'm sorry, too, Marbella. I forgive you."

She didn't reply, as if she had not heard, then her shoulders began to jerk and shake as she sobbed out her grief into his neck.

Standing just inside the door, Leta was a witness to the tender scene. She'd dressed and, after making the bed, took the tray to the kitchen. She had been about to thank them and say goodbye when she found them in an embrace. Her ankles felt weak and her throat tightened with a bitter sweetness she couldn't swallow. Marbella, tan and trim in her summer Bohemian dress, continued to rack with emotion as she held tightly to Tru's neck. Frozen to the spot, Leta was unable to pull her eyes away as much as she desired to.

A low and curious voice came from behind, interrupting her thoughts. "What do you make of it?"

Startled, Leta turned to see J.D. standing behind her. That question might have seemed natural for anyone watching Tru and Marbella's embrace. But the situation was anything but natural. It leaned more to the supernatural, and they both knew it.

"Well," Leta said, a little in awe of the situation. She felt a profound grief she would never dare verbalize, not even to her pastor. "We may be looking at the beginning of a marriage restoration." She smiled at him. "Mind giving me a ride home?" She motioned with her head toward the couple. "We need to get out of the way."

Chapter 29

When all chance of saying goodbye was gone, the door was gently closed. Leta slowed her pace and, sliding into the car, collapsed back into the seat. Closing her eyes, she tried to soothe her aching heart. It had been in New Orleans when she'd finally admitted to herself that she loved Tru. Never one to surrender control of her emotions, she'd put off the admission, wanting to protect her heart. Still, in her growing faith, she had to trust that God's will would be done. Knowing that she needed to align her feelings with that will, no matter how hard it was to accept at times.

"Where to now, Leta?" J.D. said, cranking the engine. He adjusted the rearview mirror, then glanced at her, waiting for a response. He noticed the bluish-black bruise between her eyes but decided not to comment on it. Tru had already filled him in on the incident and, in fact, that was why he'd stopped by. But one look at Leta's face and he could plainly see the reason for her pain. And it had nothing to do with the knot between her eyes.

"Home," she said quietly.

J.D. paused as he looked at the young woman. Almost hesitantly he asked, "Leta?"

Without lifting her head from the headrest, she rolled to face him.

"Feel like a little detour before I take you home?"

She thought for a moment. The prospect of having too much time to think was not appealing. "I don't mind at all. I don't care where we go or what we do, either."

"Good heavens, girl," the pastor chuckled. "I hope that bump on your head hasn't affected your judgment. That kind of thinking could land you in a lot of trouble."

"If I can't trust my pastor, I can't trust anybody," she finally managed to say. "Lead on."

He would have tried to console her, but anguish was etched in her every feature. "I want to show you something, down at the old Shiloh cemetery."

She raised a brow, then grimaced from the pain of that movement.

"I think you'll find it interesting."

To Leta's way of thinking, the opposite sex offered nothing but aggravation. Except this particular man. Though he could be direct, he had treated her with kindness and respect, looking after her spiritual condition with tenderness and compassion. If he continued with his empathy, she would be in danger of exposing her true feelings and that was something she rarely did; regardless of who did the asking.

The car dipped and bounced between the ruts on the old, sand-packed road. J.D. was quiet and Leta was glad for the silence. She needed time to come to grips with her own tangled emotions. As they rolled to a stop near the cemetery, she cut her eyes to him.

He cleared his throat and nodded. "Hmm…you know, I've come to believe that there's a certain mystery to this place."

"Mystery?" Leta searched for more words to clarify the question. "I wonder what *they* would say." She nodded toward the old headstones. "The bones of those who struggled through life in this place. If they could talk, do you think they would say this place is mysterious?"

"I do. In the everyday kind of way. Like whispered melodies and songs being hummed through the stones." He sat back in his seat and tried to explain. "I believe in the seen and the unseen, just like the old creed says. I believe in the hidden presence of God who is everywhere. Even when we think we're alone, we never are." He stopped for a moment, met her stare, and pursed his lips. "What I'm trying to say is, there is a purpose for it all." He opened the car door. "Come on, I want to show you something."

Leta got out and began following him. A limb slapped her leg as she brushed by a thicket of tangled brush.

"Watch your step," J.D. called over his shoulder. "The snakes are stirring."

With that comment, Leta hurriedly caught up with him. Walking down the path that led to the cemetery, she felt the warmth of the sun on her shoulders and tried to draw strength from it. They took the old footpath that ran along a low stone fence and then passed through the narrow opening.

The graveyard was not well-used. There were some old mossy headstones which leaned, some which had crumbled, and one in particular which sat at an angle, tilted against an ancient cedar. Sunlight filtered through the high canopy of trees, playing across the wild violets on the ground.

Leta spoke in a hushed, reverent tone. "You know,

maybe this whole humming thing is just the sound the wind makes as it moves through the cracks and shell mortar in these stone walls. They're everywhere, look!" She pointed to gaps and crevasses in the spaces between the stones. "Couldn't that make a sound like a hum if the wind was up?"

"I suppose so. But what a talent the builder must've been to lay these stones in such a way as to play a hymn. And according to the way the wind blows up from the creek too! I'd say the person was a genius."

A sad introspection fell over the face of Leta. She wandered languidly between the graves, noticing each worn name, each date. "Why are we here?" She paused for an answer.

The pastor pointed to a tilted stone, leaning against a cedar. It looked like a child, resting its head against the chest of its father.

Moving toward the gravestone, Leta stood before it and mouthed the name etched there. *August Jacobs 1837-1914.* Just below the date, in words speckled with lichen, were the words, *Our Beloved Blue Saint.*

Her sharp intake of breath was oddly broken as Leta bent down and ran a slow hand over the face of the stone. Her voice barely heard in the quiet graveyard, she said, "Who is this woman?"

J.D. leaned forward, brushed a few sticks and debris from the base of the headstone, then rubbed the cool stone beneath his thumb. Straightening, he spoke of what he'd learned. "August Jacobs. She was born a slave and spent her teenage years in fear of a cruel master who brutally molested her, leaving her with two children. The children were given to August's grandmother who lived and worked on a farm nearby."

She watched him closely, the shine of tears was in her eyes. "How do you know all this?"

J.D. laughed. "Research. The library has a good section on local history. It seems," he cleared his throat, "that she fled her plantation, knowing her chances of making it to the North were slim. She holed up in the small attic of Shiloh church. Spent seven years living in the cramped quarters and would only leave at night under the cover of darkness. Secretly, she would visit her children by paddling upstream to her grandmother's farm in an old jon boat. Some believe she made these stone walls. The pastor who was here at the time, a Scotsman named McBratton, sympathized with her and the plight of the enslaved and helped her."

"I remember Gussie telling me that a Scotsman brought in all these stones...do you think Gussie is related to this woman?"

He had the barest hint of a smile. "Could be, who knows. There are a lot of people in this area connected to the original settlers."

"Why are we the only two people who have seen Gussie?"

"Maybe we're the only two people who needed to."

Leta shivered at the thought. "What happened to her after that? August, I mean...after the seven years."

"After the Civil War, she spent the rest of her life teaching and helping all she happened upon. She was a strong and influential Christian around these parts and was known by all as Blue Saint. She was also a musician and learned a love for music while hiding out in the church. Even cared for her former master as he lay dying. He'd called for her and wouldn't rest until she came. Friends helped arrange for a meeting, but they were scared their beloved Blue Saint would be captured again, so they formed a wide circle of protection around the house with torches. They kept watch every night until the old man died. When August stepped out of the house that night, her first words to her students were, 'Love—even through anguish.'"

A long moment passed before Leta reached out a hand and rested it on the gravestone. Smiling through her tears, she said, "I love this Blue Saint, whoever she is."

***

Tru Ransome pulled away from the tight hug he had just given his ex-wife and held her at arm's length. "Be careful on the road...call me if you get into trouble." With that said, he tapped the hood of her car, watching as she backed away.

Moments later, he turned in the direction of the lane leading toward the cemetery, experiencing a rising hope as he walked along. Through the trees, he heard an airy little voice and it rooted him to the spot. He stood at the edge of the clearing and watched as Leta brush her hand lovingly over the headstone. She was mouthing words he couldn't hear. It was a deeper emotional feeling than he had expected, seeing Leta and J.D. together, as if in prayer. He slipped around to a tree and silently watched them, thankful that he had not been noticed. He wanted to take in the scene privately, without betraying the strong emotions he was experiencing.

"Speaking of a Blue Saint." J.D. motioned with his thumb. "Here comes one now."

Looking over her shoulder she saw Tru walking toward them. He was still wearing a white T-shirt; old, faded jeans; and had his hands shoved deep in his pockets. The dark stubble of his beard always gave him an air of danger, until he smiled.

There was no point in torturing herself with the thought of what could never be. She had to accept the fact that her friend's marriage had been reconciled and that was good, great even. What she had felt for him she believed to be real, but she also knew she didn't have a right to those feelings now. They would be friends—good friends and neighbors, and that was enough. She would busy herself with the work of planting and harvesting, but more importantly, growing in the newfound knowledge of her Creator.

J.D. stepped aside and waved Tru forward. "I'm going after coffee." He winked and smiled at Leta. "I trust you can find your way...home?"

Leta accepted his statement with a slight smile of her own. "I already have, preacher."

A slow grin spread across Tru's lips as he watched J.D. head for his car. He nodded toward his friend, then caught Leta in his vision and held her there. There were a hundred images of the woman in his mind, pieces of memories—the fierce, suspicious woman he'd first met; the girl who stood her ground with him and never backed down; the loving substitute mother to lost children; the hard-working flower farm girl. But now as he walked up to her, he noticed another side, one so completely different it baffled him.

"I'm sorry I left without a word. I wanted to tell you both thank you for helping me," Leta explained. "But I didn't want to interrupt."

"I'm just sorry you didn't have a chance to say goodbye to Marbella. She asked me to tell you that she hopes you recover quickly." He was calm and offhandedly casual when he reached out a hand and let the necklace, bearing three keys, fall loose from his finger and swing there, slowly. "I believe this belongs to you." He glimpsed Leta's reluctance to take it and laughed softly. "Thanks for letting me borrow it—it helped me out a little while ago."

A breeze played with the wisps of sun-lightened hair around Leta's face as she extended her hand. She felt the cool metal on her fingers, the bittersweet sorrow eking out with every determined movement. "Thank you. I've missed it."

Tru leaned down and kissed her forehead just above the bruise.

Leta pulled back. "Why did you do that?"

Tru shrugged. "Maybe it's been awhile since anyone's kissed your forehead and reminded you of how proud they are of you. But I am proud of you."

She touched the spot on her forehead then turned her head and shielded her eyes against the afternoon sun, her throat tightening by degrees. Listening, she heard the first sounds of crickets of a late spring. The sound held promise and seemed to carry a note of hope that new life was indeed about to spread across the land. "Thank you…now that all has been forgiven and your marriage restored, I'm happy for you," she said with a warmth that didn't quite reach her golden eyes.

He leaned against the cedar tree and stared reflectively down at the ground a moment. "Forgiven, yes. Restored? No."

Surprise touched Leta's face briefly as she waited for an explanation. "I don't understand."

Tru heaved a long sigh and, taking her hand, pulled her in front of him. "Is it so hard to understand, Leta?"

he asked, narrowing his eyes as he searched her face. "I have been in love with you for a while now. Even before I kissed you that day. I tried to ignore it, blamed it on a sort of fascination I had with you. Today though, I faced the truth. Oddly enough, it was Marbella who brought the truth to the surface." His eyes slowly met hers. "I don't expect you to feel the same way. It's enough for me to know my own feelings, the truth for once in my life."

Her voice was small, hesitant as she questioned, "Truth?"

"The truth is I've wasted enough time stumbling around for an excuse to be near you. When I saw you with your dad, before I knew he *was* your dad, I was heartsick. I thought I'd lost my chance for sure."

"Wait—are you asking me—you honestly want…me?" she questioned in amazement.

"I want you more than anything."

She pulled away slightly and tried to put her reeling thoughts in order. "But you don't know me—what I've done in the past, where I've been, who I was!" Her eyes filled with tears. "I'm not who you think I am. I've lived a life far from anything that you've probably experienced. I have more in common with the people you help, like those women from the wharf. You need to know that."

"I don't care about your past, Leta. Only your future. I haven't lived a perfect life either or been what you'd call successful with relationships—at least not until I learned to recognize true beauty. Beauty of the heart and soul."

"I've killed a man."

His face grew serious, and he lifted her chin until their

eyes met. With that slow, deliberate manner that reminded her so much of J.D., he asked. "And...the reason?"

"He attacked me on the street not far from my home in New Orleans, then dragged me to an abandoned building. A friend of mine, Reck Johnson, happened to be leaving our house when he saw the man grab me. Reck works as a chef for my father at The Hideaway. He fought with my attacker, knocking the gun out of his hand. The man pulled a knife from his boot and was about to stab Reck when I picked up the gun and shot him." Leta grew thoughtful, imagining what Tru must think of her now. "I was found innocent, but I don't feel innocent."

"Leta—" Tru's voice trailed off, and he fixed her with a piercing gaze. His eyes roamed over her briefly then returned to her face. Now a smile played just behind his features, and he gave a slow nod of what appeared to be approval. "You saved a man's life. That's all you need to remember."

Leta let out a sigh and realized she had been holding her breath since he had faced her. A softening warmth replaced the confusion and mellowed her emotions. After all he knew about her, could she really believe he cared for her? Could she accept the grace he offered and be the new creature she longed to be? "I want to believe you. I want to believe God when He says He forgives me too. I'm just finding it a little hard to believe."

"God often invades the people we would least expect. The one individual everyone else has given up on. It is after all, His story, and it's about what He can do with a person most think is beyond His grace. Look around you—look at the people you know who have suffered the most. God doesn't throw out the past and tell us to forget about it. He uses all the pieces, but He rearranges them, and, in His hands, it becomes something new and beautiful. I've watched you—you show that same grace to others. That's how He uses you for His glory."

Leta bowed her head in utter embarrassment. "I'm certainly no saint."

"You are—a Blue Saint. And if you open your heart to me, you'll find you have a true friend. Possibly one who will shake you up from time to time, but one who will always love you, always cherish you, every part of you."

Almost shyly she slipped her arms around his neck. Hiding her past failures was something she had done so well for so long it was hard to turn them loose. Secrets, long hidden, had been revealed and loosed from their weighty anchors of fear and pride. She took a deep breath. "I want that. I want you. My heart is open."

He rested his cheek against her soft hair as Leta nuzzled her face against his throat. Time seemed to tremble to a stop. She pulled away slightly, looking up at him, his eyes soft and caressing. Tru traced the curve of her lips with his thumb before he claimed them intensely with his own.

A wind began to swell, soft and warm, pulsing with new life. Leta closed her eyes. The faces of all the people she'd come to know passed through her mind in a quick procession. Moment by moment their lives had intertwined with hers in a grace-filled dance of providence. The light dimmed as a cloud passed over the sun and the familiar hum of the haunting hymn began a slow ascent on the wind. "God is behind it all," she whispered. "He is surely behind it all."